" Mr. Robinson," said the major, " if I may presume to make the inquiry,
is your lameness in the leg or in the foot ?"   PAGE 59.

SEBA SMITH

'Way Down East, or Portraitures of Yankee Life

The American Short Story Series

VOLUME 75

GARRETT PRESS

512-00686-5

Library of Congress Catalog Card No. 69-11916

*This volume was reprinted from the 1854 edition
published by J. C. Derby*
First Garrett Press Edition published 1969

The American Short Story Series
Volume 75
©1969

Manufactured in the United States of America

GARRETT PRESS, INC.
Publishers
250 West 54th Street, New York, N.Y. 10019

CONTENTS.

CHAPTER | PAGE

I.—JOHN WADLEIGH'S TRIAL 5

II.—YANKEE CHRISTMAS 29

III.—THE TOUGH YARN 53

IV.—CHRISTOPHER CROTCHET 76

V.—POLLY GRAY AND THE DOCTORS 99

VI.—JERRY GUTTRIDGE 125

VII.—SEATING THE PARISH 150

VIII.—THE MONEY-DIGGERS AND OLD NICK 166

IX.—PETER PUNCTUAL 216

X.—THE SPECULATOR 236

XI.—A DUTCH WEDDING 266

XII.—BILLY SNUB 280

XIII.—THE PUMPKIN FRESHET 319

XIV.—A RACE FOR A SWEETHEART 339

XV.—OLD MYERS, THE PANTHER 358

XVI.—SETH WOODSUM'S WIFE 370

"Way Down East."

CHAPTER I.

JOHN WADLEIGH'S TRIAL.

The Early Jurisprudence of New England, including a Sketch of John Wadleigh's Trial before Squire Winslow, for Sleeping in Meeting on the Lord's Day; with a brief Report of Lawyer Chandler's memorable Speech on the occasion.

THE pilgrim fathers of New England, and their children of the first and second generations, are justly renowned for their grave character, their moral uprightness, which sometimes was rather more than perpendicular, and the vigilant circumspection which each one exercised over his neighbor as well as himself. It is true that Connecticut, from an industrious promulgation of her " Blue Laws," has acquired more fame on this score than other portions of the " universal Yankee nation," but this negative testimony against the rest of New England ought not to be allowed too much weight, for wherever the light of history does gleam upon portions further "Down East," it shows a people not a whit behind Connecticut in their resolute enforcement of all the decencies of life, and their stern and watchful regard for the well-being of society. The justice of this remark will sufficiently appear by a few brief quotations from their judicial records.

In the early court records of New Hampshire, in the year 1655, may be found the following entry :

"The Grand Jury do present the wife of Mathew Giles, for swearing and reviling the constable when he came for the rates, and likewise railing on the prudenshall men and their wives. Sentenced to be whipped seven stripes, or to be redeemed with forty shillings, and to be bound to her good behavior."

Another entry upon the records the same year is as follows :

"The Grand Jury do present Jane Canny, the wife of Thomas Canny, for beating her son-in-law, Jeremy Tibbetts, and his wife ; and likewise for striking her husband in a canoe, and giving him reviling speeches. Admonished by the court, and to pay two shillings and sixpence."

If it is consistent with rational philosophy to draw an inference from two facts, we might here consider it proved, that the pilgrim ladies of 1655 had considerable human nature in them. And from the following record the same year, it would appear also that there were some of the male gender among them at that day, who still exhibited a little of the old Adam.

" Philip Edgerly, for giving out reproachful speeches against the worshipful Captain Weggen, is sentenced by the court to make a public acknowledgement three several days ; the first day in the head of the train band ; the other two days are to be the most public meeting days in Dover, when Oyster River people shall be there present ; which is to be done within four months after this present day. And in case he doth not perform as aforesaid, he is to be whipped, not exceeding ten stripes, and to be fined five pounds to the county."

The reader cannot but notice in this case, last cited, with what stern purpose and judicial acumen the severity of the penalty is made to correspond with the enormity of the offence. The crime, it will be seen, was an aggravated one. The gentleman against whom the reproachful speeches were uttered was a Captain ; and not only a Captain, but a Worshipful Captain.

Whether Captain Weggen was the commanding officer of the train band, or not, does not appear; but there was an appropriate fitness in requiring, that the crime of uttering reproachful speeches against *any Captain*, should be publicly acknowledged at the head of the *train band.* There the culprit would have to face all the officers, from the captain down to the corporal, and all the soldiers, from the top to the bottom of the company, could point the finger of scorn at him.

But as the injured party in this case was a *worshipful* captain, it was very proper that a penalty of a higher grade should be affixed to the sentence. Hence the withering exposure of the offender to make public acknowledgments on two several occasions, " to be the most public meeting days in Dover, *when Oyster River people shall be there present.*"

Whatever may be said at the present day, as to the temperance reformation being of modern origin, it may be affirmed without hazard that the good people of New England two hundred years ago, were decided and strenuous advocates of temperance. They were not tee-totallers; they did not prohibit the use of those " creature comforts " altogether; but if any one among them proved to be a wine-bibber, or abused his privilege of drinking, woe be to him, he had to feel the force of the law and good government. Witness the following court record in New Hampshire, in 1657:

"Thomas Crawlie and Mathew Layn, presented for drinking fourteen pints of wine at one time. Fined three shillings and fourpence, and two fees and sixpence."

The good people of the province of Maine in those early days have also left proof, that they were on the side of industrious and good habits and wholesome instruction. Their Grand Juries present as follows :

"We present Charles Potum, for living an idle, lazy life, following no settled employment. Major Bryant Pembleton joined with the Selectmen of Cape Porpus to dispose of Potum according to law, and to put him under family government."

So it seems there were some men, even in the early days of the Pilgrims, who enjoyed that more prevalent luxury of modern times, living *under family government*.

Again say the Grand Jury, "We present the Selectmen of the town of Kittery, for not taking care that their children and youth be taught their catechism and education according to law."

They took good care in those good old times, that the dealings between man and man should be on

1*

equitable and fair principles, and without extortion.
In 1640, the Grand Jury say—

"Imprimis, we do present Mr. John Winter, of
Richmond's Island, for extortion; for that Thomas
Wise, of Casco, hath declared upon his oath that he
paid unto Mr. John Winter a noble (six shillings and
eightpence), for a gallon of aqua vitæ, about two
months since; and further, he declareth that the said
Winter bought of Mr. George Luxton, when he was
last in Casco Bay, a hogshead of aqua vitæ for seven
pounds sterling."

The punishment inflicted on Mr. John Winter, for
extorting from his customer two hundred per cent.
profit on his merchandise, is not stated; but if one
Thomas Warnerton, who flourished in the neighborhood at that time, had any agency in fixing the
penalty, it probably went rather hard with him; for
this latter gentleman must have had a special interest
in keeping the price of the article down, inasmuch as
it is related of him, that in taking leave of a friend,
wʰo was departing for England, "he drank to him a
pint of *kill-devil*, alias rum, at a draught."

Juliana Cloyse, wife to John Cloyse, was "presented for a talebearer from house to house, setting
differences between neighbors." It was the mis-

fortune of Juliana Cloyse that she lived at too early an age of the world. Had her lot been cast in this day and generation, she would probably have met with no such trouble.

Thomas Tailor was presented "for abusing Captain F. Raynes, being in authority, for *thee-ing* and *thou-ing* of him, and many other abusive speeches."

At a town meeting in Portsmouth, March 12, 1672, "voted, that if any shall smoke tobacco in the meeting-house at any public meeting, he shall pay a fine of five shillings, for the benefit of the town."

In a previous year, September 25th, at a town meeting, it was "ordered that a cage be made, or some other means be invented by the Selectmen, *to punish such as sleep* or *take tobacco* on the Lord's day, at meeting, in the time of the public exercise."

It appears from this record that the town reposed unlimited confidence in the *inventive* powers of the Selectmen ; and it appears also that the energetic order of the town, passed on this occasion, was a few years afterwards successfully carried into practical operation. The following is preserved on the town records, July 24, 1771.

"The Selectmen agree with John Pickering *to build a cage twelve feet square, with stocks within it, and a*

*pillory on the top, a convenient space from the west
end of the meeting-house."*

Thus far we have confined ourselves to official
records ; but some of the unofficial and unwritten
records of those days are of equal importance to be
transmitted to posterity, one of which it is our present
purpose to endeavor to rescue from oblivion.

The affair of the cage, with stocks inside, and a pillory on the top, served to wake up the congregation
for a while, so that no one was caught napping or
chewing tobacco in the meeting-house during the
public exercises for several Sabbaths after this inven-
tion of the Selectmen became a "fixed fact" at the
west end of the meeting-house. As the novelty of the
thing wore off, however, the terror in some degree
seemed to depart with it. There was a visible care-
lessness on the part of several old offenders, who were
observed to relax their attention to the services, wearing very sleepy looks, sometimes yawning, and occasionally putting themselves into unseemly positions,
concealing their faces, so that the searching scrutiny
of old Deacon Winslow himself could not decide for
certainty whether they were asleep or not.

Among these delinquents, John Wadleigh seemed
to be the most conspicuous, often leaning his head so

as to hide his eyes during half sermon time. He was also gruff and stubborn when questioned on the subject. So marked was the periodical reeling of his head, that Deacon Winslow began to watch him as narrowly as a cat would a mouse. Not that the Deacon neglected the sermon; he always took care of that matter, and for his own edification, as well as an example to the congregation, he steadily kept one eye on the minister, while the other was on John Wadleigh. There began to be sundry shrugs of the shoulders among the knowing ones of the congregation, and remarks were occasionally dropt, such as " Don't you believe John Wadleigh was asleep during half the sermon yesterday?" with the reply, " Why yes, I know he was ; but he must look out, or he'll buy the rabbit, for Deacon Winslow keeps his eye upon him, and if he don't make an example of him before long, I won't guess again."

It was whispered by some, who were out of the pale of the church, that the Deacon's watchful powers with regard to Wadleigh were a little more acute in consequence of Wadleigh's having over-reached him somewhat in the sale of a cow, at which the Deacon, who prided himself on his sound judgment, it was alleged, always felt a little mortified. The Deacon however was a very upright specimen of the old puritan race, and it is not probable his sense of justice and right was much warped. True, he manifested considerable zeal in looking after the delinquencies of John Wadleigh, but his " zeal was according to knowledge ;" he knew Wadleigh to be a disregarder of the Sabbath, sleepy-headed and profane, and he did therefore feel a zealous and charitable desire to administer to him a little wholesome reproof, provided it could be done in a just, lawful, and Christian manner.

He even felt it excusable, to accomplish so good a purpose, to enter into a pious fraud with Parson Moody. He had observed that though Wadleigh generally appeared to be asleep at the close of the sermon, yet when the congregation immediately rose up to prayers, he always managed some how or other to be up with them, but with a flushed face and guilty countenance. The Deacon believed, and it was the general opinion, that Wadleigh was asleep on these occasions, and that when the congregation began to rise, it always awoke him. He therefore suggested to Parson Moody, that on the next Sabbath, at the close of the sermon, instead of immediately commencing his prayers, he should sit quietly down three or four minutes, as though he were a little fatigued, or had some notes to look over, and see whether Wadleigh would not continue to sleep on, while the attention of every one awake would of course be attracted to the Parson. This little plan was tried, but without any very satisfactory result. It added something to the presumptive testimony in the case, but nothing clear and positive. Wadleigh held his head down about half a minute after the monotonous tones of the preacher's voice had ceased to fall upon his ear, when he started suddenly, rose to his feet, looked round a moment confusedly, and sat down again.

At last, however, repeated complaints having been made to the Grand Jury, they saw fit to "present John Wadleigh for a common sleeper on the Lord's day, at the publique meeting," a thing which Deacon Winslow earnestly declared they ought to have done weeks before they did.

The Deacon was in fact the most important personage in town, being not only the first officer in the church, but also a civil magistrate, before whom most of the important causes in the place were tried. Of course the offender Wadleigh, when the Grand Jury had once caught him in their net, had a pretty fair chance of having justice meted out to him. The jury met early on Monday morning, and the first business before them was the case of Wadleigh, against whom a fresh lot of complaints had come in. They were not long in finding a bill against him as above-mentioned, and a warrant was put into the hands of Bill Cleaves, the constable, to hunt Wadleigh up, and take him before Deacon 'Squire Winslow, and summon in the witnesses for his trial.

Bill Cleaves tipped his hat to the 'Squire as he went by upon his official duties, and gave him to understand what was going on. Whereupon 'Squire Winslow proceeded to put his house in court-order, having the floor of his large open hall, where he generally held his courts, swept and newly sanded, and things all put to rights. One o'clock was the hour appointed for the trial, for as the neighborhood all dined at twelve, the 'Squire said that would give them an opportunity to go to the work with a full stomach and at their leisure.

Accordingly, at one o'clock the parties began to assemble in the hall. 'Squire Winslow, who believed that a pipe after dinner was a good settler to the stomach, and always practised accordingly, came in with a pipe in his mouth, his spectacles resting on the top of his forehead, and taking a comfortable position in his chair, placed his feet, where he had a perfect right to place them, being in a land of Liberty, and in his own house, *upon the top of the table*. The prisoner, who had been found asleep in his chair at his own dinner table, was taken away suddenly, like Cincinnatus or Putnam from the plough, and brought into court, *just as he was*, in his shirt sleeves, and placed at the other end of the table, opposite the feet of Gamaliel. Lawyer Chandler, who was always on hand to help the 'Squire along in all knotty cases, appeared with book in hand ready to lay down the law and testimony. Lawyer Stebbins was allowed by the courtesy of the court to take his seat by the side of the prisoner to see that he had fair play shown him. Bill Cleaves, the constable, took his seat a little behind the 'Squire, crossed his legs, and fell to smoking a cigar with great composure.

'Squire Winslow's faithful bull dog, Jowler, whose duty it was to keep order in the house, took his watchful station under the table, directly under his master's feet, ready for any emergency. While the constable's dog, Trip, who had done his part in running down the game and getting it housed, felt that his duties were over, and caring but little for the court scene, he had stretched himself upon the floor, and was as sound asleep as ever John Wadleigh was in church. The other witnesses and spectators present were too numerous to mention.

The indictment was read, and the prisoner called upon to answer, who, at the suggestion of Lawyer Stebbins, replied, "Not guilty;" at which Deacon 'Squire Winslow shook his head, and remarked in a low tone, "We shall see about that."

The first point made by Lawyer Chandler, was, that *the prisoner should prove his innocence;* and he argued the point with much force and eloquence. It was no easy matter to prove that a man was actually asleep, but it was easy enough for a man to prove that he was awake. Therefore, from the nature of the case, the burden of the proof ought to lay upon the prisoner. "Now, we charge that on sundry occasions, Wadleigh was asleep in church, against the laws of the town and the well-being of society. Now, if he was not so asleep, let him prove his *alibi.* A criminal always has a right to an *alibi* if he can prove it. May it please your honor, I take that ground," said Chandler, "and there I stick; I call upon the prisoner to prove his *alibi.*"

Lawyer Stebbins stoutly contended that the *alibi* could not apply in this case. He had never heard nor read of its being used in any case except murder. And the wisdom of the court finally overruled that it belonged to the prosecutors to prove the sleep.

"Well, if that be the case," said Chandler, "I move, your honor, that Solomon Young be sworn. I had no idea the burden of proof was going to lay on us, but still I've come prepared for it."

Solomon Young was sworn, and took the stand.

Question by Chandler.—Do you know that John Wadleigh sleeps in meeting?

Witness.—I guess taint no secret; I don't know anybody but what does know it.

Chandler.—Well, do *you* know it? That's the question.

Stebbins objected to the question. It was a leading question, and they had no right to put leading questions to the witness.

Chandler.—Well, then, let the court put the questions.

Justice Winslow.— *What* do you know about John Wadleigh's sleeping in meeting?

Witness.—I know *all* about it; taint no secret, I guess.

Justice.—Then tell us all about it; that's just what we want to know.

Witness (scratching his head).—Well, the long and short of it is, John Wadleigh is a hard worken man. That is, he works mighty hard doing nothing; and that's the hardest work there is done. It'll make a feller sleepy quicker than poppy leaves. So it stands to reason that Wadleigh would naterally be a very sleepy sort of a person. Well, Parson Moody's sarmons are sometimes naterally pretty long, and the weather is sometimes naterally considerable warm, and the sarmons is some times rather heavy-like.

"Stop, stop," said 'Squire Winslow, "no reflections upon Parson Moody; that is not what you were called here for."

Witness.—I don't cast no reflections on Parson Moody. I was only telling what I know about John Wadleigh's sleeping in meeting; and it's my opinion, especially in warm weather, that sarmons that are heavy-like and an hour long naterally have a tendency—

"Stop, stop, I say," said 'Squire Winslow, "if you repeat any of these reflections on Parson Moody again, I'll commit you to the cage for contempt of court."

Witness.—I don't cast no reflections on Parson Moody. I was only telling what I knew about John Wadleigh's sleeping in meeting.

'Squire Winslow.—Well, go on, and tell us all about that; you want called here to testify about Parson Moody.

Witness.—That's what I'm trying to do, if you wouldn't keep putting me out. And its my opinion in warm weather, folks is considerable apt to sleep in meeting; especially when the sarmon—I mean especially when they get pretty tired. I know I find it pretty hard work to get by seventhly and eighthly in the sarmon myself; but if I once get by there, I generally get into a kind of waking train again, and make out to weather it. But it isn't so with Wadleigh; I've generally noticed if he begins to gape at seventhly and eighthly, its a gone goose with him before he gets through tenthly, and he has to look out for another prop to his head somewhere, for his neck isn't stiff enough to hold it up. And from tenthly up to sixteenthly he's dead as a door nail; till the Amen brings the people up to prayers, and then Wadleigh comes up with a jerk, jest like opening a jack-knife.

Stebbins, cross-examining the witness.—Mr. Young, how do you *know* that Wadleigh is asleep on these occasions you speak of?

Witness.—Cause he is; everybody says he is."

Stebbins.—That won't do; we don't want you to

tell us what everybody says. You must tell *how* you know he is asleep?

Witness.—Well, cause he begins to gape at seventhly and eighthly, and props his head up at tenthly, and don't stir again till the Amen.

Stebbins.—Well how do you *know* he is asleep at that time?

Witness.—Cause when I see him settle down in that kind of way, and cover his face up so I can't see his eyes, I know he's asleep.

Stebbins.—That's no proof at all; the witness only knows he was asleep because he couldn't see his eyes.

Chandler.—Well, this witness has proved that the prisoner exhibited all the outward signs of sleep; now I will introduce one to show that he also exhibited internal evidence of being asleep. Your honor must know that it is a law in physics and metaphysics, and the universal science of medicine, that being deprived of one sense sharpens the other senses in a most wonderful degree. Now I move your honor that my blind friend here behind me, Jonathan Staples, be sworn.

Jonathan Staples was sworn accordingly.

Chandler.—Now, Staples, do you know that John Wadleigh sleeps in meeting?

Staples.—Yes, I du.

Chandler.—Do you *know* it?

Staples.—Yes, I know it.

Squire Winslow.—*How* do you know it?

Staples.—Why, don't I hear him sleep every Sabbath?

Chandler.—What is the state of your hearing?

Staples.—It is as sharp as a needle with two pints.

Chandler.—Can you always tell by a person's breathing, whether he is asleep or awake?

Staples.—Jest as easy as I can tell whether I'm asleep or awake myself.

Chandler.—Tell us where you sit in meeting, and how you know Wadleigh is asleep.

Staples.—Well, I goes to meeting of a Sabbath, and commonly takes my seat in the seventh seat at the west end of the meeting-house. And John Wadleigh he sets in the sixth seat, and that brings him almost right afore me. All the first part of the exercises he has a waking breath, till it gets along into the sarmon, say about seventhly or eighthly, and then he begins to have a sleepy breath; and when it gets along into tenthly, he commonly goes it like a porpus.

Squire Winslow.—Do you know him to be asleep at these times?

Staples.—I guess I du; I dont see how I could help it. I know him to be asleep jest as well as I know I'm awake.

Squire Winslow.—Well, that's sufficient, unless Mr. Stebbins wishes to ask any questions.

Stebbins.—Now, Staples, do you pretend to say that you can tell John Wadleigh's breath from the breath of any other person in meeting?

Staples.—Sartainly I do. Aint everybody's breath pitched on a different key? There's as much difference in breathing as there is in speaking.

Chandler.—I'm willing, your honor, to rest the cause here. I have a plenty more witnesses as good as these, but I consider the case so clearly proved that it is hardly necessary to bring on any more unless my friend Stebbins should offer anything on the other side which may need to be answered.

Stebbins.—I dont consider it necessary, may it please your honor, for me to say a single word. I dont consider that there has been the least particle of evidence offered here yet, to prove that John Wadleigh ever slept a wink in meeting in all his life. And surely your honor wont convict this man without any proof at all against him. Look at the evidence, sir; what does it amount to? One man has seen him lean his head, and another has heard him breathe; and that is the sum total. Why, sir, if you convict a man on such evidence as this, no man is safe. Every man, is liable to lean his head and to breathe in meeting. And if that is to be considered evidence of sleep, I repeat, who is safe? No, sir; as I said before, I dont consider it necessary for me to say one word on the subject, for there has been no evidence offered to prove the offence charged.

Here Lawyer Chandler rose with fire in his eyes and thunder on his tongue.

May it please your honor, said he, I am astonished, I am amazed at the hardihood and effrontery of my learned friend, the counsel on the opposite side of this cause. Why, sir, if there ever was a case made out in any court under heaven, by clear, positive, and irresistible evidence, it is this. Sir, I say, sir, evidence as clear as sunshine and irresistible as thunder. Yes, sir, as irresistible as thunder. First, sir, an unimpeachable witness swears to you, that he sees the culprit Wadleigh, the prisoner at the bar, gaping in meeting and exhibiting all the signs of going to sleep; then he sees him flatting away and muzzling about to find a prop for his head. Now, sir, men don't want a prop for their heads when they are awake. It's only

2

when they are asleep they want a prop for their heads,
sir. Well, now sir, follow the prisoner along a little
further, and what do we find, sir? Do we find him
wide awake, sir, and attending to the services as a
Christian and as a man ought to do? No, sir. We
find him from tenthly up to sixteenthly, as dead as a
door nail. Them's the witnesses' words, sir, as dead
as a door nail. What next, sir? Why, then the witness swears to you, that when the congregation rise
up to prayers, Wadleigh comes up with a jerk, jest
like opening a jack-knife. Them's the witnesses' very
words, sir. Now, sir, persons that's awake don't get
up in meeting in that kind of style. It's only them
that's waked up out of a sudden sleep, that comes up
with a jerk, like the opening of a jack-knife, sir.
What stronger proof do we need, or rather what
stronger proof could we have, of all the outward signs
of sleep, than we have from this witness? With regard
to the internal evidence of sleep, another witness
swears to you that he hears Wadleigh asleep every
Sabbath ; that he can tell when a person is asleep
or awake by his breathing, as easily as he can tell
whether he's asleep or awake himself. This witness swears to you that during the first part of the
exercises Wadleigh has a waking breath, and when

the minister gets along to seventhly and eighthly he begins to have a very sleepy breath. Well, sir, when the minister gets to tenthly, the witness swears to you that Wadleigh commonly goes it like a porpus. Yes, sir, so sound asleep, that's the inference, so sound asleep, that he goes it like a porpus.

Sir, I will not say another word. I will not waste words upon a case so strong, so clear, and so perfectly made out. If this evidence doesn't prove the culprit Wadleigh to be a common sleeper in meetin on the Lord's day, then there is no dependence to be placed in human testimony. Sir, I have done. Whether this man is to be convicted or not, I clear my skirts ; and when posterity shall see the account of this trial, should the culprit go clear, they may cry out " judgment has fled to brutish beasts and men have lost their reason ;" but they shall not say Chandler did not do his duty.

The effect of this speech on the court and audience was tremendous. It was some minutes before a word was spoken, or any person moved. All eyes still seemed to be rivetted upon Squire Chandler. At last Squire Winslow spoke.

This is a very clear case, said he ; there can be no question of the prisoner's guilt ; and he is sentenced

to be confined in the cage four hours, and in the stocks
one hour.   Constable Cleaves will take charge of the
prisoner, and see the sentence properly executed.

CHAPTER II.

YANKEE CHRISTMAS.

The autumnal holiday peculiar to New England is *Thanksgiving ;*
while in the middle and southern States the great domestic festi-
val is more generally at Christmas or New Year's. Whether the
following historical sketch, therefore, applies with more propriety
to Christmas or Thanksgiving, must depend in some degree upon
the latitude in which Mr. Solomon Briggs resides.

"NEXT Thursday is Christmas," said Mrs. Briggs,
as she came bustling out of the kitchen into the long
dining-room, and took her seat at the breakfast table,
where her husband, Mr. Solomon Briggs, and all the
children, being ten in number, were seated before
her. If Mrs. Briggs was the last at the table, the
circumstance must not be set down as an index to
her character, for she was a restless, stirring body,
and was never the last anywhere, without good
cause. From childhood she had been taught to
believe that the old adage, "the eye of the master
does more work than both his hands," applied
equally well to the mistress. Accordingly, she was

in all parts of the house at once, not only working
with her own hands, but overseeing everything that
was done by others.   Indeed, now that we have said
thus much in favor of Mrs. Briggs, a due regard to
impartial justice requires us to add, that Mr. Briggs
himself, though a very quiet sort of a man, and not
of so restless and mercurial a temperament as his
wife, could hardly be said to be less industrious.
His guiding motto through life had been—

> "He that by the plough would thrive,
> Himself must either hold or drive."

And most literally had he been governed by the
precept.   He was, in short, an industrious, thriving
New England farmer.   His exact location it is not
our purpose here to disclose.   We give our fair
readers, and unfair, if we have any, the whole range
of New England, from the shore of Connecticut to
the Green Mountains, and from Mount Hope to
Moosehead Lake, to trace him out.   But we shall
not point to the spot, lest Mr. Solomon Briggs, seeing
his own likeness brought home to his own door,
might think us impertinent for meddling with family
affairs.

To go back to our starting point—Mrs. Briggs,
who had stopped in the kitchen till the last moment,

in order to see the last dish properly prepared for breakfast, came herself at last to the table.

"Next Thursday is Christmas," said she, "and nothing done yet to prepare for it. I do wish we could ever have things in any sort of season."

At the mention of Christmas the children's eyes all brightened, from James, the eldest, who was twenty-one, down to Mary, who was but two years old, and who, of course, knew nothing about Christmas, but looked smiling and bright because all the rest did.

Mr. Briggs, however, who considered the last remark as having a little bearing upon himself, replied—"That he should think three days was time enough to get a Christmas dinner or a Christmas supper good enough for any common sort of folks."

"It would be time enough to get it," said Mrs. Briggs, "if we had anything to get it with; but we haven't a mite of flour in the house, nor no meat for the mince pies, and there aint no poultry killed yet, neither!"

"Well, well, mother," said Mr. Briggs, very moderately, and with a half smile, "just be patient a little, and you shall have as much Christmas as you want. There's a bushel of as good wheat as ever was ground, I put into a bag on Saturday; James can take a horse and carry it to mill this morning, and in two hours you may have a bushel of good flour. You've got butter enough and lard enough in the house, and if you want any plums or raisins, or any such sort of things, James may call at Haskall's store, as he comes home from mill, and get what you want. Then Mr. Butterfield is going to kill a beef critter this morning, and I'm going to have a quarter, so that before noon you can have a hundred weight of beef to make your mince pies of, and if that aint enough, I'll send to Mr. Butterfield's for another quarter. And then there is five heaping cart loads of large yellow punkins in the barn, and there is five cows that give a good mess of milk; and you've got spices and ginger, and molasses, and sugar enough in the house, so I don't see as there need be any difficulty but what we might have punkin pies enough for all hands. And as for the poultry, it'll be time enough to kill that to-morrow morning; and if two turkeys aint enough, I'll kill four, besides a bushel basket full of chickens. So now go on with your birds'-egging, and make your Christmas as fast as you please, and as much of it."

When this speech was ended, the children clapped

their hands and laughed, and said, "never fear
father—he always brings it out right at last."

From that hour forth, for three days, there was
unusual hurry and bustle throughout the house of
Solomon Briggs. In the kitchen particularly there
was constant and great commotion. The oven was
hot from morning till night, and almost from night
till morning. There was baking of pound cake, and
plum cake, and sponge cake, and Christmas cake,
and New Year's cake, and all sorts of cake that
could be found in the cook book. Then there
were ovens full of mince pies, and apple pies, and
custard pies, and all sorts of pies. The greatest
display of pies, however, was of the pumpkin tribe.
There were "punkin pies" baked on large platters for
Christmas dinner, and others on large plates for
breakfast and supper a month afterwards; and others
still, in saucers, for each of the small children. In
the next place, there was a pair of plum puddings,
baked in the largest sized earthen pots, and Indian
puddings and custard puddings to match. And then
the roastings that were shown up on the morning of
Christmas were in excellent keeping with the rest of
the preparations. Besides a fine sirloin of beef, two
fat turkeys were roasted, two geese, and a half a

2*

dozen chickens. And then another half dozen of chickens were made into an enormous chicken pie, and baked in a milk pan.

A query may arise, perhaps, in the mind of the reader, why such a profusion of food should be cooked up at once for a single family, and that family, too, not unreasonably large, though respectable in number, for it did not count over sixteen, including domestics, hired help and all. This is a very natural error for the reader to fall into, but it *is* an error nevertheless. This array of food was *not* prepared for a single family; but for a numerous company, to be made up from many families in the neighborhood. The truth was, Mr. Briggs was well to do in the world, a circumstance owing to his long course of patient industry and economical habits. Several of his children were now nearly men and women grown, full of life and fond of fun, as most young folks are. Mrs. Briggs also was very fond of society, and a little vain of her smart family of children, as well as of her good cooking. From these premises, a gathering of several of the neighbors at Mr. Briggs's house, to eat a Christmas dinner, and a still larger company of young folks towards night, to spend a Christmas evening would not be a very unnatural consequence. Such *was* the consequence, as we shall presently see.

We shall not stop to give a particular account of the dinner, as that was a transaction performed in the daytime, openly and above-board, and could be seen and understood by everybody; but the evening company, and the supper, and the frolic, as they were hid from the world by the darkness of the night, need more elucidation. We must not dismiss the dinner, however, without remarking that it fullfilled every expectation, and gave entire satisfaction to all parties. A table of extra length was spread in the long dining hall, which was graced by a goodly circle of elderly people, besides many of the middle-aged and the young. And when we state that the loin of beef was reduced to a skeleton; that two turkeys, one goose, and five chickens, vanished in the twinkling of a case-knife; that the large milk pan, containing the chicken-pie, was explored and cleared to the very bottom; and that three or four large puddings and a couple of acres of "punkin pie" were among the things lost in the *dessert*, we think it has been sufficiently shown that due respect was paid to Mrs. Briggs's dinner, and that her culinary skill should not be called in question.

"Now, James, who's coming here to-night?" said Susan, the eldest daughter, a bright, blue-eyed girl of eighteen. "Who have you asked? Jest name 'em over, will you?"

"Oh, I can't name 'em over," said James; "jest wait an hour or two and you'll see for yourself. I've asked pretty much all the young folks within a mile or two; as much as twenty of 'em I guess."

"Well, have you asked Betsy Harlow?" said Susan.

"Yes, and Ivory too, if that's what you want to know," said James.

"Nobody said anything about Ivory," said Susan, as the color came to her cheek, and she turned to go out of the room.

"Here, Suky, come back here," said James, "I've got something to tell you."

"What is it?" said Susan, turning round at the door, and waiting.

"They say Ivory is waiting on Harriet Gibbs; what do you think of that?" said James.

"I don't believe a word of it," said Susan, coloring still more deeply.

"Well, Harriet will be here this evening," said James "and then may be you can judge for yourself."

"Is her brother coming with her?" said Susan.

"George is coming," said James, "but whether she will come with him, or with Ivory Harlow, remains to be seen."

That Christmas was rather a cold day, and as night approached, it grew still colder.

"Pile on more wood," said Mr. Briggs, "get your rooms warm, so there shan't be no shiverin' or huddling about the fire this evening."

The boys were never more ready to start promptly at their father's bidding than they were on this occasion. The large fire-place in the long dining-room was piled full of round sticks of heavy wood almost up to the mantel; and the fires in the "fore room" and in the end room were renewed with equal bounty. By early candle light, the company began to drop in one after another, and by twos and threes in pretty frequent succession. There were stout boys in round jackets, and stouter boys in long-tailed coats, and rosy-cheeked girls in shawls, and blankets, and cloaks, and muffs, and tippets. Some of the middle-aged and elderly people who had remained to pass the evening, sat in the "fore room" with Mr. and Mrs. Briggs, while the young folks were huddled in' o the end room, till the supper table should be spr,ad in the long dining-hall.

"There's Ivory Harlow's bells," said James, as a sleigh came with a merry gingle up to the door; and instantly the windows were crowded with heads looking out to see who had come with him. Ivory lived about a mile and a half distant and was the only one who came with a sleigh that evening, as most of the others lived considerably nearer.

"Why, there's four of 'em, as true as I live," said Susan, as they crossed the stream of candle light, that poured from the windows and spread across the door yard. One of the younger boys had already opened the door, and in a moment more the new comers were ushered into the room, viz: Ivory Harlow and his sister Betsy, and Harriet Gibbs, and a strange gentleman, whom Ivory introduced to the company as Mr. Stephen Long, the gentleman who was engaged to keep the district school that winter. And then he turned and whispered to James, and told him that the master had arrived at their house that afternoon, as he was to begin the school the next day, so he thought he would bring him with him.

"That's jest right," said James, "I'm glad you did;" though at the same time his heart belied his words, for he felt afraid it would spoil half the fun of the evening. The boys and girls all at once put on long and sober faces, and sat and stood round the room as quiet as though they had been at a funeral. Presently Susan whispered to James and told him he ought to take the master into the "fore room," and introduce him to father and mother and the rest of the folks. "And I'd leave him there, if I was you," she added in a very suppressed whisper, lest she should be overheard.

James at once followed the suggestion of Susan, and took Mr. Stephen Long into the other room and introduced him to Mr. and Mrs. Briggs and the rest of the company, and a chair was of course set for Mr. Long, and he of course sat down in it and began to talk about the weather and other subjects of like interest, while James retreated back into the end room. The moment the master had left the room the boys and girls all began to breathe more freely, and to bustle about, and talk and laugh as merry as crickets. Not a few regrets were thrown out from one and another, that the school-master had been brought there to spend the evening, and some of them thought "Ive Harlow ought to a-known better, for he might know it would spoil half their play." But it seems they had not rightly estimated Mr. Stephen Long's social and youthful qualities, who, although two or three and twenty years old, was almost as much of a boy as any in the room. He had not been gone more than fifteen minutes before he came back into the room with the young folks again, much to the dismay of the whole company.

A cloud immediately settled upon their faces; all were whist as mice, and sober as deacons, till Mr. Stephen Long came across the room with an exceedingly droll expression of merriment upon his face, and gave James a hearty slap on the back, saying at the same time:

"Well, now, what's the order of the day here to-night? Dance, or forfeits, or blind man's bluff? I'm for improving the time."

At once the whole company burst out into a loud laugh, and several of the juniors, feeling such a burden suddenly removed from them, fell to pounding each other's shoulders, probably to prevent them in their lightness from flying of the handle.

"I guess we'll have something or other a going bime by," said James; "whatever the company likes best; but I guess we'll have supper first, for that's about ready."

The words were but just uttered when the call for supper was given, and the fore-room, and the end-room poured out their respective companies into the long dining-hall. It was soon perceived that, long as the table was, they could not all be seated at once, and there began to be some canvassing to determine who should wait. The elderly people must of course sit down, and the school-master must of course sit at the first table, and then it was decided that the youngest of the young folks should sit down too, because the eldest of the young folks chose to wait and eat by themselves. To this last arrangement there was one exception ; for Miss Harriet Gibbs, when she saw the school-master seated on one side of the table, had somehow or other, inadvertently of course, taken a seat on the other side directly opposite to him. And when, as the young folks were retiring from the room, Ivory Harlow looked at her and saw she had concluded to remain, Susan thought she saw considerable color come into Ivory's face.

When the first company at the table had eaten up two rows of pies clear round the board, including mince, apple and custard, and " punkin pies," of the largest class, together with a reasonable portion of various kinds of cakes and sweetmeats, and had given place to the second company at the table, who had gone through similar operations to a similar extent, the great dining-hall was speedily cleared of dishes, and chairs, and tables, and all such sorts of trumpery, that there might be nothing to impede the real business of the evening.

The elderly people were again seated in the fore-room, where a brisk fire was blazing so warmly that they could sit back comfortably clear to the walls; and around the hearth was a goodly array of mugs and pitchers of cider, and bowls heaped with mellow apples, red and yellow and green.

"Now, then, what shall we have to begin with?" said James.

"Blind man's buff," said George Gibbs.

"Suppose we have a quiet dance to begin with?" said Susan.

"Oh, I'd rather have something that has more life in it," said Harriet Gibbs; "let's have 'hunt the slipper,' or 'forfeits,' I don't care which.

"Oh get away with them small potatoes," said Bill Dingley; "let's go right into blind man's buff at once; that's the stuff for Christmas."

"You know we must please the ladies, Bill," said James Briggs, "I guess we'll have a sort of game at forfeits first, as Miss Gibbs proposed it."

"Well, agreed," said all hands.

Accordingly the company arranged themselves in a circle round the large hall, holding the palms of their hands together, and James took a piece of money between his hands and passed round to each one of the company, and made the motion to drop the money into the hands of each.

" Button, button, who's got the button?" said James to the head one, when he had been round the circle.

" Harriet Gibbs," was the reply.

" Button, button, who's got the button?" said James to the next.

" Betsey Harlow," answered the next.

At last, when James had been clear round the circle and questioned each one in like manner, he called out,

" Them that's got it, rise."

At once up hopped Sam Nelson, a sly little redheaded fellow about a dozen years old, whom no one suspected of having it, and of course no one had guessed him. Every one of the company, therefore, had to pay a forfeit.

" I move we redeem, before we go any further," said Ivory Harlow.

The motion was seconded all round, and the forfeits were accordingly collected, and James selecting a couple, held them over Harriet Gibbs's head.

" Whose two pawns are these ?" said he, " and what shall he and she do to redeem them ?"

" The lady shall kiss the schoolmaster," said Harriet, " and the gentleman shall go into the fore-room and kiss Mrs. Briggs.

" Miss Harriet Gibbs and Mr. Ivory Harlow go and do it," said James.

" Oh, la me ! I shant do no sich thing," said Harriet with a half scream.

" Then you don't have your ring again," said James.

" Well, then, I suppose I *must* do it, or I shall be setting a bad example to the rest," said Harriet. And away she run across the room to Mr. Stephen Long, and at once gave the whole company audible evidence that she had fully redeemed her ring.

Ivory Harlow walked leisurely into the fore-room. What he did there the young people could not certainly say, but from the hearty laugh that came from the elderly people there assembled, they inferred that he did *something*, and on his return James gave him up his pawn.

James then selected two more of the forfeits, and held them over Bill Dingley's head.

" Whose two pawns are these, and what shall he and she do to redeem them ?" said James.

"They shall kiss each other through a chair back," said Bill.

"Miss Susan Briggs and Mr. Stephen Long have got to do it," said James.

Whereupon Mr. Stephen Long readily took a chair and approached Miss Susan Briggs. But Miss Susan, when she saw the school-master coming towards her, holding a chair up to his face, and his lips poking through the back of it, colored up to the eyes and turned away.

"Do it, do it!" cried half the company, "or you shan't have your hankerchief."

Mr. Stephen Long seemed bent upon redeeming *his* pawn at any rate, and he followed Miss Susan with the chair with an earnestness that showed he did not mean to be baffled. When Miss Susan found herself cornered, and could retreat no further, she kissed her hand and tossed it at the chair.

"That wont do," cried half a dozen voices.

"I had to redeem mine," said Harriet Gibbs, "and it's no more than fair that she should redeem hers."

"Well, you may redeem mine too, if you are a mind to," said Susan, pushing the chair from her with her hand.

When Mr. Stephen Long found he could not

redeem his pawn through the chair, he declared he
would redeem it without the chair. So setting the
chair down, he commenced a fresh attack upon Miss
Susan, who held both hands tightly over her face.
After some violence, however, the company heard
the appropriate signal of triumph, but whether the
victory had been achieved upon cheek or hand,
always remained matter of doubt.

In redeeming the rest of the pawns, the penalties
were as various as the characters of the several persons who stood judges. One had to measure half a
dozen yards of love ribbon. One had to hop across
the room on one foot backwards. Another had to
kneel to the prettiest, bow to the wittiest, and kiss
the one he loved best. But when Bill Dingley stood
as judge, he declared he wasn't in favor of any half-
way punishments, and he accordingly adjudged the
delinquents to kiss every lady and gentleman in the
room ; that is, the lady to kiss the gentlemen, and the
gentleman to kiss the ladies, which penalties the
aforesaid delinquents performed according to the best
of their abilities.

When the game of pawns was over, the general
vote seemed to be in favor of blind man's buff.
James had to blind first, and he whirled about the

room, and flew from side to side, and corner to corner, with as much ease and boldness as though he had nothing over his eyes; and he kept the company continually flying from one end of the hall to the other, like a flock of frightened pigeons. He, however, killed them off pretty fast, by catching one after another, and sending them into the end room. While they were running for their lives, this way and that, Ivory Harlow couldn't help noticing that, somehow or other, Harriet Gibbs most always blundered into the same corner where the school-master was; and sometimes she would run right against him before she saw him; and then sometimes she would almost fall down, and the school-master would have to catch hold of her to keep her from falling. More than once that evening, Ivory wished he had not brought her, and more than twice he wished Susan Briggs might forget that he did bring her.

The brisk running and bustle at blind man's buff drew the elderly people to the door of the fore room, where they stood and looked on. When James had caught about half the company, Mrs. Briggs could not stand it any longer. She slipped off her shoes, and in she went right among them, and joined in the game; and she ran about lighter and quicker than any girl there. So much upon the alert was she, and moved about with such noiseless and nimble foot-steps, that she was in fact the very last to be taken. And when at last she was cornered and caught, James was a little puzzled to know who it was, for he felt almost sure he had caught all the large girls. But when he put his hand upon her head, and face, and neck, and shoulders, he exclaimed,

"Well done, mother; this is you. Now you shall blind."

"Oh, no, I can't do that, James," said Mrs. Briggs, retreating toward the fore-room.

"Yes, but you must," said James, "you are the last caught."

"Yes, yes, you must, you must," echoed the young folks from all sides.

"Well," said Mrs. Briggs at last, "if Mr. Briggs and the rest of 'em will come out and run, I'll blind."

The elderly people stood and looked at each other a minute, and at last they haw hawed right out, and then half a dozen of them came out upon the floor to join the game. The handkerchief was put upon Mrs. Briggs's eyes, and the old folks commenced running, and the old folks stepped heavy, and the young folks laughed loud, and there was a most decided racket.

Mrs. Briggs, however, soon cleared the coast, for she was spry as a cat, and caught her prey as fast as that useful animal would do when shut up in a room with a flock of mice.

When this run was over, the play went back again exclusively into the hands of the young folks, and after several of them had been blinded, it came at last to Bill Dingley's turn. Bill went into it like a day's work. He leaped upon his prey like a tiger among sheep. He ran over one, and tripped up another, knocked one this way and another that, and caught three or four in his arms at once. He made very quick work of it, and caught them all off, but when he got through, two or three were rubbing the bruises on their heads, and one was bleeding at the nose. This wound up the blind man's buff.

Mrs. Briggs then came out and told Susan to get a table out in the middle of the room. She then brought forward a couple of nice little loaves of Christmas cake, and placed them on a couple of plates, and cut them up into as many slices as there were young folks present, men and women grown.

"Now," said Mrs. Briggs, "we'll see which of you is going to be married first. These two cakes have each of 'em a Christmas ring in them; and which-

8

ever gets the slice that has the ring in it, will be married before the year is out. So all the gals over sixteen years old stand up in a row on one side, and all the young men over eighteen stand up in a row on the other side, and I'll pass the cake round."

She carried it round to the young men first, and each took a slice and commenced eating to ascertain who had the ring.

"By jings, I haven't got it," said Billy Dingley, swallowing his cake at three mouthfuls.

"May be you've swallowed it," said George Gibbs.

"Well, them that's got it," said Mrs. Briggs, "please to keep quiet till we find out which of the gals has the other."

She then passed the cake round to the young ladies. When she came to Susan, Harriet Gibbs, who was standing by her side, said:

"It's no use for any of the rest of us to try, for Susan knows which slice 'tis in, and she'll get it."

"No, that isn't fair," said Mrs. Briggs; "I put the rings in myself, and nobody else knows anything about it."

The young ladies then took their slices, and Mrs. Briggs passed on to Sally Dingley, Bill's sister, who being on the wrong side of forty, did not stand in the row, and rather declined taking the cake. Mrs. Briggs urged her, and told her she must take some; when Bill suddenly called out:

"Take hold, Sal, take hold and try your luck; as long as there's life there's hope."

Miss Sally Dingley run across the room and boxed Bill's ears, and then came back and said she'd take a piece of cake.

"For who knows," said she, "but what I shall get the ring; and who knows but what I shall be married before any of you, now?"

After the young ladies had eaten their cake, Mrs. Briggs called upon them that had the rings to step forward into the floor. Upon which, Ivory Harlow stepped out on one side, and Harriet Gibbs on the other.

"Ah, that ain't fair; that's cheatin, that's cheatin," cried out little Sam Nelson.

"Why, what do you mean by that, Sam?" said Mrs. Briggs.

"Cause," said Sam, "I see Susan, when she was eating the cake, take the ring out of her mouth, and slip it into Harriet Gibbs's hand."

At this Susan blushed, Harriet looked angry, and the company laughed.

By this time it was twelve o'clock, and the elderly people began to think it was time for them to be moving homeward.　And as soon as they were gone, the young folks put on their shawls and cloaks and hats, and prepared to follow them.　Before they went, however, Ivory Harlow got a chance to whisper to Susan Briggs, and tell her, that he supposed he should have to carry Harriet home this time, but it was the last time he should ever carry her anywhere, as long as his name was Ivory Harlow.

CHAPTER III.

THE TOUGH YARN:

Major Grant of Massachusetts was returning home
from Moosehead Lake, where he had been to look
after one of his newly-purchased townships, and to
sell stumpage to the loggers for the ensuing winter,
when he stopped for the night at a snug tavern in one
of the back towns in Maine, and having been to the
stable, and seen with his own eyes that his horse was
well provided with hay and grain, he returned to the
bar-room, laid aside his cloak, and took a seat by the
box stove, which was waging a hot war with the cold
and raw atmosphere of November.

The major was a large, portly man, well to do in
the world, and loved his comfort. Having called for
a mug of hot flip, he loaded his long pipe, and prepared for a long and comfortable smoke. He was
also a very social man, and there being but one person
in the room with him, he invited him to join him in
a tumbler of flip. This gentleman was Doctor Snow,

an active member of a temperance society, and therefore he politely begged to be excused; but having a good share of the volubility natural to his profession, he readily entered into conversation with the major, answered many of his inquiries about the townships in that section of the State, described minutely the process of lumbering, explained how it might be made profitable, and showed why it was often attended with great loss. A half hour thus passed imperceptibly away, and the doctor rose, drew his wrapper close about him, and placed his cap on his head. The major looked round the room with an air of uneasiness.

"What, going so soon, Doctor? No more company here to-night, think? Dull business, Doctor, to sit alone one of these long tedious evenings. Always want somebody to talk with; man wasn't made to be alone, you know."

"True," said the doctor, "and I should be happy to spend the evening with you; but I have to go three miles to see a patient yet to-night, and it's high time I was off. But luckily, Major, you won't be left alone after all, for there comes Jack Robinson, driving his horse and wagon into the yard now; and I presume he'll not only spend the evening with you, but stop all night."

" Well, that's good news," said the Major, " if he'll only talk. Will he talk, Doctor ?"

" Talk ? yes ! till all is blue. He's the greatest talker you ever met. I'll tell you what 'tis, Major, I'll bet the price of your reckoning here to-night, that you may ask him the most direct simple question you please, and you shan't get an answer from him under half an hour, and he shall keep talking a steady stream the whole time, too."

" Done," said the major ; "'tis a bet. Let us under-stand it fairly, now. You say I may ask him any simple, plain question I please, and he shall be half an hour answering it, and talk all the time too ; and you will bet my night's reckoning of it."

" That's the bet exactly," said the doctor.

Here the parties shook hands upon it, just as the door opened, and Mr. Jack Robinson came limping into the room, supported by a crutch, and with some-thing of a bustling, care-for-nothing air, hobbled along toward the fire. The doctor introduced Mr. Jack Robinson to Major Grant, and after the usual saluta-tions and shaking of hands, Mr. Robinson took his seat upon the other side of the stove, opposite the major.

Mr. Jack Robinson was a small, brisk man, with

a grey twinkling eye, and a knowing expression of countenance. As he carefully settled himself into his chair, resting his lame limb against the edge of the stove-hearth, he threw his hat carelessly upon the floor, laid his crutch across his knee, and looked round with a satisfied air, that seemed to say, "Now, gentlemen, if you want to know the time of day, here's the boy that can tell ye."

"Allow me, Mr. Robinson, to help you to a tumbler of hot flip," said the major, raising the mug from the stove.

"With all my heart, and thank ye too," said Robinson, taking a sip from the tumbler. "I believe there's nothing better for a cold day than a hot flip. I've known it to cure many a one who was thought to be in a consumption. There's something so"—

"And I have known it," said the doctor, shrugging his shoulders, "to kill many a one that was thought to have an excellent constitution and sound health."

"There's something so warming," continued Mr. Robinson, following up his own thoughts so earnestly that he seemed not to have heard the remark of the doctor, "there's something so warming and so nourishing in hot flip, it seems to give new life to the blood, and puts the insides all in good trim. And as for cold weather, it will keep that out better than any double-milled kersey or fearnot great coat that I ever see.

"I could drive twenty miles in a cold day with a good mug of hot flip easier than I could ten miles without it. And this *is* a cold day, gentlemen, a real cold day, there's no mistake about it. This norwester cuts like a razor. But tain't nothing near so cold as 'twas a year ago, the twenty-second day of this month. That day, it seemed as if your breath would freeze stiff before it got an inch from your mouth. I drove my little Canada grey in a sleigh that day twelve miles in forty-five minutes, and froze two of my toes on my lame leg as stiff as maggots. Them toes chill a great deal quicker than they do on t'other foot. In my well days I never froze the coldest day that ever blew. But that cold snap, the twenty-second day of last November, if my little grey hadn't gone like a bird, would have done the job for my poor lame foot. When I got home I found two of my sheep dead, and they were under a good shed, too. And one of my neighbors, poor fellow, went into the woods after a load of wood, and we found him next day froze to death, leaning up against a

beech tree as stiff as a stake. But his oxen was alive
and well. It's very wonderful how much longer a
brute critter will stan' the cold than a man will.
Them oxen didn't even shiver."

" Perhaps," said the doctor, standing with his
back towards Mr. Robinson, " perhaps the oxen had
taken a mug of hot flip before they went into the
woods."

By this time Major Grant began to feel a little
suspicious that he might lose his bet, and was setting
all his wits to work to fix on a question so direct and
limited in its nature, that it could not fail to draw
from Mr. Robinson a pretty direct answer. He had
thought at first of making some simple inquiry about
the weather; but he now felt convinced that, with
Mr. Robinson, the weather was a very copious subject.
He had also several times thought of asking some
question in relation to the beverage they were drinking; such as, whether Mr. Robinson preferred flip to
hot sling. And at first he could hardly perceive, if
the question were put direct, how it could fail to
bring out a direct yes or no. But the discursive
nature of Mr. Robinson's eloquence on flip had already
induced him to turn his thoughts in another direction
for a safe and suitable question. At last he thought

he would make his inquiry in reference to Mr. Robinson's lameness. He would have asked the cause of his lameness, but the thought occurred to him that the cause might not be clearly known, or his lameness might have been produced by a complication of causes, that would allow too much latitude for a reply. He resolved, therefore, simply to ask him whether his lameness was in the leg or in the foot. That was a question which it appeared to him required a short answer. For if it were in the leg, Mr. Robinson would say it was in his leg; and if it were in his foot, he would at once reply, in his foot; and if it were in both, what could be more natural than that he should say, in both? and that would seem to be the end of the story.

Having at length fully made up his mind as to the point of attack, he prepared for the charge, and taking a careless look at his watch, he gave the doctor a sly wink. Doctor Snow, without turning or scarce appearing to move, drew his watch from beneath his wrapper so far as to see the hour, and returned it again to his pocket.

"Mr. Robinson," said the major, "if I may presume to make the inquiry, is your lameness in the leg or in the foot?"

"Well, that reminds me," said Mr. Robinson, taking a sip from the tumbler, which he still held in his hand, "that reminds me of what my old father said to me once when I was a boy. Says he, 'Jack, you blockhead, don't you never tell where anything is, unless you can first tell how it come there.' The reason of his saying it was this : Father and I was coming in the steamboat from New York to Providence; and they was all strangers on board—we didn't know one of 'em from Adam ; and on the way, one of the passengers missed his pocket-book, and begun to make a great outcry about it. He called the captain, and said there must be a search. The boat must be searched, and all the passengers and all on board must be searched. Well, the captain he agreed to it ; and at it they went, and overhauled everything from one end of the boat to t'other ; but they couldn't find hide nor hair of it. And they searched all the passengers and all the hands, but they couldn't get no track on't. And the man that lost the pocket-book took on and made a great fuss. He said it wasn't so much on account of the money, for there wasn't a great deal in it; but the papers in it were of great consequence to him, and he offered to give ten dollars to any body that

would find it. Pretty soon after that, I was fixin' up
father's berth a little, where he was going to sleep,
and I found the pocket-book under the clothes at the
head of the berth, where the thief had tucked it
away while the search was going on. So I took it,
tickled enough, and run to the man, and told him I
had found his pocket-book. He catched it out of my
hands, and says he, 'Where did you find it?' Says
I, 'Under the clothes in the head of my father's
berth.'

" ' In your father's berth, did you?' says he, and he
give me a look and spoke so sharp, I jumped as if I
was going out of my skin.

" Says he, ' Show me the place.'

" So I run and showed him the place.

" ' Call your father here,' says he. So I run and
called father.

" ' Now Mister,' says he to father, ' I should like to
know how my pocket-book come in your berth.'

" ' I don't know nothin' about it,' says father.

" Then he turned to me and says he, ' Young man,
how came this pocket-book in your father's berth?'

" Says I, ' I can't tell. I found it there, and that's
all I know about it.'

" Then he called the captain and asked him if he

knew us. The captain said he didn't. The man
looked at us mighty sharp, first to father, and then to
me, and eyed us from top to toe. We wasn't neither
of us dressed very slick, and we could tell by his looks
pretty well what he was thinking. At last he said
he would leave it to the passengers whether, under all
the circumstances, he should pay the boy the ten
dollars or not. I looked at father, and his face was
as red as a blaze, and I see his dander begun to rise.
He didn't wait for any of the passengers to give their
opinion about it, but says he to the man, "Dod-rot
your money! if you've got any more than you want,
you may throw it into the sea for what I care; but if
you offer any of it to my boy, I'll send you where a
streak of lightning wouldn't reach you in six
months."

" That seemed to settle the business; the man didn't
say no more to father, and most of the passengers
begun to look as if they didn't believe father was
guilty. But a number of times after that, on the
passage, I see the man that lost the pocket-book whisper to some of the passengers, and then turn and look
at father. And then father would look gritty enough
to bite a board-nail off. When we got ashore, as soon
as we got a little out of sight of folks, father catched

hold of my arm and gave it a most awful jerk, and says he, " Jack you blockhead, don't you never tell where any thing is again, unless you can first tell how it come there."

" Now it would be about as difficult," continued Mr. Robinson after a slight pause, which he employed in taking a sip from his tumbler, " for me to tell to a certainty how I come by this lameness, as it was to tell how the pocket-book come in father's berth. There was a hundred folks aboard, and we knew some of 'em must a put it in ; but which one 'twas, it would have puzzled a Philadelphia lawyer to tell. Well, it's pretty much so with my lameness. This poor leg of mine has gone through some most awful sieges, and it's a wonder there's an inch of it left. But it's a pretty good leg yet ; I can almost bear my weight upon it ; and with the help of a crutch you'd be surprised to see how fast I can get over the ground."

" Then your lameness is in the leg rather than in the foot ?" said Major Grant, taking advantage of a short pause in Mr. Robinson's speech.

" Well, I was going on to tell you all the particulars," said Mr. Robinson. " You've no idea what terrible narrow chances I've gone through with this leg."

"Then the difficulty *is* in the leg, is it not?" said Major Grant.

"Well, after I tell you the particulars," said Mr. Robinson, "you can judge for yourself. The way it first got hurt was going in a swimming, when I was about twelve years old. I could swim like a duck, and used to be in Uncle John's mill-pond along with his Stephen half the time. Uncle John, he always used to keep scolding at us and telling of us we should get sucked into the floome bime-by, and break our plaguy necks under the water-wheel. But we knew better. We'd tried it so much we could tell jest how near we could go to the gate and get away again without being drawn through. But one day Steeve, jest to plague me, threw my straw hat into the pond between me and the gate. I was swimming about two rods from the gate, and the hat was almost as near as we dared to go, and the stream was sucking it down pretty fast; so I sprung with all my might to catch the hat before it should go through and get smashed under the water-wheel. When I got within about half my length of it, I found I was as near the gate as we ever dared to go. But I hated to lose the hat, and I thought I might venture to go a little nearer, so I fetched a spring with all my might, and grabbed the hat and put it on my

head, and turned back and pulled for my life. At
first I thought I gained a little, and I made my hands
and feet fly as tight as I could spring. In about a
minute I found I didn't gain a bit one way nor t'other;
and then I sprung as if I would a tore my arms off;
and it seemed as if I could feel the sweat start all over
me right there in the water. I begun to feel all at
once as if death had me by the heels, and I screamed
for help. Stephen was on the shore watching me, but
he couldn't get near enough to help me. When he
see I couldn't gain any, and heard me scream, he was
about as scared as I was, and turned and run towards
the mill, and screamed for uncle as loud as he could
bawl. In a minute uncle come running to the mill-
pond, and got there jest time enough to see me going
through the gate feet foremost. Uncle said, if he
should live to be as old as Methuselah, he should never
forget what a beseeching look my eyes had as I lifted
up my hands towards him and then sunk guggling
into the floome. He knew I should be smashed all to
pieces under the great water-wheel : but he run round
as fast as he could to the tail of the mill to be ready
to pick up my mangled body when it got through, so
I might be carried home and buried. Presently he
see me drifting along in the white foam that came out

from under the mill, and he got a pole with a hook to it and drawed me to the shore. He found I was not jammed all to pieces as he expected, though he couldn't see any signs of life. But having considerable doctor skill, he went to work upon me, and rolled me over, and rubbed me, and worked upon me, till bime-by I began to groan and breathe. And at last I come to, so I could speak. They carried me home and sent for a doctor to examine me. My left foot and leg was terribly bruised, and one of the bones broke, and that was all the hurt there was on me. I must have gone lengthways right in between two buckets of the water-wheel, and that saved my life. But this poor leg and foot got such a bruising I wasn't able to go a step on it for three months, and never got entirely over it to this day."

"Then your lameness is in the leg and foot both, is it not?" said Major Grant, hoping at this favorable point to get an answer to this question.

"Oh, it wasn't that bruising under the mill-wheel," said Mr. Jack Robinson, "that caused this lameness, though I've no doubt it caused a part of it and helps to make it worse; but it wasn't the principal cause. I've had tougher scrapes than that in my day, and I was going on to tell you what I s'pose hurt my leg more than anything else ever happened to it. When I was about eighteen years old I was the greatest hunter there was within twenty miles round. I had a first-rate little fowling-piece; she would carry as true as a hair. I could hit a squirrel fifty yards twenty times running. And at all the thanksgiving shooting-matches I used to pop off the geese and turkeys so fast, it spoilt all their fun; and they got so at last they wouldn't let me fire till all the rest had fired round three times a piece. And when all of 'em had fired at a turkey three times and couldn't hit it, they would say, 'well, that turkey belongs to Jack Robinson.' So I would up and fire and pop it over. Well, I used to be almost everlastingly a gunning; and father would fret and scold, because whenever there was any work to do, Jack was always off in the woods. One day I started to go over Bear Mountain, about two miles from home, to see if I couldn't kill some raccoons; and I took my brother Ned, who was three years younger than myself, with me to help bring home the game. We took some bread and cheese and doughnuts in our pockets, for we calculated to be gone all day, and I shouldered my little fowling-piece, and took a plenty of powder and shot and small bullets, and off we started through

the woods. When we got round the other side of
Bear Mountain, where I had always had the best luck
in hunting, it was about noon. On the way I had
killed a couple of grey squirrels, a large fat raccoon,
and a hedge-hog. We sot down under a large beech
tree to eat our bread and cheese. As we sot eating,
we looked up into the tree, and it was very full of
beechnuts. They were about ripe, but there had not
been frost enough to make them drop much from the
tree. So says I to Ned, Let us take some sticks and
climb this tree and beat off some nuts to carry home.
So we got some sticks, and up we went. We hadn't
but jest got cleverly up into the body of the tree,
before we heard something crackling among the
bushes a few rods off. We looked and listened, and
heard it again, louder and nearer. In a minute we
see the bushes moving, not three rods off from the
tree, and something black stirring about among them.
Then out come an awful great black bear, the ugliest-
looking feller that ever I laid my eyes on. He looked
up towards the tree we was on, and turned up his nose
as though he was snuffing something. I begun to
feel pretty streaked; I knew bears was terrible
climbers, and I'd a gin all the world if I'd only had
my gun in my hand, well loaded. But there was no

time to go down after it now, and I thought the only
way was to keep as still as possible, and perhaps he
might go off again about his business. So we didn't
stir nor hardly breathe. Whether the old feller smelt
us, or whether he was looking for beechnuts, I don't
know; but he reared right up on his hind legs and
walked as straight to the tree as a man could walk.
He walked round the tree twice, and turned his great
black nose up, and looked more like Old Nick than
anything I ever see before. Then he stuck his sharp
nails into the sides of the tree, and begun to hitch
himself up. I felt as if we had got into a bad scrape,
and wished we was out of it. Ned begun to cry.
But, says I to Ned, 'It's no use to take on about it;
if he's coming up we must fight him off the best way
we can.' We climb'd up higher into the tree, and
the old bear come hitching along up after us. I
made Ned go up above me, and, as I had a pretty
good club in my hand, I thought I might be able to
keep the old feller down. He didn't seem to stop for
the beechnuts, but kept climbing right up towards
us. When he got up pretty near I poked my club at
him, and he showed his teeth and growled. Says I,
'Ned, scrabble up a little higher.' We clim up two
or three limbs higher, and the old bear followed close

after. When he got up so he could almost touch my feet, I thought it was time to begin to fight. So I up with my club and tried to fetch him a pelt over the nose. And the very first blow he knocked the club right out of my hand, with his great nigger paw, as easy as I could knock it out of the hand of a baby a year old. I begun to think then it was gone goose with us. However, I took Ned's club, and thought I'd try once more; but he knocked it out of my hand like a feather, and made another hitch and grabbed at my feet. We scrabbled up the tree, and he after us, till we got almost to the top of the tree. At last I had to stop a little for Ned, and the old bear clinched my feet. First he stuck his claw into 'em, and then he stuck his teeth into 'em, and begun to naw. I felt as if 'twas a gone case, but I kicked and fit, and told Ned to get up higher; and he did get up a little higher, and I got up a little higher too, and the old bear made another hitch and come up higher, and begun to naw my heels again. And then the top of the tree begun to bend, for we had got up so high we was all on a single limb as 'twere; and it bent a little more, and cracked and broke, and down we went, bear and all, about thirty feet, to the ground. At first I didn't know whether I was dead or alive. I guess we all lay still as much as a minute before we could make out to breathe. When I come to my feeling a little, I found the bear had fell on my lame leg, and give it another most awful crushing. Ned wasn't hurt much. He fell on top of the bear, and the bear fell partly on me. Ned sprung off and got out of the way of the bear; and in about a minute more the bear crawled up slowly on to his feet, and began to walk off, without taking any notice of us, and I was glad enough to see that he went rather lame. When I come to try my legs I found one of 'em was terribly smashed, and I couldn't walk a step on it. So I told Ned to hand me my gun, and to go home as fast as he could go, and get the horse and father, and come and carry me home.

"Ned went off upon the quick trot, as if he was after the doctor. But the blundering critter—Ned always was a great blunderer—lost his way and wandered about in the woods all night, and didn't get home till sunrise next morning. The way I spent the night wasn't very comfortable, I can tell ye. Jest before dark it begun to rain, and I looked round to try to find some kind of a shelter. At last I see a great tree, lying on the ground a little ways off, that seemed to be holler. I crawled along to it, and found there was a holler in one end large enough for me to creep into. So in I went, and in order to get entirely out of the way of the spattering of the rain, and keep myself dry, I crept in as much as ten feet. I laid there and rested myself as well as I could, though my leg pained me too much to sleep. Some time in the night, all at once, I heerd a sort of rustling noise at the end of the log where I come in. My hair stood right on eend. It was dark as Egypt; I couldn't see the least thing, but I could hear the rustling noise again, and it sounded as if it was coming into the log. I held my breath, but I could hear something breathing heavily, and there seemed to be a sort of scratching against the sides of the log, and it kept working along in towards me. I clinched my fowling-piece and held on to it. 'Twas well loaded with a brace of balls and some shot besides. But whether to fire, or what to do, I couldn't tell. I was sure there was some terrible critter in the log, and the rustling noise kept coming nearer and nearer to me. At last I heerd a low kind of a growl. I thought if I was only dead and decently buried somewhere I should be glad; for to be eat up alive there by bears, or wolves, or cata- mounts, I couldn't bear the idea of it. In a minute more something made a horrible grab at my feet, and begun to naw 'em. At first I crawled a little further into the tree. But the critter was hold of my feet again in a minute, and I found it was no use for me to go in any farther. I didn't hardly dare to fire; for I thought if I didn't kill the critter, it would only be likely to make him fight the harder. And then again I thought if I should kill him, and he should be as large as I fancied him to be, I should never be able to shove him out of the log, nor to get out by him. While I was having these thoughts the old feller was nawing and tearing my feet so bad, I found he would soon kill me if I laid still. So I took my gun and pointed down by my feet, as near the centre of the holler log as I could, and let drive. The report almost stunned me. But when I come to my hearing again, I laid still and listened. Everything round me was still as death; I couldn't hear the least sound. I crawled back a few inches towards the mouth of the log, and was stopt by something against my feet. I pushed it. 'Twould give a little, but I couldn't move it. I got my hand down far enough to reach, and felt the fur and hair and ears of some terrible animal.

"That was an awful long night. And when the morning did come, the critter filled the holler up so

4

much, there was but very little light come in where I was. I tried again to shove the animal towards the mouth of the log, but I found 'twas no use,—I couldn't move him. At last the light come in so much that I felt pretty sure it was a monstrous great bear that I had killed. But I begun to feel now as if I was buried alive; for I was afraid our folks wouldn't find me, and I was sure I never could get out myself. But about two hours after sunrise, all at once I thought I heered somebody holler " Jack." I listened and I heered it again, and I knew 'twas father's voice. I answered as loud as I could holler. They kept hollering, and I kept hollering. Sometimes they would go further off and sometimes come nearer. My voice sounded so queer they couldn't tell where it come from, nor what to make of it. At last, by going round considerable, they found my voice seemed to be some where round the holler tree, and bime-by father come along and put his head into the holler of the tree, and called out, ' Jack, are you here?' ' Yes I be,' says I, ' and I wish you would pull this bear out, so I can get out myself.' When they got us out, I was about as much dead as alive; but they got me on to the horse, and led me home and nursed me up, and had a doctor to set my leg again; and it's a pretty good leg yet."

Here, while Mr. Robinson was taking another sip from his tumbler, Major Grant glanced at his watch, and, looking up to Doctor Snow, said, with a grave, quiet air, " Doctor, I give it up ; the bet is yours."

CHAPTER IV.

CHRISTOPHER CROTCHET.

YOUR New England country singing-master is a peculiar character; who shall venture to describe him? During his stay in a country village, he is the most important personage in it. The common school-master, to be sure, is a man of dignity and importance. Children never pass him on the road without turning square round, pulling off their hats, and making one of their best and most profound bows. He is looked up to with universal deference both by young and old, and is often invited out to tea. Or, if he "boards round," great is the parade, and great the preparation, by each family, when their "week for boarding the master" draws near. Then not unfrequently a well fatted porker is killed, and the spare-ribs are duly hung round the pantry in readiness for roasting. A half bushel of sausages are made up into "links," and suspended on a pole near the ceiling from one end of the kitchen to the other.

And the Saturday beforehand, if the school-master is to come on Monday, the work of preparation reaches its crisis. Then it is, that the old oven, if it be not "heaten seven times hotter than it is wont to be," is at least heated seven times; and apple-pies, and pumpkin-pies, and mince-pies are turned out by dozens, and packed away in closet and cellar for the coming week. And the "fore room," which has not had a fire in it for the winter, is now duly washed and scrubbed and put to rights, and wood is heaped on the fire with a liberal hand, till the room itself becomes almost another oven. George is up betimes on Monday morning to go with his hand-sled and bring the master's trunk; Betsey and Sally are rigged out in their best calico gowns, the little ones have their faces washed and their hair combed with more than ordinary care, and the mother's cap has an extra crimp. And all this stir and preparation for the common school-master. And yet he is but an every-day planet, that moves in a regular orbit, and comes round at least every winter.

But the *singing-master* is your true comet. Appearing at no regular intervals, he comes suddenly, and often unexpected. Brilliant, mysterious and erratic, no wonder that he attracts all eyes, and produces a tremendous sensation. Not only the children, but the whole family, flock to the windows when he passes, and a face may be seen at every pane of glass, eagerly peering out to catch a glimpse of the singing-master. Even the very dogs seem to partake of the awe he inspires, and bark with uncommon fierceness whenever they meet him.

" O, father," said little Jimmy Brown, as he came running into the house on a cold December night, with eyes staring wide open, and panting for breath. " O, father, Mr. Christopher Crotchet from Quavertown, is over to Mr. Gibbs' tavern, come to see about keeping singing-school; and Mr. Gibbs, and a whole parcel more of 'em, wants you to come right over there, cause they're goin' to have a meeting this evening to see about hiring of him."

Squire Brown and his family, all except Jimmy, were seated round the supper table when this interesting piece of intelligence was announced. Every one save Squire Brown himself, gave a sudden start, and at once suspended operations; but the Squire, who was a very moderate man, and never did anything from impulse, ate on without turning his head, or changing his position. After a short pause, however, which was a moment of intense anxiety to some members of the family, he replied to Jimmy as follows:—

"I shan't do no sich thing; if they want a singing-school, they may get it themselves. A singing-school won't do us no good, and I've ways enough to spend my money without paying it for singing." Turning his head round and casting a severe look upon Jimmy, he proceeded with increasing energy:

"Now, sir, hang your hat up and set down and eat your supper; I should like to know what sent you off over to the tavern without leave."

"I wanted to see the singing-master," said Jimmy. "Sam Gibbs said there was a singing-master over to their house, and so I wanted to see him."

"Well, I'll singing-master you," said the Squire, "if I catch you to go off so again without leave. Come, don't stand there; set down and eat your supper, or I'll trounce you in two minutes."

"There, I declare," said Mrs. Brown, "I do think it too bad. I do wish I could live in peace one moment of my life. The children will be spoilt and ruined. They never can stir a step nor hardly breathe, but what they must be scolded and fretted to death."

Squire Brown had been accustomed to these

sudden squalls about twenty-five years, they having commenced some six months or so after his marriage; and long experience had taught him, that the only way to escape with safety, was to bear away immediately and scud before the wind. Accordingly he turned again to Jimmy, and with a much softened tone addressed him as follows:—

"Come, Jimmy, my son, set down and eat your supper, that's a good boy. You shouldn't go away without asking your mother or me; but you'll try to remember next time, won't you?"

Jimmy and his mother were both somewhat soothed by this well-timed suavity, and the boy took his seat at the table.

"Now, pa," said Miss Jerusha Brown, "you *will* go over and see about having a singing-school, won't you? I want to go dreadfully?"

"Oh, I can't do anything about that," said the Squire; "it'll cost a good deal of money, and I can't afford it. And besides, there's no use at all in it. You can sing enough now, any of you; you are singing half your time."

"There," said Mrs. Brown, "that's just the way. Our children will never have a chance to be anything as long as they live. Other folks' children have a chance to go to singing-schools, and to see young company, and to be something in the world. Here's our Jerusha has got to be in her twenty-fifth year now, and if she's ever going to have young company, and have a chance to be anything, she must have it soon; for she'll be past the time bime-by for sich things. 'Tisn't as if we was poor and couldn't afford it; for you know, Mr. Brown, you pay the largest tax of anybody in the town, and can afford to give the children a chance to be something in the world, as well as not. And as for living in this kind of way any longer, I've no notion on't."

Mrs. Brown knew how to follow up an advantage. She had got her husband upon the retreat in the onset a moment before, in reference to Jimmy's absence, and the closing part of this last speech was uttered with an energy and determination, of which Squire Brown knew too well the import to disregard it. Perceiving that a storm was brewing that would burst upon his head with tremendous power, if he did not take care to avoid it, he finished his supper with all convenient despatch, rose from the table, put on his great coat and hat, and marched deliberately over to Gibbs' tavern. Mrs. Brown knew at once that she had won the victory, and that they should have a singing-school. The children also had become so well versed in the science of their mother's tactics, that they understood the same thing, and immediately began to discuss matters preparatory to attending the school.

Miss Jerusha said she must have her new calico gown made right up the next day; and her mother said she should, and David might go right over after Betsey Davis to come to work on it the next morning.

"How delightful it will be to have a singing school," said Miss Jerusha: "Jimmy, what sort of a looking man is Mr. Crotchet?"

"Oh, he is a slick kind of a looking man," said Jimmy.

"Is he a young man, or a married man?" inquired Miss Jerusha.

"Ho! married? no; I guess he isn't," said Jimmy, "I don't believe he's more than twenty years old."

"Poh; I don't believe that story," said Jerusha, a singing-master must be as much as twenty-five years old, I know! How is he dressed? Isn't he dressed quite genteel?"

"Oh, he's dressed pretty slick," said Jimmy.

"Well, that's what makes him look so young," said

Miss Jerusha; "I dare say he's as much as twenty-five years old; don't you think he is, mother?"

"Well, I think it's pretty likely he is," said Mrs. Brown; "singing-masters are generally about that age."

"How does he look?" said Miss Jerusha; "is he handsome?"

"He's handsome enough," said Jimmy, "only he's got a red head and freckly face."

"Now, Jim, I don't believe a word you say. You are saying this, only just to plague *me*."

To understand the propriety of this last remark of Miss Jerusha, the reader should be informed, that for the last ten years she had looked upon every young man who came into the place, as her own peculiar property. And in all cases, in order to obtain possession of her aforesaid property, she had adopted prompt measures, and pursued them with a diligence worthy of all praise.

"No I ain't neither," said Jimmy, "I say he has got a red head and freckly face."

"La, well," said Mrs. Brown, "what if he has? I'm sure a red head don't look bad; and one of the handsomest men that ever I see, had a freckly face."

"Well, Jimmy, how large is he? Is he a tall man or a short man?" said Miss Jerusha.

"Why, he isn't bigger round than I be," said Jimmy; "and I guess he isn't quite as tall as a hay-pole; but he's so tall he has to stoop when he goes into the door."

So far from adding to the shock, which Miss Jeru-sha's nerves had already received from the account of the red head and freckly face, this last piece of intel-ligence was on the whole rather consolatory; for she lacked but an inch and a half of six feet in height herself.

"Well, Jimmy," said Miss Jerusha, "when he stands up, take him altogether, isn't he a good-looking young man?"

"I don't know anything about that," said Jimmy; "he looks the most like the tongs in the riddle, of anything I can think of:

> 'Long legs and crooked thighs,
> Little head and no eyes.'"

"There, Jim, you little plague," said Miss Jerusha, "you shall go right off to bed if you don't leave off your nonsense. I won't hear another word of it."

"I don't care if you won't," said Jimmy, "it's all true, every word of it."

"What! then the singing-master hasn't got no eyes, has he?" said Miss Jerusha; "that's a pretty story."

"I don't mean he hasn't got no eyes at all," said Jimmy, "only his eyes are dreadful little, and you can't see but one of 'em to time neither, they're twisted round so."

"A little cross-eyed, I s'pose," said Mrs. Brown, "that's all; I don't think that hurts the looks of a man a bit; it only makes him look a little sharper."

While those things were transpiring at Mr. Brown's, matters of weight and importance were being discussed at the tavern. About a dozen of the neighbors had collected there early in the evening, and every one, as soon as he found that Mr. Christopher Crotchet from Quavertown was in the village, was for having a singing-school forthwith, cost what it would. They accordingly proceeded at once to ascertain Mr. Crotchet's terms. His proposals were, to keep twenty evenings for twenty dollars and "found," or for thirty and board himself. The school to be kept three evenings in the week. A subscription-paper was opened, and the sum of fifteen dollars was at last made up. But that was the extent to which they could go; not another dollar could be raised. Much anxiety was now felt for the arrival of Squire Brown; for the question of school or no school depended entirely on him.

"Squire Brown's got money enough," said Mr. Gibbs, "and if he only has the will, we shall have a school."

"Not exactly," said Mr. Jones; "if *Mrs.* Brown has the will, we shall have a school, let the Squire's will be what it may."

Before the laugh occasioned by this last remark had fully subsided, Squire Brown entered, much to the joy of the whole company.

"Squire Brown, I'm glad to see you," said Mr. Gibbs; "shall I introduce you to Mr. Christopher Crotchet, singing-master from Quavertown?"

The Squire was a very short man, somewhat inclined to corpulence, and Mr. Crotchet, according to Jimmy's account, was not quite as tall as a hay-pole; so that by dint of the Squire's throwing his head back and looking up, and Mr. Crotchet's canting his head on one side in order to bring one eye to bear on the Squire, the parties were brought within each other's field of vision. The Squire made a bow, which was done by throwing his head upward, and Mr. Crotchet returned the compliment by extending his arm downward to the Squire and shaking hands.

When the ceremony of introduction was over, Mr.

Gibbs laid the whole matter before Mr. Brown, showed him the subscription-paper, and told him they were all depending upon him to decide whether they should have a singing-school or not. Squire Brown put on his spectacles and read the subscription-paper over two or three times, till he fully understood the terms, and the deficiency in the amount subscribed. Then without saying a word he took a pen and deliberately subscribed five dollars. That settled the business; the desired sum was raised, and the school was to go ahead. It was agreed that it should commence on the following evening, and that Mr. Crotchet should board with Mr. Gibbs one week, with the Squire the next, and so go round through the neighborhood.

On the following day there was no small commotion among the young folks of the village, in making preparation for the evening school. New singing-books were purchased, dresses were prepared, curling-tongs and crimping-irons were put in requisition, and early in the evening the long chamber in Gibbs' tavern, which was called by way of eminence "the hall," was well filled by youth of both sexes, the old folks not being allowed to attend that evening, lest the ' boys and gals" should be diffident about "sounding the notes." A range of long narrow tables was placed round three sides of the hall, with benches behind them, upon which the youth were seated. A singing-book and a candle were shared by two, all round the room, till you came to Miss Jerusha Brown, who had taken the uppermost seat, and monopolized a whole book and a whole candle to her own use. Betsey Buck, a lively, reckless sort of a girl of sixteen, who cared for nobody nor nothing in this world, but was full of frolic and fun, had by chance taken a seat next to Miss Jerusha. Miss Betsey had a slight inward turn of one eye, just enough to give her a roguish look, that comported well with her character.

While they were waiting for the entrance of the master, many a suppressed laugh, and now and then an audible giggle, passed round the room, the mere ebullitions of buoyant spirits and contagious mirth, without aim or object. Miss Jerusha, who was trying to behave her prettiest, repeatedly chided their rudeness, and more than once told Miss Betsey Buck, that she ought to be ashamed to be laughing so much; " for what would Mr. Crotchet think, if he should come in and find them all of a giggle ?"

After a while the door opened, and Mr. Christopher Crotchet entered. He bent his body slightly, as he passed the door, to prevent a concussion of his head against the lintel, and then walked very erect into the middle of the floor, and made a short speech to his class. His grotesque appearance caused a slight tittering round the room, and Miss Betsey was even guilty of an incipient audible laugh, which, however, she had the tact so far to turn into a cough as to save appearances. Still it was observed by Miss Jerusha, who told her again in a low whisper that she ought to be ashamed, and added that " Mr. Crotchet was a most splendid man ; a beautiful man."

After Mr. Crotchet had made his introductory speech, he proceeded to try the voices of his pupils, making each one alone follow him in rising and falling the notes. He passed round without difficulty till he came to Miss Betsey Buck. She rather hesitated to let her voice be heard alone ; but the master told her she must sound, and holding his head down so close to hers that they almost met, he commenced pouring his faw, sole, law, into her ear. Miss Betsey drew back a little, but followed with a low and somewhat tremulous voice, till she had sounded three or four notes, when her risible muscles got the mastery, and she burst out in an unrestrained fit of laughter.

The master looked confused and cross ; and Miss
Jerusha even looked crosser than the master. She
again reproached Miss Betsey for her rudeness, and
told her in an emphatic whisper, which was intended
more especially for the master's ear, " that such conduct was shameful, and if she couldn't behave better
she ought to stay at home."

Miss Jerusha's turn to sound came next, and she
leaned her head full half-way across the table to meet
the master's, and sounded the notes clear through,
three or four times over, from bottom to top and
from top to bottom ; and sounded them with a
loudness and trength fully equal to that of the
master.

When the process of sounding the voices separately
had been gone through with, they were called upon
to sound together ; and before the close of the evening
they were allowed to commence the notes of some
easy tunes. It is unnecessary here to give a detailed
account of the progress that was made, or to attempt
to describe the jargon of strange sounds, with which
Gibbs' hall echoed that night. Suffice it to say, that
the proficiency of the pupils was so great, that on the
tenth evening, or when the school was half through,
the parents were permitted to be present, and were

delighted to hear their children sing Old Hundred, Mear, St. Martin's, Northfield, and Hallowell, with so much accuracy, that those who knew the tunes, could readily tell, every time, which one was being performed. Mrs. Brown was almost in ecstasies at the performance, and sat the whole evening and looked at Jerusha, who sung with great earnestness and with a voice far above all the rest. Even Squire Brown himself was so much softened that evening, that his face wore a sort of smile, and he told his wife "he didn't grudge his five dollars, a bit."

The school went on swimmingly. Mr. Crotchet became the lion of the village ; and Miss Jerusha Brown "thought he improved upon acquaintance astonishingly." Great preparation was made at Squire Brown's for the important week of boarding the singing-master. They outdid all the village in the quantity and variety of their eatables, and at every meal Miss Jerusha was particularly assiduous in placing all the good things in the neighborhood of Mr. Crotchet's plate. In fact, so bountifully and regularly was Mr. Crotchet stuffed during the week, that his lank form began to assume a perceptible fulness. He evidently seemed very fond of his boarding-place, espe-

cially at meal time; and made himself so much at
home, that Mrs. Brown and Jerusha were in a state
of absolute felicity the whole week. It was true he
spent two evenings abroad during the week, and it
was reported that one of them was passed at Mr.
Buck's. But Miss Jerusha would not believe a word
of such a story. She said " there was no young folks
at Mr. Buck's except Betsey, and she was sure Mr.
Crotchet was a man of more sense than to spend his
evenings with such a wild, rude thing as Betsey
Buck." Still, however, the report gave her a little
uneasiness; and when it was ascertained, that during the week on which Mr. Crotchet boarded at Mr.
Buck's he spent every evening at home, except the
three devoted to the singing-school, Miss Jerusha's
uneasiness evidently increased. She resolved to make
a desperate effort to counteract these untoward influences, and to teach Miss Betsey Buck not to interfere
with other folk's concerns. For this purpose she
made a grand evening party, and invited all the young
folks of the village, except Miss Buck, who was point-
edly left out. The treat was elaborate for a country
village, and Miss Jerusha was uncommonly assiduous
in her attentions to Mr. Crotchet during the evening.
But to her inexpressible surprise and chagrin, about

eight o'clock, Mr. Crotchet put on his hat and great
coat and bade the company good night. Mrs. Brown
looked very blue, and Miss Jerusha's nerves were in
a state of high excitement. What could it mean?
She would give anything in the world to know where
he had gone. She ran up into the chamber and
looked out from the window. The night was rather
dark, but she fancied she saw him making his way
toward Mr. Buck's. The company for the remainder
of the evening had rather a dull time; and Miss
Jerusha passed almost a sleepless night.

The next evening Miss Jerusha was early at the
singing-school. She took her seat with a disconsolate
air, opened her singing-book and commenced singing
Hallowell in the following words:

> "As on some lonely building's top,
>   The sparrow tells her moan,
> Far from the tents of joy and hope,
>   I sit and grieve alone."

On former occasions, when the scholars were
singing before school commenced, the moment the
master opened the door they broke off short, even if
they were in the midst of a tune. But now, when
the master entered, Miss Jerusha kept on singing.
She went through the whole tune after Mr. Crotchet

came in, and went back and repeated the latter half
of it with a loud and full voice, which caused a laugh
among the scholars, and divers streaks of red to pass
over the master's face.

At the close of the evening's exercises Miss Jerusha hurried on her shawl and bonnet, and watched
the movements of the master. She perceived he
went out directly after Betsey Buck, and she hastened
after them with becoming speed. She contrived to
get between Miss Buck and the master as they
walked along the road, and kept Mr. Crotchet in close
conversation with her, or rather kept herself in close
conversation with Mr. Crotchet, till they came to the
corner that turned down to Mr. Buck's house. Here
Mr. Crotchet left her somewhat abruptly, and walked
by the side of Miss Betsey towards Mr. Buck's.
This was more than Miss Jerusha's nerves could well
bear. She was under too much excitement to proceed on her way home. She stopped and gazed after
the couple as they receded from her; and as their
forms became indistinct in the darkness of the night,
she turned and followed them, just keeping them in
view till they reached the house. The door opened,
and to her inexpressible horror, they both went in.
It was past ten o'clock, too! She was greatly

puzzled. The affair was entirely inexplicable to her. It could not be, however, that he would stop many minutes, and she waited to see the result. Presently a light appeared in the " fore-room ;" and from the mellowness of that light, a fire was evidently kindled there. Miss Jerusha approached the house and reconnoitred. She tried to look in at the window, but a thick curtain effectually prevented her from seeing anything within. The curtain did not reach quite to the top of the window, and she thought she saw the shadows of two persons before the fire, thrown against the ceiling. She was determined by some means or other to know the worst of it. She looked round the door-yard and found a long piece of board. She thought by placing this against the house by the side of the window, she might be able to climb up and look over the top of the curtain. The board was accordingly raised on one end and placed carefully by the side of the window, and Miss Jerusha eagerly commenced the task of climbing. She had reached the top of the curtain and cast one glance into the room, where, sure enough, she beheld Mr. Crotchet seated close by the side of Miss Betsey. At this interesting moment, from some cause or other, either from her own trembling, for she was exceedingly agitated, or from the board not being properly supported at the bottom, it slipped and canted, and in an instant one half of the window was dashed with a tremendous crash into the room.

Miss Jerusha fell to the ground, but not being much injured by the fall, she sprang to her feet and ran with the fleetness of a wild deer. The door opened, and out came Mr. Crotchet and Mr. Buck, and started in the race. They thought they had a glimpse of some person running up the road when they first came out, and Mr. Crotchet's long legs measured off the ground with remarkable velocity. But the fright had added so essentially to Miss Jerusha's powers of locomotion, that not even Mr. Crotchet could overtake her, and her pursuers soon lost sight of her in the darkness of the night, and gave up the chase and returned home.

Miss Jerusha was not seen at the singing-school after this, and Mrs. Brown said she stayed at home because she had a cough. Notwithstanding there were many rumors and surmises afloat, and some slanderous insinuations thrown out against Miss Jerusha Brown, yet it was never ascertained by the neighbors, for a certainty, who it was that demolished Mr. Buck's window.

One item farther remains to be added to this veritable history ; and that is, that in three months from this memorable night, Miss Betsey Buck became Mrs. Crotchet of Quavertown.

5

CHAPTER V.

POLLY GRAY AND THE DOCTORS.

It was a dark, and rainy night in June, when Deacon Gray, about ten o'clock in the evening, drove his horse and wagon up to the door, on his return from market.

"Oh dear, Mr. Gray!" exclaimed his wife, as she met him at the door, "I'm dreadful glad you've come; Polly's so sick, I'm afraid she won't live till mornin', if something ain't done for her."

"Polly is always ailing," said the deacon, deliberately; "I guess it's only some of her old aches and pains. Just take this box of sugar in; it has been raining on it this hour."

"Well, do come right in, Mr. Gray, for you don't know what a desput case she is in; I daren't leave her a minute."

"You are always scared half to death," said the deacon, "if anything ails Polly; but you know she always gets over it again. Here's coffee and tea and

some other notions rolled up in this bag," handing her
another bundle to carry into the house.

"Well, but Mr. Gray, don't pray stop for bundles
or nothin' else. You must go right over after Doctor
Longley, and get him here as quick as you can."

"Oh, if it's only Doctor Longley she wants," said
the deacon carelessly, "I guess she aint so dangerous,
after all."

"Now, Mr. Gray, jest because Doctor Longley is a
young man and about Polly's age, that you should
make such an unfeelin' expression as that, I think is
too bad."

The deacon turned away without making a reply,
and began to move the harness from the horse.

"Mr. Gray, ain't you going after the doctor?" said
Mrs. Gray, with increasing impatience.

"I'm going to turn the horse into the pasture, and
then I'll come in and see about it," said the deacon.

A loud groan from Polly drew Mrs. Gray hastily
into the house. The deacon led his horse a quarter
of a mile to the pasture; let down the bars and turned him in; put all the bars carefully up; hunted
round and found a stick to drive in as a wedge to
fasten the top bar; went round the barn to see that
the doors were all closed; got an armful of dry straw

and threw it into the pig-pen; called the dog from his kennel, patted him on his head, and went into the house.

" I'm afraid she's dying," said Mrs. Gray, as the deacon entered.

" You are always scared half out of your wits," said the deacon, " if there's anything the matter. I'll come in as soon as I've took off my coat and boots and put on some dry ones."

Mrs. Gray ran back to attend upon Polly; but before the deacon had got ready to enter the room, Mrs. Gray screamed again with the whole strength of her lungs.

" Mr. Gray, Mr. Gray, do make haste, she's in a fit."

This was the first sound that had given the deacon any uneasiness about the matter. He had been accustomed for years to hear his wife worry about Polly, and had heard her predict her death so often from very slight illness, that he had come to regard such scenes and such predictions with as little attention as he did the rain that pattered against the window. But the word *fit* was something he had never heard applied in these cases before, and the sound of it gave him a strange feeling of apprehension. He had just thrown off his boots and put his feet into dry shoes, and held a dry coat in his hand, when this last appeal came to his ear and caused him actually to hasten into the room.

"Polly, what's the matter now?" said the deacon, beginning to be somewhat agitated, as he approached the bedside.

Polly was in violent spasms, and heeded not the inquiry. The deacon took hold of her arm, and repeated the question more earnestly and in a tender tone.

"You may as well speak to the dead," said Mrs. Gray; "she's past hearing or speaking."

The deacon's eyes looked wild, and his face grew very long.

"Why didn't you tell me how sick she was when I first got home?" said the deacon with a look of rebuke.

"I did tell you when you first come," said Mrs. Gray, sharply, "and you didn't take no notice on it."

"You didn't tell me anything about how sick she was," said the deacon; "you only spoke jest as you used to, when she wasn't hardly sick at all."

The subject here seemed to subside by mutual consent, and both stood with their eyes fixed upon

Polly, who was apparently struggling in the fierce agonies of death. In a few minutes, however, she came out of the spasm, breathed comparatively easy, and lay perfectly quiet. The deacon spoke to her again. She looked up with a wild delirious look, but made no answer.

"I'll go for the doctor," said the deacon, "It may be he can do something for her, though she looks to me as though it was gone goose with her."

Saying this, he put on his hat and coat and started. Having half a mile to go, and finding the doctor in bed, it was half an hour before he returned with Doctor Longley in his company. In the meantime Mrs. Gray had called in old Mrs. Livermore, who lived next door, and they had lifted Polly up and put a clean pillow upon the bed, and a clean cap on her head, and had been round and "slicked up" the room a little, for Mrs. Livermore said, "Doctor Longley was such a nice man she always loved to see things look tidy where he was coming to."

The deacon came in and hung his hat up behind the door, and Doctor Longley followed with his hat in his hand and a small pair of saddle-bags on his arm. Mrs. Gray stood at one side of the bed, and Mrs. Livermore at the other, and the doctor laid his hat and saddle-bags on the table that stood by the window, and stepped immediately to the bed-side.

"Miss Gray, are you sick?" said the doctor, taking the hand of the patient.

No answer or look from the patient gave any indication that she heard the question.

"How long has she been ill?" said the doctor.

"Ever since mornin'," said Mrs. Gray. "She got up with a head-ache, jest after her father went away to market, and smart pains inside, and she's been growing worse all day."

"And what have you given her?" said the doctor.

"Nothing, but arb-drink," said Mrs. Gray; "when-ever she felt worse, I made her take a good deal of arb-drink, because that, you know, is always good, doctor. And besides, when it can't do no good, it would do no hurt."

"But what sort of drinks have you given her?" said the doctor.

"Well, I give her most all sorts, for we had a plenty of 'em in the house," said Mrs. Gray. "I give her sage, and peppermint, and sparemint, and cammermile, and pennyryal, and motherwort, and balm; you know, balm is very coolin', doctor, and sometimes she'd be very hot, and then I'd make her drink a good dose of balm."

"Give me a candle," said the doctor.

The deacon brought a candle and held it over the patient's head. The doctor opened her mouth and examined it carefully for the space of a minute. He felt her pulse another minute, and looked again into her mouth.

"Low pulse, but heavy and labored respiration," said the doctor.

"What do you think ails her?" said Mrs. Gray.

The doctor shook his head.

"Do you think you can give her anything to help her?" said the deacon, anxiously.

The doctor looked very grave, and fixed his eyes thoughtfully on the patient for a minute, but made no reply to the deacon's question.

"Why didn't you send for me sooner?" at last said the doctor, turning to Mrs. Gray.

"Because I thought my arb-drink would help her, and so I kept trying it all day till it got to be dark, and then she got to be so bad I didn't dare to leave her till Mr. Gray got home."

"It's a great pity," said the doctor, turning from the bed to the table and opening his saddle-bags.

"Thousands and thousands of lives are lost only by delaying to send for medical advice till it is too late; thousands that might have been saved as well as not, if only taken in season."

"But doctor, you don't think it's too late for Polly, do you?" said Mrs. Gray.

"I think her case, to say the least, is extremely doubtful," said the doctor. "Her appearance is very remarkable. Whatever her disease is, it has made such progress, and life is so nearly extinct, that it is impossible to tell what were the original symptoms, and consequently what applications are best to be made."

"Well, now, doctor," said Mrs. Livermore, "excuse me for speakin'; but I'm a good deal older than you are, and have seen a great deal of sickness in my day, and I've been in here with Polly a number of times to-day, and sometimes this evening, and I'm satisfied, doctor, there's something the matter of her insides."

"Undoubtedly," said the doctor, looking very grave.

This new hint from Mrs. Livermore seemed to give Mrs. Gray new hope, and she appealed again to the doctor.

5*

"Well, now, doctor," said she, "don't you think Mrs. Livermore has the right of it?"

"Most unquestionably," said the doctor.

"Well, then, doctor, if you should give her something that's pretty powerful to operate inwardly, don't you think it might help her?"

"It might, and it might not," said the doctor; "the powers of life are so nearly exhausted, I must tell you frankly I have very little hope of being able to rally them. There is not life enough left to indicate the disease or show the remedies that are wanted. Applications now must be made entirely in the dark, and leave the effect to chance."

At this, Mrs. Livermore took the candle and was proceeding to remove it from the room, when the doctor, perceiving her mistake, called her back. He did not mean to administer the medicine literally in a dark room, but simply in a state of darkness and ignorance as to the nature of the disease. It was a very strange case; it was certain life could hold out but a short time longer; he felt bound to do something, and therefore proceeded to prepare such applications and remedies as his best judgment dictated. These were administered without confidence, and their effect awaited with painful solicitude. They either produced no perceptible effect at all, or very different from the ordinary results of such applications.

"I should like," said Doctor Longley to the deacon, "to have you call in Doctor Stubbs; this is a very extraordinary case, and I should prefer that some other medical practitioner might be present."

The deacon accordingly hastened to call Doctor Stubbs, a young man who had come into the place a a short time before, with a high reputation, but not a favorite with the deacon and his family, on account of his being rather fresh from college, and full of modern innovations.

After Doctor Stubbs had examined the patient, and made various inquiries of the family, he and Doctor Longley held a brief consultation. Their united wisdom, however, was not sufficient to throw any light upon the case or to afford any relief.

"Have you thought of poison?" said Doctor Longley.

"Yes," said Doctor Stubbs, "but there are certain indications in the case, which forbid that altogether. Indeed, I can form no satisfactory opinion about it; it is the most anomalous case I ever knew."

Before their conference was brought to a close, the

deacon called them, saying he believed Polly was a going. They came into the room and hastened to the bedside.

" Yes," said Doctor Stubbs, looking at the patient, " those are dying struggles ; in a short time all her troubles in this life will be over."

The patient sunk gradually and quietly away, and in the course of two hours after the arrival of Doctor Stubbs, all signs of life were gone.

" The Lord's will be done," said the deacon, as he stood by the bed and saw her chest heave for the last time.

Mrs. Gray sat in the corner of the room with her apron to her face weeping aloud. Old Mrs. Livermore and two other females, who had been called in during the night, were already busily employed in preparing for laying out the corpse.

It was about daybreak when the two doctors left the house and started for home.

" Very singular case," said Doctor Stubbs, who spoke with more ease and freedom, now that they were out of the way of the afflicted family. " We ought not to give it up so, Doctor ; we ought to follow this case up till we ascertain what was the cause of ner death. What say to a post mortem examination?"

"I always dislike them," said Doctor Longley ; "they are ugly uncomfortable jobs ; and besides, I doubt whether the deacon's folks would consent to it."

"It is important for us, as well as for the cause of the science,'" said Doctor Stubbs, "that something should be done about it. We are both young, and it may have an injurious bearing upon our reputation if we are not able to give any explanation of the case. I consider my reputation at stake as well as yours, as I was called in for consultation. There will doubtless be an hundred rumors afloat, and the older physicians, who look upon us, you know, with rather an evil eye, will be pretty sure to lay hold of the matter and turn it greatly to our disadvantage, if we cannot show facts for our vindication. The deacon's folks *must* consent, and you had better go down after breakfast and have a talk with the deacon about it."

Doctor Longley felt the force of the reasoning, and consented to go. Accordingly, after breakfast, he returned to Deacon Gray's, and kindly offered his services, if there was any assistance he could render in making preparations for the funeral. The deacon felt much obliged to him, but didn't know as there was anything for which they particularly needed his assistance. The doctor then broached the subject of the very sudden and singular death of Polly, and how important it was for the living that the causes of such a sudden death should, if possible, be ascertained, and delicately hinted that the only means of obtaining this information, so desirable for the benefit of the science and so valuable for all living, was by opening and examining the body after death.

At this the deacon looked up at him with such an awful expression of holy horror, that the doctor saw at once it would be altogether useless to pursue the subject further. Accordingly, after advising, on account of the warm weather and the patient dying suddenly and in full blood, not to postpone the funeral later than that afternoon, the doctor took his leave.

"Well, what is the result?" said Doctor Stubbs, as Doctor Longley entered his door.

"Oh, as I expected," said Doctor Longley. "The moment I hinted at the subject to the deacon, I saw by his looks, if it were to save his own life and the lives of all his friends, he never would consent to it."

"Well, 'tis astonishing," said Doctor Stubbs, "that people who have common sense should have so little sense on a subject of this kind. I won't be baffled so, Doctor Longley; I'll tell you what I'll do. What time is she to be buried?"

" This afternoon," said Doctor Longley.

" In the burying-ground by the old meeting-house up the road, I suppose," said Doctor Stubbs.

" Yes, undoubtedly," replied Dr. Longley.

" Well, I'll have that corpse taken up this night, and you may depend upon it," said Doctor Stubbs, " I'll not only ascertain the cause of her death, but I want a subject for dissection, and she, having died so suddenly, will make an excellent one."

Doctor Longley shuddered a little at the bold project of Doctor Stubbs. " You know, Doctor, there is a law against it," said he, " and besides, the burying-ground is in such a lonely place and surrounded by woods, I don't believe you can find anybody with nerve enough to go there and take up a newly buried corpse in the night."

" Let me alone for that," said Doctor Stubbs. " I know a chap that would do it every night in the week if I wanted him to ; a friend of mine down there in the college, in the senior class. He has nerve enough to go anywhere, and is up to a job of this kind at any time. The business is all arranged, Doctor, and I shall go through with it. Joe Palmer is the man for it, and Rufus Barnes will go with him. I'd go myself, but it would be more prudent for me to be at home, for in case of accident, and the thing should be discovered, suspicion would be likely to fall on me, and it would be important for me to be able to prove where I was. Rufus must go to the funeral and see whereabouts the corpse is buried, so he can find the place in a dark night, and I shall have to go down to the college the first of the evening after Joe myself, and get him started, and then come right home, and stay at home, so that I can prove an alibi in case of any questions. Don't I understand it, Doctor ?"

"Yes, full well enough," said Doctor Longley, "but I had rather you would be in the scrape than I should."

That evening, half an hour after dark, there was a light rap at Joe Palmer's door in the third story of one of the college buildings. The door was partly open, and Joe said "Come in." No one entered, but in a few moments the rap was heard again. "Come in," said Joe. Still no one entered. Presently a figure, concealed under a cloak and with muffled face, appeared partly before the door, and said something in a low voice. Joe looked wild and agitated. Some college scrape, he thought, but what was the nature of it he could not divine. The figure looked mysterious. Presently the voice was heard again, and understood to utter the word Palmer. Joe was still more agitated, and looked at his chum most inquiringly. His chum stepped to the door and asked what was wanting. The figure drew back into the darkness of the hall, and answered in a faint voice, that he wanted Palmer. At last Palmer screwed his resolution up to the sticking point and ventured as far as the door, while his chum stepped back into the room. The figure again came forward and whispered to Palmer to come out, for he wanted to speak with him.

"But who are you?" said Palmer.

The figure partially uncovered his face, and whispered "Doctor Stubbs."

Palmer at once recognized him, and stepped back as bold as a lion, and took his hat and went out. In a few minutes he returned and told his chum, with rather a mysterious air, that he was going out with a friend to be gone two or three hours, that he need not feel uneasy about him, and might leave the door unfastened for him till he returned.

Doctor Stubbs, having given Joe and Rufus full directions how to proceed, telling them to get a large wide chaise, so that they could manage to carry the corpse conveniently, and informing them where they could find spades and shovels deposited by the side of the road for the purpose, left them and hastened home.

"Well now, Rufe," said Joe, "we'll just go over to Jake Rider's and get one of his horses and chaise. But we needn't be in a hurry, for we don't want to get there much before midnight; and we'll go into the store here and get a drink of brandy to begin with, for this kind of business needs a little stimulus."

Having braced their nerves with a drink of brandy, they proceeded to Jacob Rider's.

"Jake, give us a horse and chaise to take a ride three or four hours," said Joe. You needn't mind setting up for us; we'll put the horse up when we come back, and take good care of him; we know where to put him. We don't want a nag; an old steady horse that will give us an easy, pleasant ride."

"Old Tom is jest the horse you want," said Jacob, "and there's a good easy going chaise."

"That chaise isn't wide enough," said Joe; "give us the widest one you've got."

"But that's plenty wide enough for two to ride in," said Jacob; "I don't see what you want a wider chaise than that for."

"Oh, I like to have plenty of elbow room," said Joe.

"Maybe you are going to have a lady to ride with you," said Jacob.

Joe laughed, and whispered to Rufus that Jake had hit nearer the mark than he was aware of.

Jacob selected another chaise. "There is one," said he "wide enough for three to ride in, and even four upon a pinch."

"That'll do," said Joe; "now put in old Tom."

The horse was soon harnessed, and Joe and Rufus jumped into the chaise and drove off.

"Confound these college chaps," said Jacob to himself as they drove out of the yard; "they are always a sky-larkin' somewhere or other. There's one thing in it, though, they pay me well for my horses. But these two fellows wanting such a broad chaise; they are going to have a real frolic somewhere to night. I've a plaguy good mind to jump on to one of the horses and follow, and see what sort of snuff they are up to. It's so dark I could do it just as well as not, without the least danger of their seeing me."

No sooner thought than done. Jake at once mounted one of his horses, and followed the chaise. There was no moon, and the night was cloudy and dark; but a slight rattle in one of the wheels of the

chaise enabled him easily to follow it, though
entirely out of sight. Having gone about two miles
the chaise stopped at the corner, about a hundred
rods from the house of Dr. Stubbs. Jake got off
and hitched his horse, and crept carefully along by
the side of the fence to see what was done there.
By stooping down and looking up against a clear
patch of sky, he could see one of the two leave the
chaise and go to the fence by the side of the road,
and return again, carrying something in his arms to
the chaise. He repeated this operation twice; but
what he carried Jake could not discern. Perhaps
it might be some baskets of refreshments. They
were going off to some house to have a frolic. The
chaise moved on again, and Jake mounted his horse
and followed. They went up the road till they
came to the old meeting-house; they passed it a
little, and came against the old burying-ground.
The chaise stopped and Jake stopped. The chaise
stood still for the space of about five minutes, and
there was not the least sound to be heard in any
direction. At last, from the little rattle of the chaise
wheel, he perceived they were moving at a moderate
walk. They came to the corner of the burying-
ground, and turned a little out of the road and

stopped the chaise under the shadow of a large spreading tree, where it could not be perceived by any one passing in the road, even should the clouds brush away and leave it starlight.

" It is very odd," thought Jake, " that they should stop at such a place as this in a dark night; the last place in the world I should think of stopping at."

Jake dismounted and hitched his horse a little distance, and crept carefully up to watch their movements. They took something out of the chaise, passed along by the fence, went through the little gate, and entered the burying-ground. Here a new light seemed to flash upon Jake's mind.

" I hope no murder has been committed," thought he to himself; " but it's pretty clear something is to be buried here to-night that the world must know nothing about."

Jake was perplexed, and in doubt as to what he should do. He had some conscience, and felt as though he ought to investigate the matter, and put a stop to the business if anything very wicked was going on. But then there were other considerations that weighed on the other side. If murder had been committed, it was within the range of possibility, and not very unreasonable to suppose, that murder might be committed again to conceal it. There were two of them, and he was alone. It might not be entirely safe for him to interfere. He would hardly care to be thrown into a grave and buried there that night. And then, again, Jake was avaricious, and wouldn't care to break friends with those college fellows, for they paid him a good deal of money. On the whole, he was resolved to keep quiet and see the end of the matter.

Joe and Rufus walked two-thirds of the way across the burying-ground and stopped. Jake followed at a careful distance, and when he found they had stopped, he crept slowly up on the darkest side, so near that, partly by sight and partly by sound, he could discover what took place. There was not a loud word spoken, though he occasionally heard them whisper to each other. Then he heard the sound of shovels and the moving of the gravel.

"It is true," said Jake to himself, "they are digging a grave!" and the cold sweat started on his forehead. Still he resolved to be quiet and see it all through. Once or twice they stopped and seemed to be listening, as though they thought they heard some noise. Then he could hear them whisper to each other, but could not understand what they said. After they had been digging and throwing out gravel some time, he heard a sound like the light knock of a shovel upon the lid of a coffin.

"Take care," said Joe, in a very loud whisper, "it'll never do to make such a noise as that; it could be heard almost half a mile; do be more careful."

Again they pursued their work, and occasionally a hollow sound like a shovel scraping over a coffin was heard. At length their work of throwing out gravel seemed to be completed; and then there was a pause for some time, interrupted occasionally by sounds of screwing, and wedging, and wrenching; and at last they seemed to be lifting some heavy substance out of the grave. They carried it toward the gate. Jake was lying almost upon the ground, and as they passed near him, he could perceive they were carrying some white object about the length and size of a corpse. They went out at the gate and round to the chaise; and presently they returned again, and appeared by their motions and the sound to be filling up the grave. Jake took this opportunity to go and examine the chaise; and sure enough he found there a full-sized corpse, wrapped in a white sheet, lying in the centre of the chaise, the feet resting on the floor, the body leaning across the seat, and the head resting against the centre of the back part of the chaise.

"Only some scrape of the doctor's after all," said Jake to himself, who now began to breathe somewhat easier than he had done for some time past. "But it's rather shameful business, though; this must be Deacon Gray's daughter, I'm sure; and it's a shame to treat the old man in this shabby kind of way. I'll put a stop to this, anyhow. Polly Gray was too good a sort of a gal to be chopped up like a quarter of beef, according to my way of thinking, and it shan't be."

Jake then lifted the corpse out of the chaise, carried it a few rods farther from the road, laid it down, took off the winding-sheet, wrapped it carefully round himself, went back and got into the chaise, and placed himself exactly in the position in which the corpse had been left. He had remained in that situation but a short time before Joe and Rufus, having filled up the grave and made all right there, came and seated themselves in the chaise, one on each side of the corpse, and drove slowly and quietly off.

"I'm glad it's over," said Rufus, fetching a long breath. "My heart's been in my mouth the whole time. I thought I heard somebody coming half a dozen times; and then it's such a dismal gloomy place too. You would n't catch me there again, in such a scrape, I can tell you.."

"Well, I was calm as clock-work the whole time," said Joe. "You should have such pluck as I've got, Rufe; nothing ever frightens me."

At that moment the chaise wheel struck a stone, and caused the corpse to roll suddenly against Joe. He clapped up his hand to push it a little back, and instead of a cold clammy corpse, he felt his hand pressed against a warm face of live flesh. As quick as though he had been struck by lightning, Joe dropped the reins, and with one bound sprang a rod from the chaise and ran for his life. Rufus, without knowing the cause of this strange and sudden movement, sprang from the other side with almost equal agility, and followed Joe with his utmost speed. They scarcely stopped to take breath till they had run two miles and got into Joe's room at the college, and shut the door and locked themselves in. Here, having sworn Joe's chum to secrecy, they began to discuss the matter. But concerning the very strange warmth of the corpse they could come to no satisfactory conclusion. Whether it could be, that they had not actually taken up the corpse from the grave, but before they had got down to it some evil spirit had

6

come in the shape of the corpse and deceived them, or whether it was actually the corpse, and it had come to life, or whether it was the ghost of Polly Gray, were questions they could not decide. They agreed, however, to go the next morning by sunrise on to the ground, and see what discoveries they could make.

When Jacob Rider found himself alone in the chaise, being convinced that Joe and Rufus would not come back to trouble him that night, he turned about and drove back to the burying-ground.

"Now," said Jake, "I think the best thing I can do, for all concerned, is to put Polly Gray back where she belongs, and there let her rest."

Accordingly Jake went to work and opened the grave again, carried the corpse and replaced it as well as he could, and filled up the grave and rounded it off in good order. He then took his horse and chaise and returned home, well satisfied with his night's work.

The next morning, some time before sunrise, and before any one was stirring in the neighborhood, Joe and Rufus were at the old burying-ground. They went round the inclosure, went to the tree where they had fastened their horse, and looked on every side, but discovered nothing. They went through the gate, and across to the grave where they had been the night before. The grave looked all right, as though it had not been touched since the funeral. They could see nothing of the horse or chaise, and they concluded if the corpse or evil spirit, or whatever it was in the chaise, had left the horse to himself, he probably found his way directly home. They thought it best therefore immediately to go and see Jake, and make some kind of an explanation. So they went over immediately to Jake's stable, and found the horse safe in his stall. Presently Jake made his appearance.

"Well, your confounded old horse," said Joe, "would n't stay hitched last night. He left us in the lurch, and we had to come home afoot. I see he's come home, though. Chaise all right, I hope?"

"Yes, all right," said Jake.

"Well, how much for the ride," said Joe, "seeing we did n't ride but one way?"

"Seeing you rode *part way* back," said Jake, "I shall charge you fifty dollars."

Joe started and looked round, but a knowing leer in Jake's eye convinced him it was no joke. He handed Jake the fifty dollars, at the same time placing his finger emphatically across his lips; and

Jake took the fifty dollars, whispering in Joe's ear, "dead folks tell no tales." Jake then put his finger across his lips, and Joe and Rufus bade him good morning.

CHAPTER VI.

JERRY GUTTRIDGE.

OH, for "the good old days of Adam and Eve!" when vagabond idlers were not; or the good old days of the pilgrim fathers of New England, when they were suitably rewarded! That idlers could not bide those days, there is extant the following testimony. In the early court records of that portion of the old Bay State called the District of Maine, in the year 1656, we have the following entry of a presentment by a grand jury:—

"We present Jerry Guttridge for an idle person, and not providing for his family, and for giving reproachful language to Mr. Nat. Frier, when he reproved him for his idleness.

"The Court, for his offence, adjudges the delinquent to have twenty lashes on his back, and to bring security to the Court to be of better behavior in providing for his family."—[*A True Extract from the Court Records.*]

The whole history of this affair, thus faintly shadowed forth in these few lines, has recently come to light, and is now published for the benefit of the world, as hereafter followeth.

————

"What shall we have for dinner, Mr. Guttridge?" said the wife of Jerry Guttridge, in a sad, desponding tone, as her husband came into their log hovel, from a neighboring grog-shop, about twelve o'clock on a hot July day.

"Oh, pick up something," said Jerry, "and I wish you would be spry and get it ready, for I'm hungry now, and I want to go back to the shop; for Sam Willard and Seth Harmon are coming over, by an' by, to swop horses, and they'll want me to ride 'em. Come, stir around; I can't wait."

"We have n't got anything at all in the house to eat," said Mrs. Guttridge. "What shall I get?"

"Well, *cook* something," said Jerry; "no matter what it is."

"But, Mr. Guttridge, we have n't got the least thing in the house to cook."

"Well, well, *pick up something*," said Jerry, rather snappishly, "for I'm in a hurry."

"I can't make victuals out of nothing," said the wife; "if you'll only bring me anything in the world into the house to cook, I'll cook it. But I tell you we have n't got a mouthful of meat in the house, nor a mouthful of bread, nor a speck of meal; and the last potatoes we had in the house, we ate for breakfast; and you know we didn't have more than half enough for breakfast, neither."

"Well, what have you been doing all this fore-noon," said Jerry, "that you have n't picked up some-thing? Why did n't you go over to Mr. Whitman's and borrow some meal?"

"Because," said Mrs. Guttridge, "we've borrowed meal there three times that is n't returned yet; and I was ashamed to go again till that was paid. And beside, the baby's cried so, I've had to 'tend him the whole forenoon, and could n't go out."

"Then you a'n't a-goin' to give us any dinner, are you?" said Jerry, with a reproachful tone and look. "I pity the man that has a helpless, shiftless wife; he has a hard row to hoe. What's become of that fish I brought in yesterday?"

"Why, Mr. Guttridge," said his wife, with tears in her eyes, "you and the children ate that fish for your supper last night. I never tasted a morsel of it, and have n't tasted anything but potatoe sthese two days; and I'm so faint now I can hardly stand."

"Always a-grumblin'," said Jerry; "I can't never come into the house but what I must hear a fuss about something or other. What's this boy snivelling about?" he continued, turning to little Bobby, his oldest boy, a little ragged, dirty-faced, sickly-looking thing, about six years old; at the same time giving the child a box on the ear, which laid him his length on the floor. "Now shet up!" said Jerry, "or I'll larn you to be crying about all day for nothing."

The tears rolled afresh down the cheeks of Mrs. Guttridge; she sighed heavily as she raised the child from the floor, and seated him on a bench on the opposite side of the room.

"What is Bob crying about?" said Jerry, fretfully.

"Why, Mr. Guttridge," said his wife, sinking upon the bench beside her little boy, and wiping the tears with her apron, "the poor child has been crying for a piece of bread these two hours. He's eat nothing to-day but one potatoe, and I s'pose the poor thing is half starved."

At this moment their neighbor, Mr. Nat. Frier, a substantial farmer, and a worthy man, made his appearance at the door; and as it was wide open, he

walked in and took a seat. He knew the destitute
condition of Guttridge's family, and had often relieved
their distresses. His visit at the present time was
partly an errand of charity; for, being in want of
some extra labor in his haying field that afternoon,
and knowing that Jerry was doing nothing, while his
family was starving, he thought he would endeavor to
get him to work for him, and pay him in provisions.

Jerry seated himself rather sullenly on a broken-
backed chair, the only sound one in the house being
occupied by Mr. Frier, toward whom he cast sundry
gruff looks and surly glances. The truth was, Jerry
had not received the visits of his neighbors, of late
years, with a very gracious welcome. He regarded
them rather as spies, who came to search out the naked-
ness of the land, than as neighborly visitors, calling
to exchange friendly salutations. He said not a word;
and the first address of Mr. Frier was to little Bobby.

" What's the matter with little Bobby?" said he, in
a gentle tone; "come, my little fellow, come here
and tell me what's the matter."

" Go, run, Bobby; go and see Mr. Frier," said the
mother, slightly pushing him forward with her hand.

The boy, with one finger in his mouth, and the tears
still rolling over his dirty face, edged along sidewise

6*

up to Mr. Frier, who took him in his lap, and asked him again what was the matter.

"I want a piece of bread!" said Bobby.

"And won't your mother give you some?" said Mr. Frier, tenderly.

"She ha'n't got none," replied Bobby, "nor 'taters too." Mrs. Guttridge's tears told the rest of the story. The worthy farmer knew they were entirely out of provisions again, and he forbore to ask any further questions; but told Bobby if he would go over to his house, he would give him something to eat. Then turning to Jerry, said he :—

"Neighbor Guttridge, I've got four tons of hay down, that needs to go in this afternoon, for it looks as if we should have rain to-morrow; and I've come over to see if I can get you to go and help me. If you'll go this afternoon, and assist me to get it in, I'll give you a bushel of meal, or a half bushel of meal and a bushel of potatoes, and two pounds of pork."

"I can't go," said Jerry, "I've got something else to do."

"Oh, well," said Mr Frier, "if you've got anything else to do that will be more profitable, I'm glad of it, for there's enough hands that I can get; only I thought you might like to go, bein' you was scant of provisions."

"Do pray go, Mr. Guttridge!" said his wife, with a beseeching look, "for you are only going over to the shop to ride them horses, and that won't do no good; you'll only spend all the afternoon for nothin', and then we shall have to go to bed without our supper, again. Do pray go, Mr. Guttridge, do!"

"I wish you would hold your everlasting clack;" said Jerry; "you are always full of complainings. It's got to be a fine time of day, if the women are a-goin' to rule the roast. I *shall* go over and ride them horses, and it's no business to you nor nobody else; and if you are too lazy to get your own supper, you may go without it; that's all I've got to say."

With that he aimed for the door, when Mr. Frier addressed him as follows :—

"Now I must say, neighbor Guttridge, if you are going to spend the afternoon over to the shop, to ride horses for them jockeys, and leave your family without provisions, when you have a good chance to 'arn enough this afternoon to last them nigh about a week, I must say, neighbor Guttridge, that I think you are not in the way of your duty."

Upon this Jerry whirled round, and looked Mr.

Frier full in the face, "grinning horribly a ghastly smile," and said he,

"You old, miserable, dirty, meddling vagabond! you are a scoundrel and a scape-gallows, and an infernal small piece of a man, *I* think! I've as good a mind to kick you out of doors, as ever I had to eat! Who made *you* a master over me, to be telling me what's my duty? You better go home and take care of your own brats, and let your neighbors' alone!"

Mr. Frier sat and looked Jerry calmly in the face, without uttering a syllable; while he, having blown his blast, marched out of doors, and steered directly for the grog-shop, leaving his wife to "pick up something," if she could, to keep herself and children from absolute starvation.

Mr. Frier was a benevolent man and a Christian, and in the true spirit of Christianity he always sought to relieve distress wherever he found it. He was endowed, too, with a good share of plain common sense, and knew something of human nature; and as he was well aware that Mrs. Guttridge really loved her husband, notwithstanding his idle habits, and cold, brutal treatment to his family, he forebore to remark upon the scene which had just passed; but telling the afflicted woman he would send her something to eat, he took little Bobby by the hand, and led him home. A plate of victuals was set before the child, who devoured it with a greediness that was piteous to behold.

" Poor cre'tur !" said Mrs. Frier, " why, he's half starved ! Betsey, bring him a dish of bread and milk; that will set the best on his poor, empty, starved stomach."

Betsey ran and got the bowl of bread and milk, and little Bobby's hand soon began to move from the dish to his mouth, with a motion as steady and rapid as the pendulum of a clock. The whole family stood and looked on, with pity and surprise, until he had finished his meal, or rather until he had eaten as much as they dared allow him to eat at once ; for although he had devoured a large plate of meat and vegetables, and two dishes of bread and milk, his appetite seemed as ravenous as when he first began ; and he still, like the memorable Oliver Twist, " asked for more."

While Bobby had been eating, Mr. Frier had been relating to his family the events which had occurred at Guttridge's house, and the starving condition of the inmates; and it was at once agreed that something should be sent over immediately ; for they all said

"Mrs. Guttridge was a clever woman, and it was a shame that she should be left to suffer so."

Accordingly, a basket was filled with bread, a jug of milk, and some meat and vegetables, ready cooked, which had been left from their dinner; and Betsey ran and brought a pie, made from their last year's dried pumpkins, and asked her mother if she might not put that in, "so the poor starving cre'turs might have a little taste of something that was good."

"Yes," said her mother, "and put in a bit of cheese with it; I don't think we shall be any the poorer for it; for 'he that giveth to the poor lendeth to the Lord.'"

"Yes, yes," said Mr. Frier, "and I guess you may as well put in a little dried pumpkin; she can stew it up for the little ones, and it'll be good for 'em. We've got a plenty of green stuff a-growin', to last till pumpkins come again." So a quantity of dried pumpkin was also packed in the basket, and the pie laid on the top, and George was despatched, in company with little Bobby, to carry it over.

Mr. Frier's benevolent feelings had become highly excited. He forgot his four tons of hay, and sat down to consult with his wife about what could be done for the Guttridge family. Something must be done soon; he was not able to support them all the time; and if they were left alone much longer they would starve. He told his wife he "had a good mind to go and enter a complaint to the grand jury agin' Jerry, for a lazy, idle person, that did n't provide for his family. The court sets at Saco to-morrow, and don't you think, wife, I had better go and do it?"

His wife thought he had better go over first and talk with Mrs. Guttridge about it; and if she was willing he had better do it. Mr. Frier said, he "could go over and talk with her, but he did n't think it would be the least use, for she loved Jerry, ugly as he was, and he did n't believe she would be willing to have him punished by the court."

However, after due consultation, he concluded to go over and have a talk with Mrs. Guttridge about the matter. Accordingly, he took his hat and walked over. He found the door open, as usual, and walked in without ceremony. Here he beheld the whole family, including Jerry himself, seated at their little pine table, doing ample justice to their basket of provisions which he had just before sent them. He observed the pie had been cut into pieces, and one half of it, and he thought rather the largest half, was laid on Jerry's plate, the rest being cut up into small bits, and divided among the children. Mrs. Gut-tridge had reserved none to herself, except a small spoonful of the soft part with which she was trying to feed the baby. The other eatables seemed to be distributed very much in the same proportion.

Mr. Frier was a cool, considerate man, whose pas-sions were always under the most perfect control; but he always confessed, for years afterwards, "that for a minute or two, he thought he felt a little some-thing like anger rising up in his stomach!"

He sat and looked on until they had finished their meal, and Jerry had eaten bread, and meat, and vegetables enough for two common men's dinner, and swallowed his half of the pie, and a large slice of cheese by way of dessert; and then rose, took his hat, and without saying a word, marched deliberately out of the house, directing his course again to the grog-shop.

Mr. Frier now broached the subject of his errand to Mrs. Guttridge. He told her the neighbors could not afford to support her family much longer, and unless her husband went to work he did n't see but they would have to starve.

Mrs. Guttridge began to cry. She said "she did n't know what they should do; she had talked as long as talking would do any good; but somehow Mr. Guttridge did n't seem to love work. She believed it was n't his natur' to work."

"Well, Mrs. Guttridge, do you believe the Scriptures?" said Mr. Frier, solemnly.

"I'm sure I do," said Mrs. Guttridge; "I believe all there is in the Bible."

"And don't you know," said Mr. Frier, "the Bible says, 'He that will not work, neither shall he eat.'"

"I know there's something in the Bible like that," said Mrs. Guttridge, with a very serious look.

"Then do you think it right," said Mr. Frier, "when your neighbors send you in a basket of provisions, do you think it right that Mr. Guttridge, who won't work and 'arn a mouthful himself, should sit down and eat more than all the rest of you, and pick out the best part of it, too?"

"Well, I don't suppose it's right," said Mrs. Guttridge, thoughtfully; "but somehow, Mr. Guttridge is so hearty, it seems as if he would faint away, if he didn't have more than the rest of us to eat."

"Well, are you willing to go on in this way?" continued Mr. Frier, "in open violation of the Scriptures, and keep yourself and children every day in danger of starving?"

"What can I do, Mr. Frier?" said Mrs. Guttridge, bursting into a flood of tears; "I've talked, and it's no use; Mr. Guttridge, won't work; it don't seem to be in him. Maybe if you should talk to him, Mr. Frier, he might do better."

"No, that would be no use," said Mr. Frier. "When I was over here before, you see how he took it, jest because I spoke to him about going over to the shop, when he ought to be to work, to get something for his family to eat. You see how mad he was, and how provoking he talked to me. It's no use for me to say anything to him; but I think, Mrs. Guttridge, if somebody should complain to the Grand Jury about him, the Court would make him go to work. And if you are willing for it, I think I should feel it my duty to go and complain of him."

"Well, I don't know but it would be best," said Mrs. Guttridge, " and if you think it would make him go to work, I'm willing you should. When will the Court sit?"

"To-morrow," said Mr. Frier; "and I'll give up all other business, and go and attend to it."

"But what will the Court *do* to him, Mr. Frier?" asked Mrs. Guttridge.

"Well, I don't know," said Mr. Frier, "but I expect they'll punish him; and I know they'll make him go to work."

"Punish him!" exclaimed Mrs. Guttridge, with a troubled air. "Seems to me I don't want to have him punished. But do you think, Mr. Frier, they will hurt him any?"

"Well, I think it's likely," said Mr. Frier, "they will hurt him some; but you must remember, Mrs. Guttridge, it is better once to smart than always to ache. Remember, too, you'll be out of provisions again by to-morrow. Your neighbors can't support your family all the time; and if your husband don't go to work, you'll be starving again."

"Oh dear—well, I don't know!" said Mrs. Guttridge, with tears in her eyes. "You may do jest as you think best about it, Mr. Frier; that is, if you don't think they'll hurt him."

Mr. Frier returned home; but the afternoon was so far spent that he was able to get in only one ton of his hay, leaving the other three tons out, to take the chance of the weather. He and his wife spent the evening in discussing what course was best to pursue with regard to the complaint against Mr. Guttridge; but, notwithstanding his wife was decidedly in favor of his going the next morning and entering the com-

plaint, since Mrs. Guttridge had consented, yet Mr.
Frier was undecided. He did not like to do it; Mr.
Guttridge was a neighbor, and it was an unpleasant
business. But when he arose the next morning, looked
out, and beheld his three tons of hay drenched with
a heavy rain, and a prospect of a continued storm, he
was not long in making up his mind.

"Here," said he, "I spent a good part of the day,
yesterday, in looking after Guttridge's family, to keep
them from starving; and now, by this means, I've
nigh about as good as lost three tons of hay. I
don't think it's my duty to put up with it any
longer."

Accordingly, as soon as breakfast was over, Mr.
Frier was out, spattering along in the mud and rain,
with his old great-coat thrown over his shoulders, the
sleeves flapping loosely down by his side, and his
drooping hat twisted awry, wending his way to Court,
to appear before the Grand Jury.

"Well, Mr. Frier, what do *you* want?" asked the
foreman, as the complainant entered the room.

"I come to complain of Jerry Guttridge to the
Grand Jury," replied Mr. Frier, taking off his hat,
and shaking the rain from it.

"Why, what has Jerry Guttridge done?" said the

foreman. "I didn't think he had life enough to do anything worth complaining of to the Grand Jury."

"It's because he *has n't* got life enough to do anything," said Mr. Frier, "that I've come to complain of him. The fact is, Mr. Foreman, he's a lazy, idle fellow, and won't work, nor provide nothin' for his family to eat; and they've been half starving this long time; and the neighbors have had to keep sending in something all the time, to keep 'em alive."

"But," said the foreman, "Jerry's a peaceable kind of a chap, Mr. Frier; has anybody ever talked to him about it in a neighborly way, and advised him to do differently? And maybe he has no chance to work where he could get anything for it."

"I am sorry to say," replied Mr. Frier, "that he's been talked to a great deal, and it don't do no good; and I tried hard to get him to work for me yesterday afternoon, and offered to give him victuals enough to last his family 'most a week, but I couldn't get him to, and he went off to the grog-shop to see some jockeys swop horses. And when I told him, calmly, I did n't think he was in the way of his duty, he flew in a passion, and called me an old, miserable, dirty,

meddling vagabond, and a scoundrel, and a scape-
gallows, and an infernal small piece of a man!"

"Abominable!" exclaimed one of the jury; "who
ever heard of such outrageous conduct?"

"What a vile, blasphemous wretch!" exclaimed
another; "I shouldn't a wondered if he'd a fell dead
on the spot."

The foreman asked Mr. Frier if Jerry had "used
them very words."

"Exactly them words, every one of 'em," said Mr.
Frier.

"Well," said the foreman, "then there is no more
to be said. Jerry certainly deserves to be indicted,
if anybody in this world ever did."

Accordingly the indictment was drawn up, a warrant was issued, and the next day Jerry was brought
before the Court to answer to the charges preferred
against him. Mrs. Sally Guttridge and Mr. Nat.
Frier were summoned as witnesses. When the
honorable Court was ready to hear the case, the clerk
called Jerry Guttridge, and bade him to hearken to
an indictment found against him by the grand inquest
for the District of Maine, now sitting at Saco, in the
words following, viz:—

"We present Jerry Guttridge for an idle person,

and not providing for his family; and giving
reproachful language to Mr. Nat. Frier, when he
reproved him for his idleness." "Jerry Guttridge,
what say you to this indictment? Are you guilty
thereof, or not guilty?"

"Not guilty," said Jerry, "and here's my wife can
tell you the same any day. Sally, have n't I always
provided for my family?"

"Why, yes," said Mrs. Guttridge, "I don't know
but you have as well as "——

"Stop, stop!" said the Judge, looking down over
the top of his spectacles at the witness; "stop, Mrs.
Guttridge; you must not answer questions until you
have been sworn."

The Court then directed the clerk to swear the witnesses; whereupon, he called Nat. Frier and Sally
Guttridge to come forward, and hold up their right
hands. Mr. Frier advanced, with a ready, honest air,
and held up his hand. Mrs. Guttridge lingered a
little behind; but when at last she faltered along,
with feeble and hesitating step, and held up her thin,
trembling hand, and raised her pale blue eyes, half
swimming in tears, towards the Court, and exhibited
her care-worn features, which, though sun-burned,
were pale and sickly, the Judge had in his own mind

more than half decided the case against Jerry. The witnesses having been sworn, Mrs. Guttridge was called to the stand.

"Now, Mrs. Guttridge," said the Judge, "you are not obliged to testify against your husband any more than you choose; your testimony must be voluntary. The Court will ask you questions touching the case, and you may answer them or not, as you think best. And, in the first place, I will ask you whether your husband neglects to provide for the necessary wants of his family; and whether you do, or do not, have comfortable food and clothing for yourself and children?"

"Well, we go pretty hungry a good deal of the time," said Mrs. Guttridge, trembling; "but I don't know but Mr. Guttridge does the best he can about it. There don't seem to be any victuals that he can get, a good deal of the time."

"Well, is he, or is he not, in the habit of spending his time idly when he might be at work, and earning something for his family to live upon?"

"Why, as to that," replied the witness, "Mr. Guttridge don't work much; but I don't know as he can help it; it does n't seem to be his natur' to work. Somehow, he don't seem to be made like other folks; for if he tries ever so much, he can't never work but a few minutes at a time ; the natur' don't seem to be in him."

" Well, well," said the Judge, casting a dignified and judicial glance at the culprit, who stood with his mouth wide open, and eyes fixed on the Court with an intentness that showed he began to take some interest in the matter ; " well, well, perhaps the Court will be able to *put* the natur' in him."

Mrs. Guttridge was directed to step aside, and Mr. Nat. Frier was called to the stand. His testimony was very much to the point; clear and conclusive. But as the reader is already in possession of the substance of it, it is unnecessary to recapitulate it. Suffice it to say, that when he was called upon to repeat the reproachful language which Jerry had bestowed upon the witness, there was much shuddering, and an awful rolling of eyes, throughout the court room. Even the prisoner's face kindled almost up to a blaze, and thick drops of sweat were seen to start from his forehead. The Judge, to be sure, retained a dignified self-possession, and settling back in his chair, said it was not necessary to question the witness any further; the case was clearly made out; Jerry Guttridge was unquestionably guilty of the charges preferred against him.

7

The Court, out of delicacy toward the feelings of his wife, refrained from pronouncing sentence until she had retired, which she did on an intimation being given her that the case was closed, and she could return home. Jerry was then called and ordered to hearken to his sentence, as the Court had recorded it.

Jerry stood up and faced the Court, with fixed eyes and gaping mouth, and the clerk repeated as follows :—

" Jerry Guttridge ! you have been found guilty of being an idle and lazy person, and not providing for your family, and giving reproachful language to Mr. Nat. Frier, when he reproved you for your idleness. The Court orders that you receive twenty smart lashes, with the cat-o'-nine-tails, upon your naked back, and that this sentence be executed forthwith, by the con stables, at the whipping-post in the yard adjoining the court-house."

Jerry dropped his head, and his face assumed divers deep colors, sometimes red, and sometimes shading upon the blue. He tried to glance round upon the assembled multitude, but his look was very sheepish ; and, unable to stand the gaze of the hundreds of eyes that were upon him, he settled back on a bench, leaned his head on his hand, and looked steadily upon the floor. The constables having been directed by the Court to proceed forthwith to execute the sentence, they led him out into the yard, put his arms round the whipping-post, and tied his hands together. He submitted without resistance; but when they commenced tying his hands round the post, he began to cry and beg, and promised better fashions if they would only let him go this time. But the constables told him it was too late now; the sentence of the Court had been passed, and the punishment must be inflicted. The whole throng of spectators had issued from the court-house, and stood round in a large ring, to see the sentence enforced. The Judge himself had stepped to a side window, which commanded a view of the yard, and stood peering solemnly through his spectacles to see that the ceremony was duly performed. All things being in readiness, the stoutest constable took the cat-o'-nine-tails, and laid the blows heavily across the naked back of the victim. Nearly every blow brought blood, and as they successively fell, Jerry jumped and screamed, so that he might have been heard well-nigh a mile. When the twenty blows were counted, and the ceremony was ended, he was loosed from his confinement, and told that he might go. He put on his garments, with a sullen but subdued air, and without stopping to pay his respects to the Court, or even to bid any one good-by, he straightened for home as fast as he could go.

Mrs. Guttridge met him at the door, with a kind and piteous look, and asked him if they hurt him. He made no reply, but pushed along into the house. There he found the table set, and well supplied, for dinner; for Mrs. Guttridge, partly through the kindness of Mr. Frier, and partly from her own exertions, had managed to "pick up something" that served to make quite a comfortable meal. Jerry ate his dinner in silence, but his wife thought he manifested more tenderness and less selfishness than she had known him to exhibit for several years; for, instead of appropriating the most and the best of the food to himself, he several times placed fair proportions of it upon the plates of his wife and each of the children.

The next morning, before the sun had dried the dew from the grass, whoever passed the haying field of Mr. Nat. Frier might have beheld Jerry Guttridge busily at work, shaking out the wet hay to the sun; and for a month afterward the passer-by might have seen him every day, early and late, in that and the adjoining fields, a perfect pattern of industry.

A change soon became perceptible in the condition

and circumstances of his family. His house began to wear more of an air of comfort, outside and in. His wife improved in health and spirits, and little Bobby became a fat, hearty boy, and grew like a pumpkin. And years afterward Mrs. Guttridge was heard to say that, "somehow, ever since that 'ere trial, Mr. Guttridge's natur' seemed to be entirely changed."

CHAPTER VII.

SEATING THE PARISH.

"Order, is Heaven's first law; and this confess'd,
Some are, and must be, greater than the rest."

So thought the good people of the old town of
Brookhaven, about a hundred and forty years ago,
when they enacted the law for *for seating the parish
at church*. Do any of our distant readers want information as to the locality and geography of Brookhaven?
We may as well premise in the outset, that it is on
Long island, some sixty miles or so from the city of
New York, and is the largest town in territory in
Suffolk County, containing more than a hundred
thousand acres, and stretching across the whole width
of the island. It contains seven or eight thousand
inhabitants, who are distributed in several villages
along the shores of the Sound and the Atlantic, while the
middle portions of the town still remain covered with
pine forests, abounding with deer and other wild game.

The early settlers of this part of Long Island were

mostly from New England, and the inhabitants still retain much of the primitive Puritan character of their forefathers. A company from Boston and its vicinity, commenced a settlement in Brookhaven as early as sixteen hundred and fifty-five; and in ten years the settlement had increased so much, that they called a minister of the gospel to come and reside among them. Their choice of pastor was, of course, from the good old Pilgrim stock; for where else could they go? There was no other race among men or under heaven, according to their ideas, "whereby they could be saved." Accordingly, they settled as their first minister, Rev. Nathan Brewster, a grandson of Elder William Brewster, *who came over in the May Flower.*

Thus having proved the origin of the good people of Brookhaven, it follows as a matter of course, that they were not only a pious people, a church-going people, but also great lovers of *order and decorum.* Happily, so important a conclusion does not rest for its authority on mere inference alone; it is sustained by ample and positive proof in the shape of duly authenticated records.

Like most new and remote settlements, the town might, for some time, be regarded as a sort of independent democracy. The people met together in a body, and adopted rules, and made laws, and elected magistrates and other officers, to see the laws properly executed. Their attendance at church, also, was, for many years, conducted very much on the democratic principle. Indeed this is most usually the case with churches in all new settlements. The meeting-house, as well as the nation, experiences its revolutions, and in the progress of society, passes through all the regular forms of government.

It has its period of pure democracy ; when the temple is a humble, unfinished structure, with open doors and windows, and the people come and go at all times during the hours of worship, as best suits their pleasure. Then it is, that the congregation sit on stout longitudinal planks supported by blocks of wood, and on transverse boards resting on the aforesaid planks. These planks and boards being common property, vested in the body politic, the respective seats, on the Sabbath, are seized and rightfully held, like a newly discovered country, by the first occupant ; thus affording a practical illustration at the same time both of their political and religious faith, viz. :—that the people of the parish are all equal, and that God is no respecter of persons.

In progress of time, the meeting-house glides naturally into the aristocratic form of government. Wealth has begun to make distinctions in society. A better building is erected, or the old one repaired and put in a condition more suitable to the times. Permanent fixtures take the place of the loose planks and boards, and low partition walls divide the floor into distinct compartments. This revolution has been brought on and carried out by the wealth of the few who had the means to sustain it, and they in return receive the honors and distinctions usually bestowed on the successful leaders of a revolution. The many look up to them with reverence, and stand back and give place to them whenever they appear. The affairs of the meeting-house are now principally under their management and control, and having taken possession of the most honorable seats, and provided that the most respectable among the mass should take the seats of the next highest grade, the remainder of the house is left free for promiscuous occupation.

Years pass on ; and by the diffusion of wealth and knowledge, and the increase of numbers, the society becomes ripe for another revolution. Then perhaps comes on a sort of constitutional government, not unlike that of our great Republican Union. A tasteful and costly church is erected, and the snug and

7*

elegant family pew succeeds to the former rude compartments. Each pew, like a sovereign and independent State, is governed by the head of the family, who has entire control over all matters of its internal police, subject, however, at all times, to the general and common laws of the society.

The illustration of our subject, drawn from the history of the good old town of Brookhaven, is derived from that period when the meeting-house was undergoing a change from a democratic to an aristocratic form of government. The building had been much improved, mainly by the generous liberality of Colonel Smith, who had poured out his treasure like water, to accomplish so laudable an object. By the thorough renovation it underwent at this time, including the applications of yellow ochre and oil, and the change of loose planks and boards for permanent seats, the meeting-house was much modernized, and exhibited a very respectable appearance. In front of the pulpit stood a large table of about twelve feet by four, around which, on communion days, the church gathered to partake of the supper. At the regular Sabbath services, the upper members of the parish, including, of course, Colonel Smith and his family, seated themselves at the table, as being the most honorable seat, on account of its vicinity to the pulpit, and the convenience it afforded as a resting-place for psalm-books and psalters. The rest of the floor of the meeting-house was divided into fifteen different apartments, of an oblong, bed-room sort of size and shape, which were denominated pews.

But it is hard to bring the mass of community to adopt great changes or innovations in government, or the habits of society. When our excellent federal Constitution was framed, it was a long time before a majority of the people of all the States could be induced to fall in with it, and receive it as their form of government. So it was with the parish of Brookhaven. They had been accustomed, from time immemorial, to sit promiscuously in all parts of the meeting-house wherever they pleased, and there seemed to be but little dispositon on the part of the mass of the parish, to break over the old habit. The society had become numerous, and contained many noisy and roguish boys, and not a few thoughtless and frolicking young men. Scenes of indecorum and confusion occurred almost every Sabbath, greatly to the annoyance of the more sober part of the congregation, and sometimes to the interruption of the ceremonial of worship.

At last good Parson Phillips had to stop short one day in the midst of his sermon. He stood silent for the space of a minute, looking sternly at pews number four and six, and then, shaking his finger solemnly in that direction, he said:

"If the boys in pew number four will stop that crowding and shuffling their feet, and the young men in pew number six will cease their whispering with the young women, the sermon can go on; if not, not."

The whole congregation looked thunderstruck. The old men turned their heads towards the two pews and then towards the minister, and then towards the pews again. Deacon Jones, coloring with indignation, rose on his feet, and glanced round with a look of awful rebuke upon pew number six; and Mr. Wigglesworth, who was seated at the table, went directly into pew number four, and seizing two of the boys by the shoulders in the thickest of the crowd, dragged them out of the pew, and set them down at the foot of the pulpit stairs. These decided demonstrations in favor of good order were not without their influence, and the services again proceeded without any material interruption till the close. When Parson Phillips was about to pronounce the benediction, Deacon Jones was observed to rise sooner than he was accustomed to do, and before any of the rest of the congregation ; and he was observed, also, to stand during that ceremony, with his back to the minister, and looking round upon the audience, a thing which he was never seen to do before. The congregation, therefore, were prepared to expect something out of the usual course, from Deacon Jones. As soon as the amen had dropped from the minister's lips, the deacon stretched out his hand, and began to address the audience.

" I think," said he, " the scenes we have witnessed here to-day, as well as on several Sabbaths heretofore, admonish us that we have a duty to perform which has been too long neglected. If we have any regard for our character, as an orderly and well-behaved people ; if we have any respect for the house of God, and the holy religion we profess, I think it is high time we took a decided stand, and adopted some strong measures to secure order and decorum during the hours of public worship. I feel impelled by a sense of duty to invite a general meeting to be held at this place to-morrow, to take the subject into consideration. And I hope that all the heads of families in town, and all who vote and pay taxes, will meet here to-morrow at ten o'clock for this purpose."

Colonel Smith spoke, and said he approved of the
suggestion of Deacon Jones, and hoped there would
be a general attendance.   The congregation then dis-
persed, some moving silently and thoughtfully homeward, and some loitering by the way and leaning over
the fences, in companies of three or four together, and
discussing earnestly the events of the day, and proposing plans to be presented at the meeting to-
morrow.

Punctually at ten o'clock, the next day, there was
a very general gathering of the inhabitants at the
meeting-house.   On motion of Deacon Jones, Colonel
Smith was unanimously appointed "moderator," or
chairman of the meeting, and on assuming the chair,
he stated in a few pertinent remarks, the general
object of the meeting, and said they were now ready
to hear any observations or suggestions on the subject.
A minute or two passed in perfect silence, and no one
seemed disposed to rise.   At last, the chairman said,
perhaps Squire Tallmadge would favor the meeting
with his views of the matter.   The eyes of all were
now turned toward Squire Tallmadge, who after a
little pause, rose slowly, and addressed the chair as
follows.

" For one, Mr. Moderator, I feel the importance of

the subject upon which we are met; and for one, I
am prepared to go into strong measures to remedy
the evil, which has been so common of late. The
evil is great, and must be corrected. We had a
specimen yesterday of the noise and indecorum which
sometimes interrupts the course of worship. And
that is not all, nor the worst of it. The young men
and the boys have got in the habit of going in early
sometimes, before services begin, and crowding into
the best seats, and occupying the chairs round the
table; so that the older people, the pillars of the
church, and those who bear most of the expense of
supporting the gospel, have to go into the back seats
or stow themselves round in the corners, wherever
they can find a chance. This is the difficulty, and it
seems to me the remedy would lie in some entirely
new arrangement for seating the parish. I think the
inhabitants should be properly divided into classes,
and each class assigned to a different pew, having
reference to the rank and respectability of each class,
and the respective proportions they contribute to the
support of the gospel."

As Squire Tallmadge sat down, Mr. Wigglesworth
and Doctor Wetmore rose nearly at the same time.
The chair finally decided that Mr. Wigglesworth had

the floor, whereupon Mr. Wigglesworth made the following remarks.

"Mr. Moderator; I agree with all that Squire Tallmadge has said, exactly; only I don't think he's stated the audacious conduct half strong enough. I think, if the young men have courting to do, they should do it at home and not in church. Why, Mr. Moderator, I've seen a young man, that I won't call by name, now, though he's here in this meeting, set with his arm round the girl that sot next to him half sermon time." Here the heads of the audience were turned in various directions, 'till their eyes rested on four or five young men, who, with unusual modesty, had taken some of the back seats, and one of whom was observed to color deeply.

"I think," continued Mr. Wigglesworth, "the people at church ought to be sifted out, and divided, each sort by itself. What's the use of having these 'ere pews, if it aint to divide the people into them according to their sorts? I have a calf-pen and a sheep-pen in my barn-yard, and I put the calves into one, and the sheep into 'tother, and then I put the bars up, and don't let 'em run back and forth into each other's pen, jest as they are a mind to. I've no more to say, Mr. Moderator, only I hope now we've begun, we shall make thorough work of it."

Doctor Wetmore then rose, and made a few remarks. He fully agreed with the suggestions thrown out by Squire Tallmadge. He had witnessed the evils complained of, and had been mortified by them a good many times; and he believed the proper remedy would be, as Squire Tallmadge suggested, in some thorough change and some regular system, with regard to seating the parish at church. He would move therefore, that the subject be referred to the trustees, or selectmen of the town, and that they be requested to draw up an ordinance, to be adopted as a town law for seating the people in a proper and orderly manner at church, according to their proper rank, and also having special reference to the sums contributed by each for the support of the gospel.

Mr. Wigglesworth seconded the motion, and it was put and carried unanimously. Deacon Jones then moved that the trustees be requested to give thorough attention to the work the present week, and bring their ordinance in the next Sabbath morning, and have it read from the pulpit, and go into immediate operation. This motion was also seconded and carried, and the meeting adjourned.

This week was an anxious week at Brookhaven, and one on which an unusual amount of talking was done. The subject was canvassed and discussed in every possible shape by all classes and in all families. The old ladies were rejoicing at the prospect of more quiet and orderly meetings, and the young ladies were in fidgets to know where they were to sit. Several persons came forward with surprising liberality during this week, and added ten, fifteen, and some as high as twenty shillings, to their annual subscription, for the support of the ministry.

At last, the important Sunday morning came round. It was a pleasant morning, and the people went uncommonly early to church, and the meeting-house was fuller than it had been seen for many months before. None, however, seemed disposed to take seats as they entered, and all were standing, when Parson Phillips came in. When the Reverend gentleman came up to the pulpit, the chairman of the trustees handed him the ordinance, and requested him to read it from the pulpit, in order that the parish might be seated accordingly before the services commenced.

Parson Phillips accordingly ascended the pulpit, and unfolded the paper, and while the whole congregation stood in profound silence, with their eyes fixed on the speaker, he read as follows.

" At a meeting of the Trustees of Brookhaven, August 6, one thousand seven hundred and three : Whereas, there hath been several rude actions of late happened in our church by reason of people not being seated, which is much to the dishonor of God and the discouragement of virtue ; For preventing the like again, it is *ordered*, that the inhabitants be seated after the manner and form following : All freeholders that have or shall subscribe within a month to pay forty shillings to Mr. Phillips towards his salary shall be seated at the table, and that no *women* are permitted to set there, except *Colonel Smith's lady*, nor any *woman kind ;* And that the President for the time being shall sit in the right-hand seat under the pulpit, and the clerk on the left ; the trustees in the front seat, and the Justices that are inhabitants of the town are to be seated at the table, whether they pay forty shillings or less. And the pew number one, all such persons as have or shall subscribe twenty shillings ; and the pew number two, such as subscribe to pay fifteen shillings; in pew number three, such as subscribe to pay ten shillings; number four, eight shillings; number five, twelve shillings; number six, nine shillings; number seven, for the young men; number eight, for the boys; number nine, for ministers' widows and wives; and for those women whose husbands pay forty shillings, to sit according to their age; number eleven, for those men's wives that pay from twenty to fifteen shillings. The alley fronting the pews to be for such maids whose parents or selves shall subscribe, for two, six shillings; number twelve, for those men's wives who pay from ten to fifteen shillings; number thirteen, for maids; number fourteen, for girls; and number fifteen, for any. Captain Clark and Joseph Tooker to settle the inhabitants according to the above orders." *

When the reading was finished, Captain Clark and Mr. Tooker entered upon the duties of their office; and after about an hour's marching and counter-marching, and whispering, and pulling and hauling, and referring to the parish subscription books, the congregation was seated, quiet was restored, and the services of the day were performed without interrup-

* True extract from old records.

tion. The next Sabbath, each one knew his own place, and the new order of things was found to work well, and answered a good purpose for many long years after that, 'till in the progress of human events the parish became ripe for another reform.

CHAPTER VIII.

THE MONEY-DIGGERS AND OLD NICK.

THIS is a money digging world of ours; and, as it is said, "there are more ways than one to skin a cat," so are there more ways than one of digging for money. But, in some mode or other, this seems to be the universal occupation of the sons of Adam. Show me the man who does not spend one half of his life long in digging for money, and I will show you an anomaly in the human species. "Hunger will break through a stone wall," but love of money will compass earth and sea, and even brave heaven and hell, in pursuit of its object. The dark and bloody highwayman, in the silent hours of night, seeks a lonely pass on the public road, waits the approach of the coming travel-ler, puts a pistol to his breast and a hand to his pocket, takes his treasure, and flies to seek another spot and another opportunity for a repetition of his crime, and that is *his* mode of digging for money. The less dar-ing robber takes his false keys, and makes his way at midnight into the store of the merchant, or the vaults of the bank, bears away his booty, and hides it in the earth; then, pale and haggard, creeps away to his restless couch, and rises in the morning to tremble at every sound he hears, and to read *suspicion* on the countenance of every one that approaches him—and that is *his* mode of digging for money.

Step with me into the courts of justice. Listen to that learned barrister, pleading for his client. What eloquence! what zeal! what power! How admirably does he " make the worse appear the better reason!" The patient judges sit from morning till night, waiting for his conclusion, and still it comes not. The evening waxeth late, and still he goes on citing case after case, and rule after rule, diving into huge piles of old volumes and musty records of the law, as eagerly as if his own life depended on the issue of the trial. What is it that impels him to all this exertion? I trow he is digging for money.

And then, do you see that restless politician? The whole weight of the government is resting on his shoulders. The salvation of the country depends upon the election of his candidates. How he rides from town to town, stirring up the voters! How he claps the speakers at the public caucus, and with what assiduity does he seize his neighbor by the button and lead him to the polls! What is it that gives such fire to his patriotic zeal, and keeps him in such continual commotion? The answer is short; he is only digging for money.

And so it is with all; the merchant in his counting-house, the mechanic in his workshop, and the farmer in his field, all are digging for money.

But, laying aside all figures of speech, and all circumlocution, let us speak of money-diggers proper—*bonâ fide* money-diggers—men who dig holes in the ground, and delve deep into the bowels of the earth, in search of pots of money and kettles of gold and silver coin. For such there are, and probably have been in all countries and all ages.

On the rough and rocky coast of Maine, about ten miles to the eastward of Portland harbor, lies Jewell's Island. It is a bright and beautiful gem on the ocean's breast, full of various and romantic scenery. It has its green pastures, its cultivated fields, and its dark shaggy forests. Its seaward shore is a high and precipitous mass of rock, rough, and ragged, and projecting in a thousand shapes into the chafing ocean, whose broken waves dash and roll into its deep fissures, and roar and growl like distant thunder. On the inland side of the island, there is a grassy slope down to the water's edge, and here is a little, round, quiet, harbor, where boats can ride at anchor, or rest on the sandy beach in in perfect security. The island has been inhabited by a few fishermen, probably for a century, and, recently works have been erected upon it for the manufacture of copperas and alum, the mineral from which these articles are produced having been found there in great abundance.

This island has been renowned as a place for money-digging ever since the first settlements were planted along the coast; and wild and romantic are the legends related by the old dames, in the cottages of the fishermen, when some wind-bound passenger, who has left his vessel to spend the evening on shore, happens to make any inquiry about the money-diggers. But of all these wild legendary narratives, probably there is none more authentic, or supported by stronger or more undoubted testimony, than the veritable history herein recorded and preserved.

Soon after the close of the revolutionary war, when the country began to breathe somewhat freely again, after its long deathlike struggle, and the industry of the inhabitants was settling down into its accustomed channels, a sailor, who had wandered from Portland

8

harbor some forty or fifty miles back into the country, called at the house of Jonathan Rider, and asked for some dinner. "But shiver my timbers," he added, "if I've got a stiver of money to pay for it with. The last shot I had in the locker went to pay for my breakfast."

"Well, never mind that," said Jonathan, "I never lets a fellow creetur go away hungry as long as I've got anything to eat myself. Come, haul up to the table here, and take a little of such pot-luck as we've got. Patty, hand on another plate, and dip up a little more soup."

The sailor threw his tarpaulin cap upon the floor, gave a hitch at his waistband, and took a seat at the table with the family, who had already nearly finished their repast.

"What may I call your name, sir, if I may be so bold?" said Jonathan, at the same time handing a bowl of soup to the sailor.

"My name is Bill Stanwood, the world over, fair weather or foul; I was born and brought up in old Marblehead, and followed fishing till I was twenty years old, and for the last ten years I've been foreign viges all over the world."

"And how happens you to get away so far from the

sea now, jest as the times is growing better, and trade is increasing?"

"Oh, I had a bit of a notion," said Bill, "to take a land tack a few days up round in these parts."

"Maybe you've got some relations up this way," said Jonathan, "that you are going to visit?"

"Oh no," said Bill, "I haint got a relation on the face of the arth, as I know on. I never had any father, nor mother, nor brother, nor sister. An old aunt, that I lived with when I was a little boy, was all the mother that ever I had; and she died when I was on my last fishing cruise; and there wasn't nobody left that I cared a stiver for, so I thought I might as well haul up line and be off. So I took to foreign viges at once, and since that I have been all round the West Indies, and to England, and France, and Russia, and South America, and up the Mediterranean, and clear round the Cape of Good Hope to China, and the deuce knows where."

"But you say you haint got no relations up this way?"

"No."

"Nor acquaintances nother?"

"No."

"Then, if I may be so bold, what sent you on a

cruise so fur back in the country, afoot and alone, as
the gal went to be married?"

"Oh, no boldness at all," said Bill; "ask again, if
you like. Howsomever," he added, giving a knowing
wink with one eye, "I come on a piece of business
of a very particular kind, that I don't tell to everybody."

"I want to know!" said Jonathan, his eyes and
mouth beginning to dilate a little. "Maybe, if you
should tell me what 'tis, I might give you a lift about
it."

"By the great hocus pocus!" said Bill, looking his
host full in the face, "If I thought you could, I'd be
your servant the longest day I live."

"You don't say so?" said Jonathan, with increasing interest; "it must be something pretty particular
then. I should like mighty well to know what 'tis.
Maybe I might help you about it."

"Well, then," said Bill, "I'll jest ask you one
question. Do you know anything of an old school-
master, about in these parts, by the name of Solomon
Bradman?"

"No—why?"

"Never heard anything of him?" said Bill, with
earnestness.

"Not a word," said Jonathan? "why, what about him?"

"It is deuced strange," said Bill, "that I never can hear a word of that man. I'd work like a slave a whole year for the sake of finding him only one hour. I was told, the last he was heard on, he was in some of these towns round here, keeping school."

"Well, I never heard of him before," said Jonathan; "but what makes you so mighty anxious to find him? Did you go to school to him once, and have you owed him a licking ever since? Or does he owe you some money?"

"No, I never set eyes on him in my life," said Bill; "but there's nobody in the world I'd give half so much to see. And now we've got along so fur, jest between you and me, I'll ask you one more question; but I wouldn't have you name it to anybody for nothing."

"No, by jings," said Jonathan, "if you're a mind to tell me, I'll be as whist about it as a mouse."

"Well, then," said Bill, "I want to know, if you know of anybody, that knows how to work *brandy-way?*"

"Brandy-way? what's that?" said Jonathan. "If you mean anybody that can *drink* brandy-way, I

guess I can show you one," he continued, turning to
a stout, red-faced, blowzy looking man, who sat at his
right hand at table. "Here's my neighbor, Asa
Sampson, I guess can do that are sort of business as
fast as anybody you can find. Don't you think you
can, Asa?"

Asa Sampson was a hard one. He was helping
Mr. Rider do his haying. He had been swinging the
scythe, through a field of stout clover, all the fore-
noon, during which time he had taken a full pint of
strong brandy, and now had just finished a hearty hot
dinner. Mr. Sampson's face, therefore, it may well
be supposed, was already in rather a high glow. But
at this sudden sally of Mr. Rider, the red in Asa's
visage grew darker and deeper, till it seemed almost
ready to burst out into a blue flame. He choked and
stammered, and tried to speak. And at last he did
speak, and says he :—

"Why, yes, Mr. Rider, I guess so ; and if you'll
jest bring your brandy bottle on, I'll try to show you
how well I can do that are sort of business."

Mr. Rider, thinking his joke upon Asa was rather
a hard one, as the most ready means of atoning for
it, called upon Mrs. Rider to bring forward the bottle
at once.

"Come," said Mr. Rider, "let's take a drop," turn-ing out a glass himself, and then passing the bottle to the sailor and Mr. Sampson.

"I can drink brandy all weathers," said Bill Stan-wood, filling up a good stiff glass ; "but if I could only jest find somebody that could show me how to work brandy-way, I should rather have it than all the brandy that ever was made in the world."

"But what do you mean by this brandy-way you talk about ?" said Jonathan. "Seems to me that's a new kind of a wrinkle ; I don't understand it."

"Why, I mean," said Bill, "I want to know how to measure brandy-way ; that is, how to measure off so many rods on the ground brandy-way. I never heard of but one man that fully understood it, and that was Master Bradman ; and I've been told that he knew it as well as he did the multiplication table. I've been hunting for that man a fortnight, all round in these towns about here, and it's plaguey strange I can't hear nothing of him."

"Well, I don't know anything about your measur-ing brandy-way," said Jonathan, "and as for Master Bradman, I'm sure there haint nobody by that name kept school in this town these twenty years. For I've lived here twenty years, and know every schoolmaster that's kept school here since I came into the town. But, if I may be so bold, what makes you so anxious to learn about this brandy-way business?"

"Why, I've reasons enough," said Bill; "I'll tell you what 'tis, shipmate," he added, giving Jonathan a familiar slap on the shoulder, "if I could only learn how to measure fifteen rods brandy-way, I would n't thank king George to be my grandfather. I should have as much money as I should want, if I should live to be as old as Methusaleh."

"You don't say so?" said Jonathan, his eyes evidently growing larger at the recital. "I should like mighty well to know how that's done."

"Well, I should a good deal rather see the money than hear about it," said Asa Sampson, whose ideas were somewhat *waked up* by the effects of the brandy.

"Then you don't believe it, do you?" said Bill. "I could convince you of it in five minutes, if I'd a mind to; for I've got the evidence of it in my pocket. If I could only measure brandy-way, I know where I could go and dig up lots and lots of money, that have been buried in the earth by pirates."

"Are you in arnest?" said Jonathan.

"To be sure I am; I never was more in arnest in my life."

" Well, now do tell us all about it, for if it's true, and you'll give me a share of it, I would n't valley taking my old horse and wagon, and going round a few days with you to help hunt up Master Bradman. And if we can't find him, perhaps we can find somebody else that knows how to do it. But do you know pretty near where the money is ?"

" Yes, I know within fifteen rods of the very spot."

" And you are sure there's money buried there ?"

" Yes, I'm sure of it. I've got the documents here in my pocket that tells all about it. I'm most tired of hunting alone for it, and, if you're a mind to take hold and follow it up with me, I've a good mind to let you into the secret, and let you go snacks with me; for, somehow or other, I kind of take a liking to you, and don't believe I shall find a cleverer fellow if I sail the world over."

" That's what you wont," said Mrs. Rider, who began to feel a strong interest in the conversation of the sailor. " I've summered and wintered Mr. Rider, and know just what he is ; and I don't think you'll find anybody that would help you more in looking for the money, or any cleverer man to have a share of it after you've found it."

"Well, that's jest what I want," said Bill; "so, if you say so, it's a bargain."

"Well, I say so," said Jonathan; "now let's see your documents."

Bill Stanwood deliberately drew from his pocket an old rusty pocket-book, carefully tied together with a piece of twine. He opened it, and took from its inmost fold a paper much worn and soiled.

"There," said he, "that's the secret charm. That's worth more than King George's crown; if 'twasn't for that plaguey little botheration about measuring fifteen rods brandy-way. Now I'll tell you how I come by this ere paper. About three years ago, we was on a vige round the Cape of Good Hope, and we had an old Spanish sailor with us that was a real dark faced old bruiser. He was full of odd ways. It seemed as if he'd got tired of the world and every body in it, and didn't care for nobody nor nothin'. And every soul on board almost hated him, he was so crabbed-like. At last he was took sick, and grew very bad. Day after day he lay in his berth, and only grew worse. The captain used to send him some medicine every day, but never would go near him, and none of the hands didn't go nigh him, only jest to hand him the medicine when the captain sent it.

And he would take the medicine without saying a
word, and then lay down again, and you wouldn't
know but what he was dead all day, if it wasn't once
in a while you would hear him fetch a hard breath,
or a groan. I began to pity him, and I went and
stood, and looked on him. The cold sweat stood in
drops on his forehead, he was in so much distress.
And says I, 'Diego, can't I do something for you?'
And I s'pose I looked kind of pitiful on him, for he
opened his eyes and stared in my face a minute, as if
he heard some strange sound, and then the tears
come into his eyes, and his chin quivered, and says
he,

" ' Bill, if you'll only jest get me a drink of cold
water, for I'm all burning up inside.'

" And I went and got him some water, and he
drinked it, and it seemed to revive him a little. And
says he to me, 'Bill, I'm jest going off upon my last
long vige.' And then he put his hand in his pocket,
and took out this very paper, and handed it to me;
and says he,

" ' I meant to have kept this in my pocket, and let
it be throwed with my old carcase into the sea; but
you have been kind to me, and you may have it; and
if ever you go into that part of the world again, it

will show you where you can get as much money as you want.'

"That night poor Diego died, and we took and wrapped him in his blanket, and put a stone to his feet, and threw him overboard ; and that was the end of poor Diego."

"Poor soul," said Mrs. Rider, brushing a tear from her eye, "how could you bear to throw him overboard ?"

"Oh, we could n't do nothin' else with him, away off there to sea. When a poor fellow dies a thousand miles from land, there's no other way but to souse him over, and let him go. I pitied the creetur at the last, but no doubt he'd been a wicked wretch, and I suppose had lived among pirates. He had scars on his face and arms, that showed he'd been in some terrible battles."

"Well, what was in the paper ?" said Jonathan, beginning to grow a little impatient for the documents.

"I'll read it to you," said Bill.

So saying, he opened the paper, which was so much worn at the folds as to drop into several pieces, and read from it as follows :—

In the name of Captain Kidd, Amen.—On Jewell's

So saying, he opened the paper, which was so much worn at the folds as to drop into several pieces, and read from it as follows:—

Island, near the harbor of Falmouth, in the District of Maine, is buried a large iron pot full of gold, with an iron cover over it, and also two large iron pots full of silver dollars and half dollars, with iron covers over them ; and also one other large iron pot, with an iron cover over it, full of rich jewels, and gold rings and necklaces, and gold watches of great value. In this last pot is the paper containing the agreement of the four persons who buried these treasures, and the name of each one is signed to it with his own blood. In that agreement it is stated that this property belongs equally to the four persons who buried it, and is not to be dug up or disturbed while the whole four are living, except they be all present. And in case it shall not be reclaimed during the lifetime of the four, it shall belong equally to the survivors, who shall be bound to each other in the same manner as the four were bound. And in case this property shall never be dug up by the four, or any of them, the last survivor shall have a right to reveal the place where it is hid, and to make such disposition of it as he may think proper. And in that same paper, the evil spirit of darkness is invoked to keep watch over this money, and to visit with sudden destruction any one of the four who may violate his agreement. This property was buried at the hour of midnight, and only at the hour of midnight can it ever be reclaimed. And it can be obtained only in the most profound silence on the part of those who are digging for it. Not a word or syllable must be uttered from the time the first spade is struck in the ground, till a handful of the money is taken out of one of the pots. This arrangement was entered into with the spirit of darkness, in order to prevent any unauthorized persons from obtaining the money. I am the last survivor of the four. If I shall dispose of this paper to any one before my death, or leave it to any one after I am gone, he may obtain possession of this great treasure by observing the following directions. Go to the north side of the island, where there is a little cove, or harbor, and a good landing on a sandy beach. Take your compass and run by it due south a half a mile, measuring from high-water mark. Then run fifty rods east by compass, and there you will find a blue stone, about two feet long, set endwise into the ground. From this stone, measure fifteen rods brandy-way, and there, at the depth of five feet from the surface of the ground, you will find the pots of money.   (Signed)

DIEGO ZEVOLA.

When Bill Stanwood had finished reading his 'document,' there was silence in the room for the space of two minutes. Jonathan's eyes were fixed in a sort of bewildered amazement upon the sailor, and Mrs. Rider's were riveted intently upon her husband; while Asa Sampson's were rolling about with a strange wildness, and his mouth was stretched open wide enough to swallow the brandy bottle whole. At last, says Bill,

"There you have it in black and white, and there's no mistake about it. It's all as true as the book of Genesis. I've been on to the ground, and I've measured off the half a mile south, and I've measured the fifty rods east, and I've found the blue stone, but how to measure the fifteen rods brandy-way, I'll die if I can tell."

"Well, that's a tremendous great story," said Asa Sampson; "but, according to my way of thinking, I should rather have it in black and white, than to have it in red and white. Somehow or other, I never should want to have anything to do with papers that are signed with men's blood. I should n't like to be handling that paper that's buried up in one of them pots."

"Poh, that paper's nothing to us," said Bill; "we

did n't write it. I should as lives take that paper up and read it, as to read the prayer-book."

"Mercy on us," said Mrs. Rider; "read a paper that's writ with men's blood, and when the old Nick is set to watch it too? I would n't do it for all the world, and husband shan't do it neither."

"But does it say we must have anything to do with the paper, in order to get the money?" said Jonathan.

"Not a word," said Bill. "I tell you that paper has no more to do with us, than it has with the man in the moon."

"But," said Mrs. Rider, "it does say the old evil one is set there to watch the money. And do you think I'd have my husband go and dig for money right in the face and eyes of old Nick himself? I should rather be as poor as Job's cat all the days of my life."

"There's no trouble about that," said Bill; "all we've got to do is to hold our tongues, while we're digging, and the old feller 'll keep his distance, and won't say a word to us. At any rate, I'm determined to have the money, if I can find it, devil or no devil.

"But that confounded brandy-way, I don't know

how to get over that. That's worse than forty Old
Nicks to get along with."

" Well, I'll tell you what 'tis," said Jonathan, " if
you can get within fifteen rods of the money, I can
find it without any help of your brandy-way, that you
tell about."

" You can?" said Bill, eagerly.

" Yes; if you'll carry me within fifteen rods of
where the money is, I'll engage to find the very spot
where it is buried in less than one hour."

" You will?" said Bill, springing on his feet, and
giving Jonathan a slap on his shoulder, " Can you
do it? Do tell us how."

" Yes, I can find it with a mineral rod."

" What's a mineral rod?" said Bill. " Now none
of your humbugs; but if you *can* do it, tell us how."

" There's no humbug about it," said Jonathan,
tartly. " I know how to work a mineral rod, and I
believe I can find the money."

" But what *is* a mineral rod?" said Bill.

" Why, don't you know? It's a green crotched
branch of witch-hazel, cut off about a foot and a half
or two foot long. And them that has the power to
work 'em, takes the ends of the branches in each hand,
and holds the other end, where the branches are

joined together, pointing up to the sky. And when they come near where there's minerals, or gold, or silver, buried in the ground, the rod will bend that way; and when they get right over the spot, the rod will bend right down and point towards the ground."

"Now, is that true?" said Bill.

"True? yes, every word of it. I've seen it done many a time, and I've done it myself. The mineral rod won't work in everybody's hands, but it 'll work in mine, and once I found a broad-axe by it that was lost in the meadow."

"Well, then," said Bill, "let us be off forthwith, and not let that money lie rusting in the ground any longer. Why not start off to-night?"

"Well, I don't know but we could start towards night," said Jonathan; "but I shall have to go out first and hunt up a witch-hazel tree to get some mineral rods."

"It's my opinion," said Asa Sampson, "you had better wait a day or two, and finish getting in your hay before you go; for if you should come back with your wagon filled with money, you'll be too confounded lazy ever to get it in afterwards."

"No, you shan't stir one step," said Mrs. Rider, "till that hay is all got in. There's two loads out that's made enough to get in now, and you know there's as much as one load to mow yet."

Mrs. Rider's will was all the law or gospel there was about the house. Of course her husband did not undertake to gainsay her dictum, but told Bill they could not possibly get ready to start before the next night, as that hay would have to be taken care of first.

"Well, then," said Bill, "call all hands, and let's go at it. Come, where's your scythe? I'll go and finish mowing that grass down in the first place."

"But can you mow?" said Jonathan, doubtingly.

"Mow? I guess you'd think so, if you should see me at it. I worked on a farm six weeks once, when I was a boy, and learnt to pull every rope in the ship."

All hands repaired to the field. Bill Stanwood took a scythe and went to thrashing about as though he were killing rattlesnakes. He soon battered up one scythe against the rocks, and presently broke another by sticking it into a stump. It was then agreed that he should change works with Asa Sampson, and help get the hay into the barn, while Asa mowed. The business then went on briskly. The boys and girls were out spreading and raking hay, and Mrs. Rider

herself went on to the mow in the barn to help stow
it away. The next day the haying was finished, and
all things were in preparation to start for Jewell's
Island. Mrs. Rider, however, whose imagination had
been excited by the idea of Old Nick being set to
guard the money, was still unwilling her husband
should go; and it was not till he had solemnly
promised to bring her home a new silk gown, and a
new pair of morocco shoes, and some stuff to make
her a new silk bonnet, that she finally gave her consent. When the matter was finished, she took a large
firkin and filled it with bread and cheese, and boiled
beef, and doughnuts, for them to eat on their way;
and Bill said there was a great plenty to last till they
got down to the pots of money, and after that they
could buy what they wanted.

Asa Sampson, who was at work for Mr. Rider,
agreed to go with them for his regular daily pay, with
this proviso: if they got the money, they were to
make him a present outright of a hundred dollars,
which he said would be as much money as he should
ever know what to do with.

As a parting caution, Mrs. Rider charged them to
remember and not speak while they were digging,
and told them, lest some word might slip out before

they thought of it, they had better each of them tie a
handkerchief over their mouths when they begun to
dig, and not take it off till they got down to the
money. They all agreed that it would be an excellent plan, and they would certainly do it.

Mr. Rider's old horse was tackled into the wagon,
the baggage was put on board, and the three fortune
hunters jumped in and drove off for Falmouth. It
was a long and lonesome road, but the bright visions
of the future, that were dancing before their eyes,
made it seem to them like a journey to Paradise.

" Now, Mr. Rider," said Bill, " what do you mean
to do with your half of the money, when we get it ?"

" Well, I think I shall take two thousand dollars of
it," said Jonathan, " and buy Squire Dickinson's
farm, that lives next neighbor to me. He's always
looked down upon me with a kind of contempt, because I was n't so well off in the world as he was ; and
I should like mighty well to get him out of the neighborhood. And I guess he's drove for money too, and
would be glad to sell out. And now, neighbor Stanwood, I'll tell you what I think *you* better do. You
better buy a good farm right up there alongside of
me, and we'll build each of us a large nice house, just
alike, and get each of us a first rate horse, and we'll

live together there, and ride about and take comfort."

" By the hocus pocus!" said Bill, " I hope you don't call that taking comfort. No, none of your land-lubber viges for me. I'll tell you what I mean to do. As soon as I get my money I mean to go right to Boston and buy the prettiest ship I can find—one that will sail like the wind—and I'll have three mates, so I shan't have to stand no watch, but go below just when I like ; and I'll go cap'n of her, and go away up the Mediterranian, and up the Baltic. And then I'll make a vige straight round the world, and if I don't beat Captain Cook all to nothin', I think it's a pity. And now you better sell out your old farm up there among the bushes, and go with me. I'll tell you what 'tis, shipmate, you'd take more comfort in one month aboard a good vessel, than you could on a farm in a whole year. What comfort is there to be found on a farm, where you never see any thing new, but have the same thing over and over forever ? No variety, no change but everything always the same—I should get as tired as death in a month."

" Well, now, neighbor," said Jonathan, " you are as much mistaken, as if you had burnt your shirt.

There's no business in the world that has so much variety and so many new things all the time, as farming. In the first place, in the spring comes ploughing time, and then comes planting time, and after that hoeing and weeding; and then comes haying time; and then reaping time; and then getting in the corn and potatoes. And then, to fill up with a little fun once in a while, we have sheep washing in the spring, and huskings in the fall, and breaking out the roads after a snow storm in the winter; and something or other new most all the time. When your crops are growing, even your fields look new every morning; while at sea you have nothing new, but the same things over and over, every day from morning till night. You do nothing but sail, sail, all the time, and have nothing to look at but water from one week's end to another."

Here Bill Stanwood burst into a broad loud laugh, and says he:—

"Well done, shipmate. I must say you are the greenest horn I've met with this long time. No variety and nothing new to be seen in going to sea! If that aint a good one! The very place, too, to see everything new and to learn everything that there is in the world. Why, only jest in working the ship

there's more variety and more to be seen than there
is in working a whole farm, to say nothing about going
all over the world, and seeing everything else.   Even
in a dead calm you can see the whales spouting and
the porpoises rolling about.   And when the wind is
slack, you have enough to do to stick on your canvas.
You run up your topgallan-sels, and your rials, and
out with your studden-sels, and trim your sheets, and
make all the sails draw.   And then you walk the
deck and watch the changes of the wind, and if a
vessel heaves in sight what a pleasure there is in
taking your spy-glass and watching her motions till
she's out of sight again ; or, if she comes near enough,
how delightful 'tis to hail her and learn where she's
from, and where she's bound, and what her captain's
name is !   And when it comes on a blow, what a
stirring time there is !   All hands are out to take in
the light sails ; down goes the topgallan' yards ; and
if the wind increases you begin to reef ; and if it
comes on to blow a real snorter, you furl all sails and
scud away under bare poles.   And sometimes, when
the storm is over, you come across some poor fellows
on a wreck, half starved or half froze to death, and
then you out with your boat and go and take 'em off,
and nurse 'em up and bring 'em to.   Now here's some

life in all this business, some variety, and something
interesting, compared with what there is on a farm.
You better pull up stakes when we get our money,
sell your old farm and go to sea along with me."

"Well," said Jonathan, "I'll tell you what 'tis
neighbor, I'll leave it out to Mr. Sampson here to say
which is the best and pleasantest business, farming or
going to sea. If he says farming, you shall pay the
toddy at the next tavern, and if he says going to sea,
I'll pay it."

"Done," said Bill. "Now, Asa, give us your
opinion."

"Well," said Asa, "all I can say is, if going to sea
isn't pleasanter business than farming there isn't much
pleasure in it, that's all."

"But that aint deciding anything at all," said Bill;
"you must tell us right up and down which is the best
business."

"Well, if I must say," said Asa, "I should say
going to sea was the best and the pleasantest."

"There, I told you so," said Bill. "Now how fur
is it to the next tavern? I want that toddy."

"It's jest to the top of this hill," said Jonathan;
"and bein' the hill's pretty steep, we'll jump out and
walk up, and give the old horse a chance to breathe."

9

So out they jumped, and Jonathan drove the horse up the hill, while Bill and Asa loitered along a little behind.

"How upon arth," said Bill, "come you to decide in favor of going to sea? Did you ever go to sea?"

"I? No I never set foot aboard a vessel in all my life."

"Then how come you to know so much about going to sea?"

"Poh!" said Asa, "all I knew about it was, I knew Mr. Rider had some money, and I knew you had n't, and I wanted the toddy. How *could* I decide any other way?"

"True enough," said Bill; "you was exactly right."

When they reached the tavern, Mr. Rider paid the toddy, and, after giving the old horse a little provender and a little time to breathe, the trio pursued their journey with renewed spirits and livelier hopes. When they reached the sea-shore at Falmouth, the sun was about an hour high. They immediately hired a small row boat for two or three days, leaving their horse and wagon in pawn for it, and prepared to embark for Jewell's Island, which was about ten miles distant. Jonathan was a little fearful about being out upon the water in the night, and was for waiting till

next morning and taking the day before them for the
voyage to the island. But Bill said no, "they could
go half the distance before sunset, and as there was a
good moon, there would be no difficulty in going the
other half after sunset; and he was determined to be
on the island that night, let the consequence be what
'twould."

They accordingly put their baggage on board, and
jumped in, and rowed off. Bill first took the helm,
and Jonathan and Asa sat down to the oars. But
being totally unaccustomed to a boat, they made sad
work of rowing, and in spite of all of Bill's teaching
and preaching, scolding and swearing, their ears
splashed up and down alternately in the water, resem-
bling more in their operation two flails upon the barn
floor than two oars upon the ocean. Their little bark
made but slow headway, and Bill soon got out of
patience, and told Jonathan to take the helm and he
would row himself. Jonathan, however, succeeded
no better at the helm than at the oar; for the boat
was soon heading in all directions, and making as
crooked a track as was ever made by the veritable
sea-serpent himself. So that Bill was obliged to call
Jonathan from the helm, and manage to keep the boat
as straight as he could by rowing. The slow progress

they made under all these disadvantages brought it to midnight before they reached the island. They however succeeded at last in gaining the little harbor, and it being about high water they drew their boat upon the beach, and walked up on the island towards a fisherman's hut, which Bill had frequented upon his former visit to the place. The moon had set, and the night was now somewhat dark. As they wound their way along through the bushes and under the tall trees, not a sound was to be heard, save the low sullen roar of the ocean, which came like delicious music to the ears of Bill Stanwood, while to Jonathan and Asa it added a still deeper gloom to the silence and darkness of the night.

They had walked but a short distance when a dim light glittered through the trees, and told them that the fisherman's hut was near.

" Ah," said Bill, "old Mother Newbegin is up. I believe she never goes to bed ; for go there what time of night you will, you will always find her padding about the room with an old black night-cap on, putting dishes to rights in the closet, or sweeping up the floor, or sitting down and mending her husband's clothes. She looks more like a witch than she does like a human creetur, and sometimes I've almost thought she had something to do about guarding the money that's buried on the island."

"Well, ain't there some other house about here," said Asa, "that we can go to? Somehow, it seems to me I should n't like to get quite so near that old hag, if there's any witchcraft about her."

"There's no other house very near," said Bill; "and, besides, I think it's best to go in and see old Mother Newbegin. For if she is a witch, it's no use to try to keep out of the way of her; and if we keep the right side of her and don't get her mad, maybe she may help us a little about finding the money."

They approached the house, and as they passed the little low window, they saw by the red light of a pitch knot, that was burning on the hearth, the old woman sitting and roasting coffee, which she was stirring with a stout iron spoon. They stopped a little and reconnoitered. The glare of the light fell full on the old woman's face, showing her features sharp and wrinkled, her skin brown, and her eyes black and fiery. Her chin was leaning on one hand, and the other was busily employed in stirring the coffee, while she was talking to herself with a solemn air, and apparently with much earnestness. Her black night-cap was on, and fastened with a piece of twine under her chin, and the tight sleeves of her frock sat close to her long bony arms, while her bare feet and bird-claw toes projected out in full view below the bottom of her dress.

"I swow," said Asa, "I believe she has got a cloven foot. Let's be off; I should rather go back and sleep in the boat than to go in here to-night."

"Poh!" said Bill, "that's only the shadow of her foot you see on the floor; she has n't got any more of a cloven foot than you have. Come, I'm going in whether or no."

With that he gave a loud rap at the door.

"Who's there?" screamed the old woman.

"A friend," said Bill.

"Well, who be ye? What's your name? I shan't open the door till I know who you be."

"Bill Stanwood," said the sailor.

"Oh, is it you, Bill? Come in then," said the old woman unfastening the door, and throwing it open.

"So you're after money again, aint ye?" said the old woman, as they entered the house; "and you've brought these two men with you to help you, and that's what you are here for this time of night."

"I swow," said Asa, whispering to Bill Stanwood, "let's be off, she knows all about it."

"Hold your tongue, you fool," said Bill; "if she

knows all about us we may as well be here as any where else."

Asa trembled a little, but finally took a seat on a bench near the door, ready to run, in case matters should grow desperate.

"Well," said the old woman, "if you get the money, you'll have to work hard for it. There's been a good many tried for it before you; and there's been two men here hunting all over the island since you was here before. They dug round in a good many places, and my old man thinks they found some, for they give him half a dollar for fetching their boat back when she went adrift, and he said the half dollar was kind of rusty, and looked as though it had been buried in the ground. But I've no idea they got a dollar. It isn't so easy a matter; Old Nick takes better care of his money than all that comes to."

"Where is your old man," said Bill. "Seems to me he's always away when I come."

"The Lord knows where he is," said the old woman; "he's been out a fishing this three days, and was to a been home last night. I've been down to the shore three times to day to see if his boat was in sight, but could n't see nothin' of him."

"Well, aint you afraid he's lost?" said Bill.

"What! old Mike Newbegin, my old man, lost? No, not he. The wind always favors him when he gets ready to come home, let it be blowing which way 'twill. If it's blowing right dead ahead, and he pulls up anchor and starts for home, it will come round in five minutes and blow a fair wind till he gets clear into the harbor."

Here Asa whispered to Bill again, declaring his opinion that the old woman was a witch, if nothing worse, and proposing to leave the house and seek shelter for the night somewhere else. But Bill resolutely opposed all propositions of the kind, and Asa, being too timid to go alone, was compelled to stay and make the best of it."

"Well, come, old lady," said Bill, "you can give us a berth to lay down and take a nap till morning."

"Why, yes," said the old woman, "there's room enough in 'tother room. If anybody wants to sleep, I always let 'em, though, for my part, I can't see what good it does 'em. I think it's throwing away time. I don't think there's any need of any body's sleeping more than once or twice a week, and then not more than an hour at once; an hour of sleep is as good as a month at any time."

This strange doctrine about sleep caused Asa's

knees to tremble worse than ever, as he followed Bill
and Jonathan into the other room, where they found
a mattress of straw and some blankets, and laid down
to rest. Bill and Jonathan soon fell into a comfortable snore; but Asa thought if there was no sleep for
Mother Newbegin there was none for him. At least
he felt little inclined to trust himself asleep in the
house while she was awake. Accordingly he turned
and rolled from side to side, for two long hours, but
could get no rest. He sat up in bed. By a crack
under the door he perceived there was a faint light
still glimmering in the other room. He walked softly
towards the door and listened. He could occasionally hear the catlike footsteps of the old woman padding across the floor. Once he thought she came
close to the door, and he drew back lightly on his tip-
toes to the bedside. He wondered how Bill and
Jonathan could sleep so quietly, and stepping to the
other side of the room, he seated himself on a chest
by a low window containing three panes of seven by
nine glass, the rest of the space being filled up with
boards. Here he sat revolving over in his mind the
events of the day, and of the night thus far, and more
and more wishing himself safely at home, money or
no money. The night was still dark and gloomy, but

9*

he could now and then see a star as he looked from
the little window, and—

> Oft to the east his weary eyes he cast,
> And wish'd the lingering dawn would glimmer forth at last.

And at last it did glimmer forth ; and presently the
grey twilight began to creep into the room, and trees,
and bushes, and rocks, as he looked from the window,
began to appear with distinctness.   Asa roused his
companions, and they prepared to sally forth for their
day's enterprise.   In leaving the house, they had to
go through the room in which they had left mother
Newbegin when they retired.   On entering this room
they found the old woman appearing precisely as they
had left her, gliding about like a spirit, apparently
busy, though they could hardly tell what she was
doing.   She seemed a little surprised at their rising
so early, and told them if they would wait half an
hour she would have some breakfast for them.   They
gave her many thanks, but told her they had provisions with them, and, as their business was important,
they must be moving.

" Ah, that money, that money," said the old woman
shaking her head ; " look out sharp, or Old Nick will
make a supper of one of you to-night."

The party left the house and started for the little harbor. Asa seemed rather wild at this last remark of the old woman, and looked back over his shoulder as they departed, till they had gone several rods from the house. When they reached the harbor, they found the boat and all things as they had left them, and proceeded forthwith to commence the important work of the day. They set their compass at high-water mark at the highest point of the harbor, and took a rod pole and measured off half a mile from that point due south. They then set their compass at this place and measured off fifty rods due east. And here they found the blue stone, as described in the " documents " which Bill Stanwood had received from the pirate. The eyes of the whole party brightened as they came to it.

" There 'tis," said Bill, " so fur, exact as I told you, aint it?"

" Yes, fact, to a hair's breadth," said Jonathan.

" Well, now if you can get the fifteen rods brandy-way, you'll find the rest jest as I told you," said Bill.

They then measured of fifteen rods from the blue stone in various directions, and set up little stakes, forming a sort of circle round the stone at fifteen rods distance from it.

"Now," said Jonathan, "I'll take my mineral rod and walk round on this ring, and if the money is here I shall find the spot."

He then took his green crotched witch-hazel bough, and holding the top ends of the twigs in his hand, so that the part where they joined would point upward, began his mysterious march round the circle, while Bill and Asa walked, one on each side of him, at a little distance, and watched the mineral rod. Sometimes it would seem to incline a little one way, and sometimes a little the other, but nothing very remarkable occurred till they had gone about three-quarters round the circle, when the rod seemed to be agitated somewhat violently, and began to bend perceptibly towards the ground, and at last it bent directly downwards.

"There," said Jonathan, "do you see that? My gracious, how strong it pulls! Here's the place for bargains; drive down a stake."

"I swow," said Asa, "I never see the like of that before. I begin to think there's something in it now."

"Something in it!" said Bill Stanwood, slapping his hands together; "didn't I tell you if we could only find the fifteen rods brandy-way, I wouldn't

thank King George to be my grandfather? Now, Mr.
Rider, jest hand out your brandy bottle. We have n't
had a drop to-day; and since we've worked brandy-
way so well your way, I should like now to work it
in Asa's way a little."

"I second that motion," said Asa, "for I'm as dry
as a herrin'."

They accordingly took a social drink of brandy and
water, and drank health and success to him who
should first hit the pot of money; and having sat
down under a tree and eaten a hearty meal from their
basket, they returned to mother Newbegin's to prepare for the labors of the coming night. They
brought from their boat three shovels, a pick-axe, and
a crowbar. The old woman eyed these preparations
askance, and as she turned away, Asa thought he
could discern on her features the deep workings of a
suppressed laugh. The afternoon wore away slowly,
for they were impatient to behold their treasures; and
twice they walked to the spot, which was to be the
scene of their operations, to consult and decide on
the details to be observed. They concluded, in order
to be sure of hitting the pots, it would be best to
make their excavation at least ten or twelve feet in
diameter, and in order to afford ample time to get

down to them at about midnight, they decided to commence operations soon after dark.

" And now, about not speaking after we begin to dig," said Bill; "how shall we work it about that? for, you know, if one of us happens to speak a word, the jig is up with us."

"I think the safest way would be," said Asa, "to cut our tongues out, and then we shall be sure not to speak. Howsomever, whether we cut our tongues out or not, if you won't speak, I'll promise you I won't; for I've no idea of giving the old feller a chance to carry me off, I can tell you."

"Well," said Jonathan, "I guess we better tie some handkerchiefs tight round our mouths, as my wife said, and we shan't be so likely to forget ourselves."

This arrangement was finally concluded upon, and they returned to the house. That night they took supper with mother Newbegin, and endeavored, by paying her a liberal sum for the meal, and by various acts of courtesy, to secure her good graces. She seemed more social than she had been before, and even, at times, a sort of benevolent expression beamed from her countenance, which caused Asa to pluck up a comfortable degree of courage. But when it became dark, and they shouldered their tools to depart, the old woman fixed her sharp eyes upon them with such a wild sort of a look, that Asa began to cringe and edge along towards the door, and when she added, with a grave shake of the head, that they had better look out sharp, or the Old Nick would have them before morning, his knees trembled, and he once more wished himself at home.

The party arrived at the spot. And first, according to previous arrangements, they tied handkerchiefs over their mouths. They then measured a circle round the stake, of twelve feet in diameter, and took their shovels and commenced throwing out the earth. The night was still and calm, and though the atmosphere was not perfectly clear, the starlight was sufficient to enable them to pursue their labors with facility. They soon broke ground over the whole area which they had marked out, and diligently, shovelful by shovelful, they raised the gravelly soil and threw it beyond the circle. In half an hour they had sunk their whole shaft nearly two feet, and were getting along so far quite comfortably, with bright hopes and tolerably quiet nerves. No sound broke upon the stilness around them, save the sound of their own shovels against the stones and gravel, and

the distant roar of the chafing ocean. But at this
moment there rose a wild and powerful wind, which
brushed down upon them like a tornado. The trees
bent and quivered before it, the leaves flew, and dust
and gravel, and light substances on the ground, were
whirled into the air, and carried aloft and abroad
with great rapidity. Among the rest, Asa Sampson's
straw hat was snatched from his head and flew away
like a bird in the air. Asa dropt his shovel, and
sprang from the pit, and gave chase with all his
might. After following it about fifty rods, it touched
the ground, and he had the good fortune to catch it.
He returned to his companions, whom he found standing awe-struck, holding their own hats on, and rubbing the dust from their eyes. It was but a few
minutes, however, before the extreme violence of the
wind began to abate and they were enabled to pursue
their labors. Still the wind was wild and gusty.
They had never known it to act so strangely, or to cut
up such mad pranks before. Sometimes it would be
blowing strongly in one direction, and in one minute
it would change and blow as powerfully in the other ;
and sometimes it would whisk round and round them
like a whirlwind, making the gravel they had thrown
but fly like hailstones. Black, heavy, and angry look-

ing clouds kept floating by, and sometimes they heard
the distant rumbling of thunder. They had never
seen such clouds before. They appeared to them like
huge living animals, that glared at them, as they flew
over, with a hundred eyes. Asa sometimes thought
they looked like monstrous great sea-turtles, and he
fancied he could see huge legs and claws extending
from their sides; and once he was just on the point
of exclaiming to his companions, and telling them to
look out, or that monstrous turtle would hit them with
his claw as he went over; but the handkerchief over
his mouth checked him, and reminded him that he
must not speak, and he only sank down close to the
bank where he was digging. The clouds grew thicker
and darker, but instead of adding to the darkness of
the night, they seemed to emit a sort of broken, flick-
ering twilight, sufficient to enable them to see the
changes in each other's countenances, and to behold
objects rather indistinctly at some rods' distance.
Each perceived that the others were pale and trembling, and each endeavored, by signs and gestures,
and plying his shovel with firmness and resolution, to
encourage his fellows to perseverance.

It was now about eleven o'clock, and having measured the depth they had gone they found it to be

good four feet. One foot more would bring them to
the money; and they fell to work with increased
vigor. At this moment a heavy crash of thunder
broke over their heads, and big drops of rain began
to spatter down. Though nearly stunned by the
report, they recovered in a minute and pursued their
labors. The rain increased rapidly, and now began
to pour down almost in one continued sheet.
Although the earth below them was loose and open,
and drank in the water very fast, still so powerfully
did the rain continue to descend, that in a short time
they found it standing six inches round their feet.
One of them now took a pail and dipped out water,
while the others continued to shovel gravel. Their
resolution seemed to increase in proportion to the
obstacles they met, and gravel and water were thrown
out in rapid succession. The force of the rain soon
began to abate, and they would in a short time have
accomplished the other foot of digging, had not the
loose soil on the sides of the shaft begun to come in by
means of the wet, and accumulate at the bottom faster
than they could throw it out. Several times it gained
upon them, in this way, to the depth of some inches.
While they were battling with this difficulty, and
looking up at the bank to see where it would come in

next, a tremendously great black dog came and stood upon the brink, and opened his deep red jaws, and began to bark with terrific power. They shrunk back from the hideous animal, and raised their shovels to fright him off; but a second thought told them they had better let him alone and stick to their work.

They measured their depth again, and found it in some places four feet and a half, and in others almost five. They again plied their shovels with all diligence, and as they stepped to and fro at their work, that deep-mouthed dog kept up his deafening bark, and leaping round the verge of the pit, and keeping on the side nearest them, whenever they approached the side to throw out a shovelful of earth, he would spring and snap at their heads like a hungry lion. Asa seized the pickaxe, partly with a view of defending himself against the dog, and partly for the purpose of striking it down to see if he could hit the pots. He commenced driving the sharp point of it into the earth, passing round from one side of the pit to the other, till at last he hit a solid stone; and striking round for some distance they perceived the stone was large and flat. Bill and Jonathan made their shovels fly, and soon began to lay the surface of the stone bare. They noticed when they first struck the stone that the dog began to bark with redoubled fierceness, and as they proceeded to uncover it, he seemed to grow more and more enraged. As he did not jump down into the pit, however, they continued to keep out of his reach and pursue their work. Having laid the stone bare, and dug the earth away from the edges, they found it to be smooth and flat, about four feet square, and six or eight inches in thickness. They got the crow-bar under one side, and found they could pry it up. They gradually raised it about six inches, and putting something under to hold it, they began, by means of a stick, to explore the cavity beneath it. In moving the stick round amongst the loose sand under the stone, they soon felt four hard round substances, which they were sure must be the four iron pots. Presently they were enabled to rattle the iron covers, which gave a sound that could not be mistaken. At last they got the stick under one of the covers and shoved it into the pot, and they heard the jingle of money. Each one took hold of the stick and tried it; there was no mistake; they all poked the money with the stick, and they all heard it jingle. All that now remained was to remove the great stone. It was very heavy, but they seized it with resolute determination, and all got hold on one side with the intention of turning it up on the edge. They lifted with all their might, and were but just able to start it. They however made out to raise it slowly till they could rest it a little on their knees, where it became stationary. It seemed doubtful whether they would possibly be able to raise it on the edge, and it seemed almost equally difficult to let it down without crushing their own feet. To add to their embarrassment, the dog was barking and snapping more fiercely than ever, and seemed just upon the point of springing upon them. At this critical moment, a person came up to the edge of the pit, and bid the dog "Get out." The dog was hushed, and drew back.

"I say, neighbors," continued the stranger, "shall I give you a lift there?"

"Yes, quick," said Asa, "I can't hold on another minute."

The stranger jumped down behind them and put his hand against the stone. In a moment the ponderous weight of the stone was changed to the lightness of a dry pine board, and it flew out of the pit, carrying the three money diggers with it, head over heels, to the distance of two rods.

They picked themselves up as speedily as they

could, and ran for their lives towards the house
When they arrived they found mother Newbegin up,
as usual, and trotting about the room. They called
to her and begged her to open the door as quick as
possible. As the old woman let them in, she fixed
her sharp eyes upon them and exclaimed,

"Well, if you've got away alive you may thank
me for it. I've kept the Bible open for you, and a
candle burning before it, ever since you left the house;
and I knew while the candle was shining on the Bible
for you he couldn't touch you."

They were too much agitated to enter into conversation on the subject, and being exceedingly
exhausted, they laid down to rest, but not to sleep.
The night passed wearily away, and morning came.
The weather was clear and pleasant, and after taking
some refreshments they concluded to repair again to
the scene of their labors, and see if the money was
still there and could be obtained. Asa was very
reluctant to go, "He didn't believe there was a
single dollar left." But Bill Stanwood was resolute.
Go he would. Jonathan said "he might as well die
one way as another, for he never should dare to go
home again without carrying his wife's new gown
and morocco shoes."

So, after due consultation, they started again for the money-hole. On arriving there, they found their tools and the general appearance of the place just as they had left them. There was the great flat stone, lying about two rods from the pit. And on looking into the pit, they observed, under the place where the stone had laid, four large round holes in the sand, all of which were much stained with iron rust. They got down and examined the place. There had evidently been iron vessels there; but they were gone, money and all.

"Come," said Asa, "this place smells rather too strong of brimstone; let us be going."

CHAPTER IX.

PETER PUNCTUAL.

The names used in the following narrative are of course fictitious;
but the incidents all occurred substantially as here related, and the
parties are respectable gentlemen recently living and doing business in this bustling city of New York. The writer had the account
directly from the lips of the principal actor.

SOME few years ago, Peter Punctual, an honest and
industrious young fellow from Yankee land—I say
Yankee land, but I freely confess that is merely an
inference of mine, drawn from circumstances of this
story itself; but if my readers, after perusing it, do
not come to the same conclusion, they may set him
down as coming from any other land they please; but
for myself, were I on a jury, and under oath, I would
bring him in a Yankee. This same Peter Punctual,
some few years ago, came into New York, and
attempted to turn a penny and get an honest living by
procuring subscribers to various magazines and peri-
odicals, on his own hook. That is, he would receive a
quantity of magazines from a distant publisher, at a

discount, and get up his own list of subscribers about the city, and serve them through the year at the regular subscription price, which would leave the amount of the said discount a clear profit in his pocket, or rather a compensation for his time and labor. There are many persons in this city who obtain a livelihood in the same way.

Peter's commissions being small, and his capital still smaller, he was obliged to transact his business with great care and circumspection, in order to make both ends meet. He adopted a rule, therefore, to make all his subscribers pay their year's subscription in advance. Such things could be done in those days when business was brisk, and the people were strangers to "hard times." In canvassing for subscribers, one day, through the lower part of the city, and in the principal business streets, he observed a store which had the air of doing a heavy business, and read upon the sign over the door, "Solomon Sharp, Importer." The field looked inviting, and in Peter went with his samples under his arm, and inquired for Mr. Sharp. The gentleman was pointed out to him by the clerks, and Peter stepped up and asked him if he would not like to subscribe for some magazines.

10

"What sort of ones have you got there?" said Mr. S.

"Three or four different kinds," said Peter, laying the specimens on the desk before him—"please to look at them and suit yourself."

Sharp tumbled them over and examined them one after another, and at last took up "Buckingham's New England Magazine," published at Boston.

"What are your terms for this?" said he; "I don't know but I would subscribe for this."

"Five dollars a year in advance," said Peter, "to be delivered carefully every month at your store or house."

"But I never pay in advance for these things," said Sharp. "It's time enough to pay for a thing when you get it. I'll subscribe for it, if you have a mind to receive your pay at the end of the year, and not otherwise."

"That's against my rule," said Peter; "I have all my subscribers pay in advance."

"Well, it's against my rule to pay for anything before I get it," said Sharp; "so if you have n't a mind to take my subscription, to be paid at the end of the year, you won't get it at all. That's the long and the short of the matter."

Peter paused a little, and queried with himself as to what he had better do. The man was evidently doing a large business, and was undoubtedly rich—a wholesale dealer and an importer—there could not possibly be any danger of losing the subscription in such a case: and would it not be better to break over his rule for once, than to lose so good a subscriber.

"Well, what say?" said Sharp; "do as you like; but those are my only terms. I will not pay for a thing before I get it."

"On the whole," said Peter, "I have a good mind to break over my rule this time, for I don't like to lose a good subscriber when I can find one. I believe I'll put your name down, sir. Where will you have it left?"

"At my house," said Mr. Sharp, which was about a mile and a half from his store, away up town.

The business being thus concluded, Peter took up his magazines, bade Mr. Sharp good morning, and left the store. No further personal intercourse occurred between them during the year. But Peter, who was his own carrier, as well as canvasser, regularly every month delivered the New England Magazine at Mr. Sharp's door. And in a few days after the year expired, he made out his bill for the five dollars, and called at Mr. Sharp's store for the money. He entered with as much confidence that he should receive the chink at once, as he would have had in going with a check for the like sum into the Bank of the United States, during that institution's palmiest days. He found Mr. Sharp at his desk, and presented him the bill. That gentleman took it and looked at it, and then looked at Peter.

"Oh! ah, good morning," said he, "you are the young man who called here on this business nearly a year ago. Well, the year has come round, has it?"

"Yes, I believe it has," said Peter.

"Well, bills of this kind," said Mr. Sharp, "are paid at the house. We don't attend to them here; you just take it to the house, any time when you are passing, and it will be settled."

"Oh, very well, sir," said Peter, bowing, and left the store. "Doing too large a business at the store, I suppose," he continued, to himself, as he walked up the street, "to attend to little things of this kind. Don't like to be bothered with 'em, probably."

But Peter thought he might as well make a finish of the business, now he was out; so he went directly to the house, and rung at the door. The servant girl soon made her appearance.

" Mrs. Sharp within ?" said Peter.

"Yes, sir," said the girl.

" Jest carry this bill to her, if you please, and ask her if she will hand you the money for it."

The girl took the bill into the house, and presently returned with the answer, that " Mrs. Sharp says she does n't pay none of these 'ere things here—you must carry it to the store."

" Please to carry it back to Mrs. Sharp," said Peter, " and tell her Mr. Sharp desired me to bring the bill here, and said it would be paid at the house."

This message brought Mrs. Sharp herself to the door, to whom Peter raised his hat and bowed very politely.

" I have n't nothing at all to do with the bills here at the house," said the lady ; ' they must be carried to the store—that's the place to attend to them."

" Well, ma'am," said Peter, " I carried it to the store, and presented it to Mr. Sharp, and he told me to bring it to the house and you would pay it here, and that he could n't attend to it at the store."

" But he could n't mean that I should pay it," said Mrs. Sharp, " for he knows I have n't the money."

" But he said so," said Peter.

" Well then there must be some mistake about it," said the lady.

"I beg your pardon, ma'am," said Peter, "it's possible there may be," and he put the bill in his pocket, bowed, and left the house.

"It is very queer," thought Peter to himself as he walked away a little vexed. "I can't conceive how there could be any mistake about it, though it is possible there may be. There could n't be any mistake on my part, for I'm sure I understood him. Maybe he thought she had money at the house when she had n't. I guess it will all come out right enough in the end."

Consoling himself with these reflections, Peter Punctual thought he would let Mr. Sharp rest two or three days, and not show any anxiety by calling again in a hurry. He would not be so unwise as to offend a good subscriber, and run the hazard of losing him, by an appearance of too much haste in presenting his bills. Accordingly, in about three days, he called again at Mr. Sharp's store, and asked him in a low voice, so that no one should overhear, if it was convenient for him to take that little bill for the magazine to-day.

"But I told you," said Mr. Sharp, "to carry that bill to the house; I can't attend to it here."

"Yes, sir, so I understood you," said Peter, "and I

carried it to the house, and Mrs. Sharp said she could n't pay it there, for she had no money, and I must bring it to the store."

"Oh, strange!" said Mr. Sharp; "well, she did n't properly understand it then. But I am too much engaged to attend to you to-day; you call again, or call at the house sometime, when I am there."

Upon this, he turned to his desk and began to write with great earnestness, and Peter left the store. The affair began to grow a little vexatious, and Peter felt a little nettled. Still, he supposed that people doing such very large business *did* find it difficult to attend to these little matters, and doubtless it would be set right when he should call again.

After waiting patiently a couple of weeks, Peter called again at Mr. Sharp's store. When he entered the door, Mr. Sharp was looking at a newspaper; but on glancing at Peter, he instantly dropped the paper, and fell to writing at his desk with great rapidity. Peter waited respectfully a few minutes, unwilling to disturb the gentleman till he should appear to be a little more at leisure. But after waiting some time without seeing any prospect of Mr. Sharp's completing the very pressing business before him, he approached him with deference, and asked if it would be conve-

nient for him to take that little bill for the magazine
to-day. Sharp turned and looked at Peter very sternly.

"I can't be bothered with these little things," said
he "when I am so much engaged. I am exceedingly
busy to-day—a good many heavy orders waiting—
you must call at the house, and hand the bill to me or
my wife, no matter which." And he turned to his
desk, and continued to write, without saying anything
more.

Peter began to think he had got hold of a hard
customer : but he had no idea of giving up the chase.

He called at the house several times afterward, but
Mr. Sharp never happened to be at home. Once he
ventured to send the bill again by the girl to Mrs.
Sharp, who returned for answer, that she had nothing
to do with such bills ; he must carry it to the store.

At last, after repeated calls, he found Mr. Sharp
one day at home. He came to the door, and Peter
presented the bill. Mr. Sharp expressed some surprise and regret that he had come away from the
store, and forgot to put any money in his pocket.
Peter would have to call some other day. Accordingly, Peter Punctual retired, with a full determination to call some other day, and that not very far
distant ; for it had now been several months that he

had been beaten back and forth like a shuttle-cock between Mr. Sharp's store and Mr. Sharp's house, and he was getting to be rather tired of the game.

Having ascertained from the girl at what hour the family dined, he called the next day precisely at the dinner hour. He rung at the door, and when the girl opened it, Peter stepped into the hall.

" Is Mr. Sharp in?" said Peter.

" Yes, sir," said the girl; " he's up stairs. I'll speak to him if you want to see him."

" Yes," said Peter, " and I'll take a seat in the parlor till he comes down."

As he said this, Peter walked into the parlor and seated himself upon an elegant sofa. The parlor was richly furnished with Brussels carpet, the best of mahogany furniture, a splendid piano, &c., &c. ; and in the back parlor, to which folding doors were open, everything appeared with corresponding elegance. A table was there spread, upon which dinner seemed to be nearly ready. Presently the girl returned from the chamber, and informed Peter, that Mr. Sharp said " it was jest the dinner hour now, and he would have to call again."

" Please to go and tell Mr. Sharp," said Peter, " that I must see him, and I'll wait till he comes down."

10*

The girl carried the message, and Mr. Sharp soon made his appearance in the parlor. A frown passed over his brow as he looked at Peter and saw him sitting so much at ease, and apparently so much at home, upon the sofa. Peter rose and asked him politely if it was convenient for him to take that little bill to-day.

"No," said Sharp, "it is not; and if it was, I would n't take it at this hour. It's a very improper time to call upon such an errand just as one is going to sit down to dinner. You must call again; but don't call at dinner time; or you may drop into the store sometime, and perhaps I may find time to at tend to it there."

"Well, now, Mr. Sharp," said Peter, with rather a determined look, "I can't stand this kind of business any longer, that's a fact. I'm a poor man, and I suppose you are a rich one. I can't afford to lose five dollars, and I'm too poor to spend any more time in running after it and trying to collect it. I must eat, as well as other folks, and if you can't pay me the five dollars to-day, to help me pay my board at my regular boarding-house, I'll stay here and board it out at your table."

"You will, will you?" said Sharp, looking daggers,

and stepping toward Peter. "If you give me a word of your impudence, you may find it'll be a long time before you collect your bill."

"It's been a long time already," said Peter, "and I can't afford to wait any longer. My mind is made up; if you don't pay me now, I'm going to stay here and board it out."

Sharp colored, and looked at the door, and then at Peter.

"Come, come, young man," said he advancing, with rather a threatening attitude, toward Peter, "the sooner you leave the house peaceably the better."

"Now, sir," said Peter, fixing his black eyes upon Sharp, with an intenseness that he could not but feel, "I am a small man, and you are considerable of a large one; but my mind is made up. I am not going to starve, when there's food enough that I have an honest claim upon."

So saying, he took his seat again very deliberately upon the sofa. Sharp paused; he looked agitated and angry; and after waiting a minute, apparently undecided what to do, he left the parlor and went up stairs. In a few minutes, the servant rung for dinner. Mrs. Sharp came into the dining room and took her seat at the head of the table. Mr. Sharp followed,

and seated himself opposite his lady; and between
them, and on the right hand of Mrs. Sharp, sat another
lady, probably some friend or relative of the family.
When they were well seated, and Mr. Sharp was
beginning to carve, Peter walked out of the parlor,
drew another chair up to the table, and seated himself
very composedly opposite the last-mentioned lady.
Mr. Sharp colored a good deal, but kept on carving.
Mrs. Sharp stared very wildly, first at Peter and then
at her husband.

"What in the world does this mean?" said she.
"Mr. Sharp, I did n't know we were to have company
to dinner."

"We are not," said the husband. "This young
man has the impudence to take his seat at the table
unasked, and says he is going to board out the amount
of the bill."

"Well, really, this is a pretty piece of politeness,"
said Mrs. Sharp, looking very hard at Peter.

"Madam," said Peter, "hunger will drive a man
through a stone wall. I must have my board somewhere."

No reply was made to this, and the dinner went on
without any further reference to Peter at present.
Mr. Sharp helped his wife, and then the other lady,

and then himself, and they all fell to eating. Peter
looked around him for a plate and knife and fork, but
there were none on the table but what were in use.
Peter, however, was not to be baffled. He reached a
plate of bread, and tipping the bread upon the table
cloth, appropriated the plate for his own convenience.
He then took possession of the carving knife and fork,
helped himself bountifully to meat and vegetables,
and commenced eating his dinner with the greatest
composure imaginable. These operations on the part
of Peter, had the effect to suspend all operations for
the time on the part of the rest of the company. The
ladies had laid down their knives and forks, and were
staring at Peter in wild astonishment.

"For mercy's sake, Mr. Sharp," said the lady of the
house, " can't we pick up money enough about the
house to pay this man his five dollars and send him
off? I declare this is too provoking. I'll see what I
can find."

With that she rose and left the room. Mr. Sharp
presently followed her. They returned again in a
minute, and Mr. Sharp laid a five dollar bill before
Peter, and told him he would thank him to leave the
house. Peter examined the bill to see if it was a good
one, and very quietly folded it and put it into his

pocket. He then drew out a little pocket inkstand and a piece of paper, laid it upon the table before him, wrote a receipt for the money, which he handed to Mr. Sharp, rose from the table, bowed to the company and retired, thinking as he left the house that he had had full enough of the custom of Solomon Sharp, the importer.

Peter Punctual still followed his vocation of circulating magazines. He had no intention of ever darkening the door of Mr. Solomon Sharp's store again, but somehow or other, two or three years after, as he was canvassing for subscribers in the lower part of the city, he happened to blunder into the same store accidentally, without noticing the name upon the door. Nor did he discover his mistake, until he had nearly crossed the store and attracted the attention of Mr. Sharp himself, who was at his accustomed seat at the desk where Peter had before so often seen him. Peter thought, as he had got fairly into the store, he would not back out; so he stepped up to Mr. Sharp without a look of recognition, and asked if he would not like to subscribe for some magazines. Mr. Sharp, who either did not recognize Peter, or chose not to appear to recognize him, took the magazines and looked at them, and found a couple he said he would like to take, and inquired the terms. They were each three dollars a year in advance.

" But I don't pay in advance for anything," said Sharp. " If you have a mind to leave them at my house, to be paid for at the end of the year, you may put me down for these two."

"No," said Peter, " I don't wish to take any subscribers, but those who pay in advance."

Saying this, he took up his specimens, and was going out the door, when Mr. Sharp called him back.

" Here young man, you may leave these two at any rate," said he, " and here's your advance," handing him the six dollars.

" Where will you have them left ?" said Peter.

" At my house, up town," said Mr. Sharp, describing the street and number.

The business being completed, Peter retired, much astonished at his good luck. He again became a monthly visitor at Mr. Sharp's door, where he regularly delivered to the servant girl the two magazines. Two or three months after this, when he called one day on his usual round, the girl told him that Mr. Sharp wanted to see him, and desired he would call at the store. Peter felt not a little curious to know what Mr. Sharp might have to say to him; so in the course of the same day he called at Mr. Sharp's store.

"Good morning," said Mr. Sharp as Peter entered; "come, take a chair, and sit down here."

Peter, with a "good morning, sir," did as he was desired.

"Ain't you the young man," said Mr. Sharp, with a comical kind of a look, "who set out to board out a subscription to the New England Magazine at my house two or three years ago."

"Yes," said Peter, "I believe I'm the same person who once had the honor of taking board at your house."

"Well," said Mr. Sharp, "I want to give you a job."

"What is it?" said Peter.

"Here, I want you to collect these bills for me," said Mr. Sharp, taking a bundle from his desk, "for I'll be hanged if *I* can; I've tried till I'm tired."

Whereupon he opened the bundle and assorted out the bills, and made a schedule of them, amounting, in the aggregate, to about a thousand dollars.

"There," said he, "I will give upon that list ten per cent. commission on all you collect; and on that

list I'll give you twenty-five per cent. on all you collect. What say you? will you undertake the job?"

"Well, I'll try," said Peter, "and see what I can
do with them. How soon must I return them?"

"Take your own time for it," said Mr. Sharp;
"I've seen enough of you to know pretty well what
you are."

Peter accordingly took the bills and entered on his
new task, following it up with diligence and perseverance. In a few weeks he called again at Sharp's
store.

"Well," said Mr. Sharp, "have you made out to
collect anything on those bills?"

"Yes," said Peter.

"There were some of the ten per cent. list that I
thought it probable you might collect," said Mr.
Sharp. "How many have you collected?"

"All of them," said Peter.

"All of them!" said Mr. Sharp; "well, fact, that's
much more than I expected. The twenty-five per
cent. list was all dead dogs, was n't it? You got
nothing on them, I suppose, did you?"

"Yes, I did," said Peter.

"Did you though? How much?" said Sharp.

"I got them all," said Peter.

" Oh, that's all a joke," said Sharp.

"No, it is n't a joke," said Peter. "I've collected every dollar of them, and here's the money," taking out his pocket-book, and counting out the bills.

Mr. Sharp received the money with the most perfect astonishment. He had not expected one-half of the amount would ever be collected.

He counted out the commissions on the ten per cent. list, and then the commissions on the twenty-five per cent. list, and handed the sum over to Peter. And then he counted out fifty dollars more, and asked Peter to accept that as a present; "partly," said he, "because you have accomplished this task so very far beyond my expectations, and partly because my acquaintance with you has taught me one of the best lessons of my life. It has taught me the value of perseverance and punctuality. I have reflected upon it much ever since you undertook to board out the bill for the magazine at my house."

" Why yes," said Peter, "I think perseverance and punctuality are great helps in the way of business."

" If every person in the community," said Mr. Sharp, "would make it a point to pay all of his bills promptly, the moment they become due, what a vast improvement it would make in the condition of society all round. That would put people in a condition, at all times, to be *able* to pay their bills promptly."

We might add, that Peter Punctual afterward opened a store in the city, in a branch of business which brought Mr. Sharp to be a customer to him, and he has been one of his best customers ever since, paying all of his bills promptly, and whenever Peter requires it, even paying in advance.

CHAPTER X.

THE SPECULATOR.

In the autumn of 1836, while travelling through a portion of the interior of the State of Maine, I stopped at a small new village, between the Kennebec and Penobscot rivers, nearly a hundred miles from the sea-board, for the purpose of giving my horse a little rest and provender, before proceeding some ten miles farther that evening. It was just after sunset; I was walking on the piazza, in front of the neat new tavern, admiring the wildness of the surrounding country, and watching the gathering shadows of the grey twilight, as it fell upon the valleys, and crept softly up the hills, when a light one-horse wagon, with a single gentleman, drove rapidly into the yard, and stopped at the stable door.

"Tom," said the gentleman to the ostler as he jumped from his wagon, "take my mare out, rub her down well, and give her four quarts of oats. Be spry, now, Tom; you need n't give her any water, for she sweats like fury. I'll give her a little when I am ready to start."

Tom sprang with uncommon alacrity to obey the orders he had received, and the stranger walked toward the house. He was a tall, middle-aged gentleman, rather thin, but well proportioned, and well dressed. It was the season of the year when the weather began to grow chilly, and the evenings cold; and the frock-coat of the stranger, trimmed with fur, and buttoned to the throat, while it insured comfort, served also to exhibit his fine elastic form to the best advantage. His little wagon, too, had a marked air of comfort about it; there were the spring-seat, the stuffed cushions, and buffalo robes; all seemed to indicate a gentleman of ease and leisure; while, on the other hand, his rapid movements and prompt manner, betokened the man of business. As he stepped on to the piazza, with his long and handsome driving-whip in his hand, the tavern-keeper, who was a brisk young man, and well understood his business, met him with a hearty shake of the hand, and a familiar "How are you, Colonel? Come, walk in."

There was something about the stranger that strongly attracted my attention, and I followed him into the bar-room. He stepped up to the bar, laid his whip on the counter, and called for a glass of brandy and water, with some small crackers and cheese.

"But not going to stop to supper, Colonel ? Going farther to-night ?" inquired the landlord, as he pushed forward the brandy bottle.

"Can't stop more than ten minutes," replied the stranger; "just long enough to let the mare eat her oats."

"Is that the same mare," asked the host, "that you had when you were here last ?"

"Yes," answered the colonel: "I've drove her thirty miles since dinner, and am going forty miles farther, before I stop."

"But you'll kill that mare, colonel, as sure as rates," said the landlord; "she's too likely a beast to drive to death."

"No, no," was the reply; "she's tough as a pitch-knot; I feed her well; she'll stand it, I guess. I go to Norridgewock before I sleep to-night."

With a few more brief remarks, the stranger finished his brandy, and crackers and cheese; he threw down some change on the counter, ordered his carriage brought to the door, and bidding his landlord good night, jumped into his wagon, cracked his whip and was off like a bird. After he was gone, I ventured to exercise the Yankee privilege of asking " who he might be."

" That's Colonel Kingston," said the landlord; " a queer sort of a chap he is, too; a real go-ahead sort of a fellow as ever I met with; does more more business in one day than some folks would do in a year. He's a right good customer; always full of money, and pays well."

" What business or profession does he follow?" I asked.

" Why, not any particular business," replied the landlord; " he kind o' speculates round, and sich like."

" But," said I, " I thought the speculation in timber lands was over; I did n't know that a single person could be found, now, to purchase lands."

" Oh, it is n't exactly that kind of speculation," said the landlord; " he's got a knack of buying out folks' farms; land, house, barn, live stock, hay, and provisions, all in the lump."

" Where does he live ?" said I.

" Oh, he's lived round in a number of places, since he's been in these parts. He's been round in these towns only a year or two, and it's astonishing to see how much property he's accumulated. He stays in Monson most of the time, now. That's where he came from this afternoon. They say he's got a number of excellent farms in Monson, and I'll warrant he's got some deeds of some more of 'em with him, now, that he's going to carry to Norridgewock to-night, to put on record."

I bade the landlord good evening, and proceeded on my journey. What I had seen and heard of Colonel Kingston, had made an unwonted impression on my mind; and as Monson lay in my route, and I was expecting to stop there a few days, my curiosity was naturally a little excited, to learn something more of his history. The next day I reached Monson; and as I rode over its many hills, and along its fine ridges of arable land, I was struck with the number of fine farms which I passed, and the evidences of thrift and good husbandry that surrounded me. As this town was at that time almost on the extreme verge of the settlements in that part of the state, I was surprised to find it so well settled, and under such good cultivation. My surprise was increased, on arriving at the centre of the town, to find a flourishing and bright-looking village, with two or three stores, a variety of mechanics' shops, a school-house, and a neat little

church, painted white, with green blinds, and sur-
mounted by a bell. A little to the westward of the
village, was one of those clear and beautiful ponds,
that greet the eye of the traveller in almost every
hour's ride in that section of the country; and on its
outlet, which ran through the village, stood a mill, and
some small manufacturing establishments, that served
to fill up the picture.

"Happy town!" thought I, "that has such a
delightful village for its centre of attraction, and happy
village that is supported by surrounding farmers of
such thrift and industry as those of Monson!" All
this, too, I had found within a dozen or fifteen miles
of Moosehead Lake, the noblest and most extensive
sheet of water in New England, which I had hitherto
considered so far embosomed in the deep, trackless
forest, as to be almost unapproachable, save by the
wild Indian or the daring hunter. A new light seemed
to burst upon me; and it was a pleasant thought that
led me to look forward but a few years, when the rug-
ged and wild shores of the great Moosehead should
resound with the hum and the song of the husband-
man, and on every side rich farms and lively vilages
should be reflected on its bosom.

I had been quietly seated in the village inn but a

11

short time, in a room that served both for bar and sitting-room, when a small man, with a flapped hat, an old brown "wrapper," a leather strap buckled round his waist, and holding a goad-stick in his hand, entered the room, and took a seat on a bench in the corner. His bright, restless eye glanced round the room, and then seemed to be bent thoughtfully toward the fire, while in the arch expression of his countenance I thought I beheld the prelude to some important piece of intelligence, that was struggling for utterance. At last, said he, addressing the landlord, " I guess the colonel ain't about home to-day, is he ?"

" No," replied Boniface, " he's been gone since yesterday morning; he said he was going up into your neighborhood. Have n't you seen anything of him ?"

" Yes," said the little man with the goad-stick, " I see him yesterday afternoon about two o'clock, starting off like a streak, to go to Norridgewock."

" Gone to Norridgewock !" said the landlord; " what for ? He did n't say nothing about going when he went away."

" More deeds, I guess," said the little teamster. " He's worried Deacon Stone out of *his* farm, at last."

" He han't got Deacon Stone's farm, has he ?" exclaimed the landlord.

"He *has n't* got Deacon Stone's farm, has he?" exclaimed the landlord.

"Deacon Stone's farm!" reiterated an elderly, sober-looking man, drawing a long pipe from his mouth, which he had until now been quietly smoking in the opposite corner.

"Deacon Stone's farm!" uttered the landlady, with upraised hands, as she entered the room just in season to hear the announcement.

"Deacon Stone's farm!" exclaimed three or four others, in different parts of the room, all turning an eager look toward the little man with the goad-stick. As soon as there was a sufficient pause in these exclamations, to allow the teamster to put in another word, he repeated:

"Yes, he's worried the deacon out, at last, and got hold of his farm, as slick as a whistle. He's been kind o' edging round the deacon this three weeks, a little to a time; jest enough to find out how to get the right side of him; for the deacon was a good deal offish, and yesterday morning the colonel was up there by the time the deacon had done breakfast; and he got them into the deacon's fore room, and shet the door; and there they staid till dinner was ready, and had waited for them an hour, before they would come out.

And when they had come out, the job was all done;
and the deed was signed, sealed, and delivered. I'd
been there about eleven o'clock, and the deacon's
wife and the gals were in terrible fidgets for fear of
what was going on in t'other room. They started to
go in, two or three times, but the door was fastened,
so they had to keep out. After dinner I went over
again, and got there just before they were out of the
fore room. The deacon asked the colonel to stop to
dinner, but I guess the colonel see so many sour looks
about the house, that he was afraid of a storm abrew-
ing; so he only ketched up a piece of bread and
cheese, and said he must be a-goin'. He jumped into
his wagon, and give his mare a cut, and was out of
sight in two minutes."

" How *did* poor Mrs. Stone feel?" asked the landlady; "I should thought she would a-died."

"She looked as if she'd turn milk sour quicker than
a thunder-shower," said the teamster: " and Jane
went into the bedroom, and cried as if her heart
would break. I believe they did n't any of 'em make
out to eat any dinner, and I thought the deacon felt
about as bad as any of 'em, after all; for I never see
him look so kind o' riled in my life. ' Now Mrs.
Stone,' said he to his wife, ' you think I've done

wrong; but after talking along with Colonel Kingston, I made up my mind it would be for the best.'
She did n't make him any answer, but begun to cry,
and went out of the room. The deacon looked as if
he would sink into the 'arth. He stood a minute or
two, as if he was n't looking at nothing, and then he
took down his pipe off the mantel, and sat down in
the corner, and went to smoking as hard as he could
smoke.

"After a while, he turned round to me, and says he,
'Neighbor, I don't know but I've done wrong.'
'Well,' says I, 'in my opinion, that depends upon
what sort of a bargain you've made. If you've got a
good bargain out of the colonel, I don't see why his
money is n't worth as much as anybody's, or why
another farm as good as your'n is n't worth as much.'
'Yes,' said the deacon, 'so it seems to me. I've
got a good bargain, I know; it's more than the
farm is worth. I never considered it worth more
than two thousand dollars, stock, and hay, and all;
and he takes the whole jest as 'tis, and gives me three
thousand dollars.' 'Is it pay down?' says I. 'Yes,'
says he, 'it's all pay down. He gives me three
hundred dollars in cash; I've got it in my pocket;
and then he gives me an order on Saunders' store for

two hundred dollars; that's as good as money, you know; for we are always wanting one thing or another out of his store. Then he gives me a deed of five hundred acres, of land, in the upper part of Vermont, at five dollars an acre. That makes up three thousand dollars. But that is n't all; he says this land is richly worth seven dollars an acre; well timbered, and a good chance to get the timber down; and he showed me certificates of several respectable men, that had been all over it, and they said it was well worth seven dollars. That gives me two dollars clear profit on an acre, which on five hundred acres makes a thousand dollars. So that instead of three thousand dollars, I s'pose I've really got four thousand for the farm. But then it seems to work up the feelings of the women folks so, to think of leaving it, after we've got it so well under way, that I don't know but I've done wrong.' And his feelings came over him so, that he begun to smoke away again as hard as he could draw. I did n't know what to say to him, for I did n't believe he would ever get five hundred dollars for his five hundred acres of land, so I got up and went home."

As my little goad-stick teamster made a pause here, the elderly man in the opposite corner, who had sat all this time knocking his pipe-bowl on the thumbnail of his left hand, took up the thread of discourse.

"I'm afraid," says he, looking up at the landlord, "I'm afraid Deacon Stone has got tricked out of his farm for a mere song. That Colonel Kingston, in my opinion, is a dangerous man, and ought to be looked after."

"Well, I declare!" said the landlord, "I'd no idee he would get hold of Deacon Stone's farm. That's one of the best farms in the town."

"Yes," replied the man with the pipe, "and that makes seven of the "best farms in town that he's got hold of already; and what 'll be the end of it, I don't know; but I think something ought to be done about it."

"Well, there," said the landlady, "I *do* pity Mrs. Stone from the bottom of my heart; she'll never get over it the longest day she lives."

Here the little man with the goad-stick, looking out the window, saw his team starting off up the road, and he flew out of the door, screaming " Hush! whoa! hush!" and that was the last I saw of him. But my curiosity was now too much excited, with regard to Colonel Kingston's mysterious operations, and my sympathies for good Deacon Stone, and his fellow-sufferers, were too thoroughly awakened, to allow me to rest without farther inquiries.

During the days that I remained in the neighborhood, I learned that he came from Vermont; that he had visited Monson several times within a year or two, and had made it his home there for the last few months. During that time he had exercised an influence over some of the honest and sober-minded farmers of Monson, that was perfectly unaccountable. He was supposed to be a man of wealth, for he never seemed to lack money for any operation he chose to undertake. He had a bold, dashing air, and rather fascinating manners, and his power over those with whom he conversed had become so conspicuous, that it was regarded as an inevitable consequence in Monson, if a farmer chanced to get shut up in a room with Colonel Kingston, he was a " gone goose," and sure to come out well stripped of his feathers. He had actually got possession of seven or eight of the best farms in the town, for about one quarter part of their real value.

It may be thought unaccountable, that thriving, sensible farmers could in so many instances be duped; but there were some extraneous circumstances that helped to produce the result. The wild spirit of speculation, which had raged throughout the country for two or three years, had pervaded almost every mind, and rendered it restless, and desirous of change. And then the seasons, for a few years past, had been cold and unfavorable. The farmer had sowed and had not reaped, and he was discouraged. If he could sell, he would go to a warmer climate. These influences, added to his own powers of adroitness and skill in making "the worse appear the better reason," had enabled Colonel Kingston to inveigle the farmers of Monson out of their hard-earned property, and turn them, houseless and poor, upon the world.

The public mind had become much excited upon the subject, and the case of Deacon Stone added fresh fuel to the fire. It was in this state of affairs that I left Monson, and heard no more of Colonel Kingston until the following summer, when another journey called me into that neighborhood, and I learned the sequel to his fortunes. The colonel made but few more conquests, after his victory over Deacon Stone; and the experience of a cold and cheerless winter, which soon overtook them, brought the deluded farmers to their senses. The trifling sums of money which they received in hand, were soon exhausted in providing necessary supplies for their families; and

11*

the property which they had obtained, as principal payment for their farms, turned out to be of little value, or was so situated that they could turn it to no profitable account. Day after day, through the winter, the excitement increased, and spread, and waxed more intense, as the unfortunate condition of the sufferers became more generally known. "Colonel Kingston" was the great and absorbing topic of discussion, at the stores, at the tavern, at evening parties, and sleigh-rides, and even during intermission at church, on the Sabbath.

The indignation of the people had reached that pitch which usually leads to acts of violence. Colonel Kingston was now regarded as a monster, preying upon the peace and happiness of society, and various were the expedients proposed to rid the town of him. The schoolboys, in the several districts, discussed the matter, and resolved to form a grand company, to snowball him out of town, and only waited a nod of approbation from some of their parents or teachers, to carry their resolutions into effect. Some reckless young men were for seizing him, and giving him a public horse-whipping, in front of the tavern at mid-day, and in presence of the whole village. Others, equally violent, but less daring, proposed catching him out, some dark evening, giving him a good coat of tar-and-feathers, and riding him out of town on a rail. But the older, more experienced, and sober-minded men, shook their heads at these rash projects, and said : " It is a bad plan for people to take the law into their own hands ; as long as we live under good laws, it is best to be governed by them. Such kind of squabbles as you young folks want to get into, most always turn out bad in the end."

So reasoned the old folks ; but they were nevertheless as eager and as determined to get rid of Colonel Kingston, as were the young ones, though more cautious and circumspect as to the means. At last, after many consultations and much perplexity, Deacon Stone declared one day, with much earnestness, to his neighbors and townsmen, who were assembled at the village, that " For his part, he believed it was best to appeal at once to the laws of the land ; and if *they* would n't give protection to the citizen, he did n't know what would. For himself, he verily believed Colonel Kingston might be charged with swindling, and if a complaint was to be made to the Grand Jury he did n't believe but they would have him indicted and tried in Court, and give back the people their farms again." The deacon spoke *feelingly*, on the subject, and his words found a ready response in the hearts of all present. It was at once agreed to present Colonel Kingston to the Grand Jury, when the Court should next be in session at Norridgewock. Accordingly, when the next Court was held, Monson was duly represented before the grand inquest for the county of Somerset, and such an array of facts and evidence was exhibited, that the Jury, without hesitation, found a bill against the colonel for swindling, and a warrant was immediately issued for his apprehension.

This crisis had been some months maturing, and the warm summer had now commenced. The forest trees were now in leaf; and though the ground was yet wet and muddy, the days began to be hot and uncomfortable. It was a warm moonlight evening, when the officer arrived at Monson with the warrant. He had taken two assistants with him, mounted on fleet horses, and about a dozen stout young men of the village were in his train as volunteers. They approached the tavern where Colonel Kingston boarded, and just as they were turning from the road up to the house, the form of a tall, slim person was seen in the bright moonlight, gliding from the back-door, and crossing the garden.

"There he goes!" exclaimed a dozen Monson voices at once; "that's he!—there he goes!"

And sure enough, it was he! Whether he had been notified of his danger, by some traitor, or had seen from the window the approach of the party, and suspected mischief was at hand, was never known. But the moment he heard these exclamations, he sprang from the ground as if a bullet had pierced his heart. He darted across the garden, leaped the fence at a bound, and flew over the adjacent pasture with the speed of a race-horse. In a moment the whole party were in full pursuit; and in five minutes more, a hundred men and boys, of all ages, roused by the cry that now rang through the village, were out, and joining in the race. The fields were rough, and in some places quite wet, so that running across them was rather a difficult and hazardous business. The direction which Kingston at first seemed inclined to take, would lead him into the main road, beyond the corner, nearly a half a mile off. But those who were mounted put spurs to their horses, and reaching the spot before him, headed him off in another direction. He now flew from field to field, leaping fence after fence, and apparently aiming for the deep forest, on the eastern part of the town. Many of his pursuers were athletic young men, and they gave him a hot chase. Even Deacon Stone, who had come to the village that evening to await the arrival of the officer—even the deacon, now in the sixty-first year of his age, ran like a boy. He kept among the foremost of the pursuers, and once getting within about a dozen rods of the fugitive, his zeal burst forth into words, and he cried out, in a tremulous voice: "Stop! you infernal villain!—stop!" This was the nearest approach he had made to profanity for forty years; and when the sound of the words he had uttered fell full on his ear, his nerves received such a shock that his legs trembled and he was no longer able to sustain his former speed.

The colonel, however, so far from obeying the emphatic injunction of the deacon, rather seemed to be inspired by it to new efforts of flight. Over log, bog and brook, stumps, stones and fences, he flew like a wild deer; and after a race of some two miles, during which he was at no time more than twenty rods from some of his pursuers, he plunged into a thick dark forest. Hearing his adversaries close upon him, after he had entered the wood, and being almost entirely exhausted, he threw himself under the side of a large fallen tree, where he was darkly sheltered by a thick clump of alders. His pursuers rushed furiously on, many of them within his hearing, and some of them passing over the very tree under which he lay. After scouring the forest for a mile round, without finding any traces of the fugitive, they began to retreat to the opening, and Kingston heard enough of their remarks, on their return, to learn that his retreat from the woods that night would be well guarded against, and that the next day Monson would pour out all its force, "to hunt him to the ends of the 'arth, but what they would have him!"

Under this comfortable assurance, he was little disposed to take much of a night's rest, where he would be sure to be discovered and overtaken in the morning. But what course to take, and what measures to adopt, was a difficult question for him to answer. To return to Monson opening, he well knew would be to throw himself into the hands of his enemies; and if he remained in the woods till next day, he foresaw there would be but a small chance of escape from the hundreds on every side, who would be on the alert to take him. North of him was the new town of Elliotville, containing some fifteen or twenty families, and to the south, lay Guilford, a well-settled farming town; but he knew he would be no more safe in either of those settlements than he would in Monson. East of

him lay an unsettled and unincorporated wild township, near the centre of which, and some three or four
miles to the eastward of where he now lay, dwelt a
solitary individual by the name of Johnson, a singular
being, who, from some unknown cause, had forsaken
social life, and had lived a hermit in that secluded spot
for seven or eight years. He had a little opening in a
fine interval, on the banks of Wilson River, where
he raised his corn and potatoes, and had constructed
a rude hovel for a dwelling. Johnson had made his
appearance occasionally at the village, with a string
of fine trout, a bear-skin, or some other trophy of his
Nimrod propensities, which he would exchange at the
stores for "a little rum, and a little tobacco, and a
little tea, and a jack-knife, and a little more rum,"
when he would plunge into the forest again, return to
his hermitage, and be seen no more for months.

After casting his thoughts about in vain for any
other refuge, Kingston resolved to throw himself upon
the protection of Johnson. Accordingly, as soon as
he was a little rested, and his pursuers were well out
of hearing, he crept from his hiding-place, and taking
his direction by the moon, made the best of his way
eastward, through the rough and thick wood. It is
no easy matter to penetrate such a forest in the day-

time; and in the night, nothing but extreme despera-
tion could drive a man through it. Here pressing his
way through dark and thick underbrush, that constantly required both hands to guard his eyes; there
climbing over huge windfalls, wading a bog, or leaping a brook; and anon working his way, for a quarter
of a mile, through a dismal, tangled cedar-swamp,
where a thousand dry and pointed limbs, shooting out
on every side, clear to the very ground, tear his clothes
from his back, and wound him at every step. Under
these impediments, and in this condition, Kingston
spent the night in pressing on toward Johnson's camp;
and after a period of extreme toil and suffering, just
at daylight, he came out to the opening. But here
another barrier was before him. The Wilson River,
a wild and rapid stream, and now swollen by a recent
freshet, was between him and Johnson's dwelling, and
he had no means of crossing. But cross he must, and
he was reluctant to lose time in deliberation. He
selected the spot that looked most likely to admit of
fording, and waded into the river. He staggered
along from rock to rock, and fought against the current, until he reached nearly the middle of the stream,
when the water deepened and took him from his feet!
He was but an indifferent swimmer, and the force of

the current carried him rapidly down the stream. At last, however, after severe struggles, and not without imminent peril of his life, he made out to reach the bank, so much exhausted, that it was with difficulty he could walk to Johnson's camp. When he reached it, he found its lonely inmate yet asleep. He roused him, made his case known to him, and begged his protection.

Johnson was naturally benevolent, and the forlorn, exhausted, ragged, and altogether wretched appearance of the fugitive, at once touched his heart. There was now.—

> "No SPECULATION in those eyes
> Which he did glare withal,"

but fear and trembling blanched his countenance, and palsied his limbs. Possibly the hermit's benevolence might have been quickened by a portion of the contents of the colonel's purse; but be that as it may, he was soon administering to the comfort of his guest. In a few minutes he had a good fire, and the exhausted wanderer took off his clothes and dried them, and tried to fasten some of the flying pieces that had been torn loose by the hatchel-teeth limbs in the cedar-swamps. In the meantime Johnson had provided some roasted potatoes, and a bit of fried bear-meat, which he served up, with a tin dipper of strong tea, and Kingston ate and drank, and was greatly refreshed.

They now set themselves earnestly to work to devise means of retreat and security against the pursuit of the enraged Monsonites, "who," Kingston said, "he was sure would visit the camp before noon." Under a part of the floor, was a small excavation in the earth, which his host called his potato-hole, since, being near the fire, it served in winter to keep his potatoes from freezing. This portion of the floor was now entirely covered over with two or three barrels, a water-pail, a bench, and sundry articles of iron and tin-ware. It was Johnson's advice, that the colonel should be secreted in this potato-hole. He was afraid, however, that they would search so close as to discover his retreat. Yet the only alternative seemed between the plan proposed and betaking himself again to the woods, exposed to toil and starvation, and the chance of arrest by some of the hundreds who would be scouring the woods that day, eager as bloodhounds for their prey. Something must be done immediately, for he was expecting every hour to hear the cry of his pursuers; and relying on Johnson's ingenuity and skill to send them off on another scent should they come to his camp, he concluded to retreat to the potato-hole.

Accordingly, the superincumbent articles were hastily removed, a board was taken up from the floor, and the gallant colonel descended to his new quarters. They were small to be sure, but under the circumstances very acceptable. The cell was barely deep enough to receive him in a sitting posture, with his neck a little bent, while under him was a little straw, upon which he could stretch his limbs to rest. Johnson replaced all the articles with such care that no one would have supposed they had been removed for months.

This labor had just been completed, when he heard shouts at a distance, and beheld ten or a dozen people rushing out of the woods, and making toward his camp. He was prepared for them; and when they came in, they found him seated quietly on his bench, mending his clothes.

" Have you seen anything of Colonel Kingston?" inquired the foremost of the company with panting eagerness.

" Colonel Kingston?" asked Johnson, looking up with a sort of vacant, honest stare.

" Yes—he's run for't," replied the other, " and we are after him. The Grand Jury has indicted him, and the Sheriff's got a warrant, and all Monson, and

one half of Guilford, is out a hunting for him. Last
night, just as they were going to take him, he run
into the woods this way. Ha'n't you seen nothin' of
him?"

Johnson sat with his mouth wide open, and listened
with such an inquiring look that any one would have
sworn it was all news to him. At last he exclaimed
with the earnestness inspired by a new thought,
"Well, there! I'll bet that was what my dog was
barking at, an hour or so ago! I heard him barking
as fierce as a tiger, about half a mile down the river.
I was busy mending my trowsers, or I should have.
gone down to see what he'd got track of."

The company unanimously agreed that it must
have been Kingston the dog was after; and in the
hope of getting upon his track, they hurried off in
the direction indicated, leaving Johnson as busily
engaged as if, like

"Brian O'Linn, he'd no breeches to wear,"

until he had finished repairing his tattered inexpressi-
bles.

The fugitive now breathed freely again ; but while
his pursuers were talking with his host, his respiration had hardly been sufficient to sustain life, and

"cold drops of sweat stood on his trembling flesh."
He did not venture to leave his retreat for two days;
for during that day and most of the next, the woods
were scoured from one end of the township to the
other, and several parties successively visited the
camp, who were all again successively despatched to
the woods by the adroitness of its occupant.

After two days the pursuers principally left the
woods and contented themselves with posting senti-
nels at short intervals on the roads that surrounded
the forest, and in the neighboring towns, hoping to
arrest their victim, when hunger should drive him
forth to some of the settlements. Kingston felt that
it was unsafe for him to remain any longer under the
protection of Johnson, and he knew it would be
exceedingly difficult to make his escape through any
of the settlements of Maine. Upon due reflection he
concluded that the only chance left for him was to
endeavor to make his way to Canada.

He was now a dozen or fifteen miles from the foot
of Moosehead lake. There was a foot-path to Elliottville, where there were a few inhabitants. Through
this settlement he thought he might venture to pass
in the night; and he could then go a few miles to the
westward, and meet the road leading from Monson to

the lake. Once across or around the foot of the lake, he believed he could make his way into the Canada road, and escape with safety. Having matured his plan he communicated it to Johnson, who aided it in the best manner he could by providing him with a pack of potatoes and fried bear-meat, accompanied with an extra Indian "johnny-cake," a jack-knife, and a flint and tinder for striking fire.

It was late in the night, when all things were prepared for the journey, and Kingston bade an affectionate adieu to his host, declaring that he should never forget him, and adding, with much originality of thought and expression, that "a friend in need was a friend indeed." He had nearly a mile to go through the woods, before reaching the path that led through the township of Elliotville ; and when he passed the Elliottville settlement the day began to dawn. A stirring young man, who was out at that early hour, saw him cross the road at a distance and strike into the woods. Satisfied at once who he was, and suspecting his object, he hastened to rouse his two or three neighbors, and then started toward Monson village with all the speed his legs could give him. Kingston, observing this movement from a hill-top in the woods, was convinced that he should be

pursued, and redoubled his exertions to reach the
lake.

When the messenger reached Monson and communicated his intelligence, the whole village was roused
like an encamped army at the battle-call; and in
twenty minutes every horse in the village was mounted
and the riders were spurring with all speed toward the
lake, and Deacon Stone among the foremost. As
they came in sight of the Moosehead, the sun, which
was about an hour high, was pouring a flood of warm
rays across the calm, still waters, and some half a mile
from land, they beheld a tall, slim man, alone in a
canoe, paddling toward the opposite shore.

For a moment the party stood speechless, and then
vent was given to such oaths and execrations as habit
had made familiar. Something was even swelling in
Deacon Stone's throat, well-nigh as sinful as he had
uttered on a former occasion, but he coughed, and
checked it before it found utterance. They looked
around, and ran on every side, to see if another boat,
or any other means of crossing the lake could be
found; but all in vain. The only skiff on that arm
of the lake had been seized by the colonel in his
flight. His pursuers were completely baffled. Some
were for crossing the woods, and going round the

southwest bay of the lake over the head waters of
the Kennebec River, and so into the great wilderness
on the western side of the lake. But others said,
"No; it's no use; if he once gets over among them
swamps and mountains, you might as well look for a
needle in a hay-mow!"

This sentiment accorded with the better judgment
of the party, and they turned about and rode quietly
back to Monson—Deacon Stone consoling himself on
the way by occasionally remarking: "Well, if the
heathen is driven out of the land, thanks to a kind
Providence, he has n't carried the land with him!"

12

CHAPTER XI.

A DUTCH WEDDING.

" You can often get over the difficulty, when you can't get over the river," said my friend John Van Ben Schoten.

" Why don't you begin your name with a Sam ?" said I; " it would give it more fulness and roundness; a more musical sound. I do like a full, harmonious name, I don't care what nation it belongs to. Only see how much better it would sound—Sam John Van Ben Schoten—I *would* make that little addition, if I was you."

" Why that is my boy's name," said my friend John Van Ben Schoten. " You Yankees are always one generation ahead of us Hollanders. Wait till my boy grows up, and he'll be just what you want. " But don't let us be disputing about names"——

Our disputes were always of the good-natured sort, and generally confined to the relative advantages of Yankee enterprise and Dutch perseverance.

"Don't let us be disputing about names," said he, "when you ought to be planning how to pay that note to-morrow. You say your draft has come back protested, and you have no other means of raising the money."

This was too true; I had been in a perfect fever all the morning; the return of the draft was most unexpected; those, of whom I had been accustomed to receive accomodations, were out of town, and the note in question would do me much injury by lying over. As a last resort I had applied to my friend John Van Ben Schoten for advice in the matter.

"I tell you," said John Van Ben Schoten, "you can often get over the difficulty, when you can't get over the river."

"Yes," said I, "but *how?* You can do most anything if you only know how."

"Well," said he, "go into my counting-room and sit down a minute, and I'll tell you how."

We went in, and took a seat in the shadiest corner, near the window. John, before sitting down, reached up over his desk and took down his long pipe. He then opened a little drawer and filled his pipe with fine dry tobacco, and pulling a lens out of his pocket he stepped into the sunshine to light it.

"You don't need that glass," said I, "you just hold your pipe in the sun, and if it don't light in half a minute without the glass, I'll engage to eat it."

"There 'tis again," said John Van Ben Schoten, "you are always showing the Yankee. Our fathers always lit their pipes with sun glasses, and now you want to contrive some other way to do it. If I knew I could light it in half the time without the glass, still I would use the glass out of respect to my ancestors."

"Well, come," said I, "this is n't telling me how to get over the difficulty."

"Wait till I get my little steam-engine a-going," said John, still holding the glass in the sun.

"But have n't you any loco foco matches?" said I, growing somewhat impatient.

"No," said John, "I never allow those new-fangled dangerous things to come into my counting room."

"But how do you get a fire when the sun don't shine?" said I.

"I use a flint and steel," said he, "the safest and surest way in the world."

At last, his pipe began to burn, and John with the utmost complacency sat down in his large arm-chair and began to smoke.

"Well, now," said I, "I suppose you are ready to open your mind upon this matter, and tell me if you can contrive any plan to help me over this difficulty."

"Why, yes," said John, "you can oftentimes get over the difficulty, when you can't get over the river. Did you ever know how Peter Van Horn got married?"

"No," said I.

"Well, I'll tell you," said John, taking the pipe from his mouth and puffing out a cloud of smoke that almost concealed his head from my view.

"Oh, now, don't stop for any of your long yarns," said I; "it is getting toward the close of business hours, and it's very important that this business of mine should be attended to."

"You Yankees are always too impatient," said John; "there's never anything lost by taking time to consider a matter. It is driving the steamboat too fast, and trying to go ahead of somebody else, that makes her burst her boiler."

At that he put his pipe in his mouth and went to smoking again.

"Well, come," said I, "the sooner you begin to tell how Peter Van Horn got married, the sooner you'll get through with it."

"I know it," said he, "and if you won't interrupt me, I'll go on."

"Yes," says I, "a Dutchman must always have his own way; go ahead."

"Well, then," said John Van Ben Schoten, throwing himself back into the chair, and leisurely blowing the smoke in a long, steady, quiet roll from his mouth; "about a hundred years ago, Peter Van Horn lived at Schenectady, or near where Schenectady now is, for it was a kind of wilderness place then. You've been at Schenectady, have n't you?"

"No" said I, "I never have."

"Well, it is about fifteen or twenty miles from Albany; you've been at Albany, of course."

"No, I have n't," said I.

"Not been at Albany?" said John, staring at me with rather an incredulous look; "then you have n't seen much of the world yet."

"Why, no," said I, "perhaps not a great deal on this side of it; though I have seen something of the other side of it, and a little of both eends."

John laughed, and went on with his story.

"Peter Van Horn lived near Schenectady, on one of the little streams that empty into the Mohawk. His father was one of the first settlers in that region;

and the old gentleman brought up a nice family, a fine set of hardy, industrious fellows; every one of them as steady as a mill horse: no wild oats—they were men before they were boys. The consequence was, they picked up the money and always had a comfortable share of this world's goods.

"Well, Peter, he grew up to be a smart young man, and at last he got it into his head, that he wanted to be married. You know how 'tis; young men now-a-days are apt to get such notions into their heads, and it was just so in old times. I don't know as Peter was to blame for that; for there was living a little ways up the hill, above his father's, Betsey Van Heyden, a round, rosy-cheeked, blue eyed girl, as neat as a new pin, and as smart as a steel-trap. Every time Peter saw her, his feelings became more interested in her. Somehow, he could not seem to keep his mind off of her. Sometimes, when he was hoeing corn in the field, the first thing he would know, his father would call out to him, 'Peter, what do you stand there leaning over your hoe-handle for?' And then he would start, and color up to the eyes, and go to work. He knew he had been thinking of Betsey Van Heyden, but how long he had been standing still he could n't tell.

" At last things grew worse and worse, and he found he could n't live without Betsey Van Heyden no how ; so he went and popped the question to her ; and Betsy said she was willing if mother was—gals in them days were remarkably well brought up, in comparison of what they are now-a-days—so after a while Peter mustered up courage enough to go and ask the old folks, and the old folks, after taking two days to consider of it, said yes; for, why should n't they ? Peter was one of the most industrious young men in the whole valley of the Mohawk.

" And now that the road was all open and plain before him, Peter was for hurrying ahead ; he did n't see any use at all in waiting.

" Betsey was for putting it off two months, till she could get another web out of the loom ; but Peter said no, he did n't care a snap about another web ; they'd be married first and make the cloth afterward. Betsey at last yielded the point ; she said she did want to make up a few articles before they were married, but she supposed they might get along without them. So they finally fixed on Thursday of the following week for the wedding. The work of preparation was soon commenced, and carried out in a liberal style. Everything requisite for a grand feast was collected, cooked, and arranged in apple-pie order. The guests were all invited, and Parson Van Brunt was engaged to be there precisely at three o'clock, in order that they might get through the business, and have supper out of the way in season for all to get home before dark.

"Thus far, up to the evening before the wedding day, everything looked fair and promising. Peter retired to bed early, in the hope of getting a good night's rest; but somehow or other he never was so restless in his life. He shut his eyes with all his might, and tried to think of sheep jumping over a wall; but do all he could, sleep would n't come. Before midnight the doors and windows began to rattle with a heavy wind. Peter got up and looked out; it was dark and cloudy. Presently flashes of lightning were seen, and heavy thunder came rolling from the clouds and echoing among the hills. In half an hour more a heavy torrent of rain was beating upon the house. 'It will be soon over,' thought Peter, 'and the air will be beautiful to-morrow, as sweet as a rose; what a fine day we shall have.'

"Hour after hour passed away, and the rain still came down in a flood. Peter could not sleep a wink all night. He got up and walked the floor till day-

12*

light, and when he looked out upon the roads and
the fields the water was standing in every hollow and
running down the hillsides in rivulets. Nine, ten,
and eleven o'clock passed, and still it rained. Peter
had been up to Mr. Van Heyden's twice through
the rain to see how affairs went on there; the family
looked rather sad, but Betsey said she had faith to
believe that it would hold up before three o'clock ;
and sure enough about twelve o'clock, while the
families were at dinner, it did hold up, and the clouds
began to clear away.

"About two o'clock the wedding guests began to
assemble at Mr. Van Heyden's, and the faces of all
began to grow shorter and brighter. All this time it
had not entered Peter's head, or the heads of any of
the rest of the company, that there might be any
difficulty in the way of Parson Van Brunt's coming
to their aid in completing the marriage ceremony.
They had all this time forgotten that they were on
one side of the Tomhenick stream and Parson Van
Brunt on the other; that there was no bridge over
the stream, and that it was now so swollen by the
flood, and the current was so rapid, that it was almost
as much as a man's life was worth to attempt to cross
it at the usual fording-place, or swim it on horseback.

" At last, about half-past two o'clock, Parson Van Brunt, true to his promise, was seen riding down the hill on the opposite side of the river and approaching the ford.

"There he is," said old Mrs. Van Heyden, who had been upon the lookout for the last half hour, " there's the dear good man; now let us all take our seats and be quiet before he comes in."

" While they were still lingering at the doors and windows, and watching the parson as he came slowly down the hill, he reached the bank of the river and stopped. He sat upon his horse some minutes, looking first up the stream and then down the stream, and then he rode his horse a few rods up and down the bank, and returned again to the ford.

" ' What can he be waiting there for ?' said Peter ; ' sure he has seen the river often enough before, that he need n't stand there so long to look at it.'

" ' I can tell you what the difficulty is,' said old Mr. Van Heyden, ' the river is so high he can't get across.'

" The truth now fell like a flash upon the minds of the whole company.

" ' Do you think so ?' said Mr. Van Horn.

" ' I know so,' said Mr. Van Heyden ; ' you can see from here the water is up the bank two rods farther than it commonly is, and must be as much as ten feet deep over the ford just now.'

"'What shall we do?' said old Mrs. Van Heyden; 'the things will all be spoilt if we don't have the wedding to-day.'

"Betsey began to turn a little pale. Peter took his hat and started off upon a quick walk toward the river; and presently all the men folks followed him. The women folks waited a little while, and seeing Parson Van Brunt still sitting on his horse upon the other side of the river without any attempt to cross, they all put on their bonnets and followed the men. When they got to the bank, the reason of the parson's delay was as clear as preaching. The little river was swollen to a mighty torrent, and was rushing along its banks with the force and rapidity of a cataract. The water had never been so high before since the neighborhood had been settled, and it was still rising. To ford the river was impossible, and to attempt to swim it on horseback was highly dangerous.

"'What shall we do?' said Peter, calling to the parson across the river.

"'Well, I think you will have to put it off two or three days, till the river goes down,' said Parson Van Brunt.

" 'Tell him we can't put it off,' said old Mrs. Van Heyden, touching Peter by the elbow : ' for the pies and cakes and things will all be spoilt.'

" ' Ask him if he don't think his horse can swim over,' said Betsey in a half whisper, standing the other side of Peter.

" Peter again called to the parson ; told him what a disappointment it would be if he did n't get over, and that it was the general opinion his horse could swim over with him if he would only try. Parson Van Brunt was devoted to the duties of his profession, and ready to do anything, even at the risk of his life, for the good of his flock. So he reined up his horse tightly, gave him the whip, and plunged into the stream. The current was too rapid and powerful for the animal ; the horse and rider were carried down stream with fearful speed for a about a dozen rods, when they made out to land again on the same side from which they started. All were now satisfied that the parson could not get over the river. The experiment already made was attended with such fearful hazard as to preclude all thought of its repetition.

" ' Oh dear, what shall we do?' said Mrs. Van Heyden ; ' was there ever anything so unlucky ?

"Betsey sighed, and Peter bit his lips with vexation. Peter's mother all this while had not uttered a syllable. She was a woman that never talked, but she did up a great deal of deep thinking. At last, very much to the surprise of the whole company, she spoke out loud, and said:

"'It seems to me, if Parson Van Brunt can't get over the river, he might get over the difficulty somehow or other.'

"'Well, how in the world can he do it?' said Peter.

"'Why, you jest take hold of Betsey's hand,' said his mother, 'and stand up here, and let the parson marry you across the river.'

"This idea struck them all very favorably; they didn't see why it couldn't be done. Peter again called to Parson Van Brunt, and stated to him the proposition, and asked him if he thought there was anything in the law or in the Bible that could go against the match if it was done in that way. Parson Van Brunt sat in a deep study about five minutes, and then said he couldn't see anything in the way, and told them they might stand up and take hold of hands. When they had taken their proper positions, and old Mrs. Van Heyden had put her handkerchief to her face to hide the tears that began to start from her eyes, the parson read over, in a loud and solemn tone, the marriage ceremony, and pronounced them man and wife.

"Peter then threw a couple of silver dollars across the river, which Parson Van Brunt gathered up and put in his pocket, and then mounted his horse and started for home, while the company upon the other side of the river returned to the house of Mr. Van Heyden to enjoy the wedding feast."

By this time John Van Ben Schoten's pipe had gone out, and he started to the window again with his lens to re-light it.

"Well," said I, "I understand, now, how Peter Van Horn got over his difficulty, but I'll be hanged if I can see any clearer how I am to get over mine."

"None so blind as them that won't see," said John, turning to his desk and pulling out his old rusty yellow pocket book. He opened it, and counted out the sum of money which I lacked.

"There," said he, "go and pay your note, and remember you can sometimes get over the difficulty, when you can't get over the river."

CHAPTER XII.

BILLY SNUB.

WHEN the biographer has a subject of unusual magnitude and importance to deal with, it becomes him to lay out his work with circumspection, and preserve a careful method in the arrangement. He must dig deep, and lay his foundation firmly, before he attempts to rear his edifice. He must not thrust his hero at once and unceremoniously in the face of his reader, standing alone and erect, like a liberty-pole on the naked common of a country meeting-house. He must keep him for a while in the background, and with a careful and skilful progression drag him slowly up from the dark and misty slough of antiquity, to the full light of day. It is not sufficient to commence with the father, nor even with the grandfather; propriety requires that the ancestral chain should be examined to the very topmost link.

Unfortunately for the cause of letters, the origin and early history of the Snubs are veiled in the deep-

est obscurity. The most indefatigable researches
have been sufficient to trace them back but a few
generations. Their family name is not found in the
list of the hardy adventurers who came over in the
Mayflower, nor yet among the early colony planted
by Captain John Smith. But though history retains
no record of the precise point of time when they
migrated to the Western continent, it is certain they
were among the early settlers of the New World,
and many respectable traditions are extant of their
ancient standing and influence in some of the older
towns in New England. There is some doubt as to
what nation may rightfully claim the honor of sup-
plying the blood that flows in their veins, and it is
probable the question at this late day can never be
settled with entire satisfaction. Though the claims
of England, France, and Germany, might each and
all be urged with so much force as to incline the historian to believe that their blood is of mixed origin,
yet the prevailing testimony ought to be considered
sufficient to establish the point that John Bull is the
father of the Snub family; a conclusion which
derives no small support from the general pugnacity
of their character. It is much to be lamented that
the ancient history of this ancient family is lost

to the world; but, alas! they had no poet, no historian.

The ancestors of Billy Snub can be traced in a direct line only to the fourth generation. The great-grandfather was a lawyer of thrift and respectability; a man of talents and influence; and tradition says, if he was not a younger son, he was the nephew of a younger son of an English earl. It cannot, therefore, with any propriety, be thrown in the face of the Snubs, that

> "Their ancient but ignoble blood
> Has crept through scoundrels ever since the flood."

But this Lawyer Snub, whose first name was William, had not the faculty or the talents to bring up his children to maintain the standing and dignity of their father. His son William was nothing more than a plain, respectable country farmer, who planted his potatoes, and hoed his corn, and mowed his hay, and milked his cows very much as other farmers do, without ever doing anything to become distinguished in the history of his times. He also was destined to see his posterity still in the descendant, for *his* son William was a village shoemaker, who sat on his bench, and drew his thread, and hammered his lapstone from morning till night, the year in and year out, with the occasional variation of whistling while paring off a shoe, and singing a song of an evening to the loungers in his shop. The tendency in the Snub family, however, was still downwards; even the shoemaker was not at the bottom of the hill, for *his* son was Billy Snub the newsboy. The direct family line, as far back as authentic history goes, running thus :

First generation, William Snub, Esquire.

Second generation, Mr. William Snub, the farmer.

Third generation, Bill Snub, the shoemaker.

Fourth generation, Billy Snub, the newsboy.

There is a tide in families, as well as "in the affairs of men." They rise and fall, though not as regularly, yet as surely as the spring and neap tides of the ocean. And Billy Snub, after kicking and floundering about upon the flats at low water, has at last caught the flood, and there is no knowing to what height of fortune he may yet be carried. His posterity will undoubtedly be in the ascendant, and it may not be too much to expect that in a few generations ahead, we shall have his Excellency, William Snub, Governor, &c., and perhaps William Snub, the eighteenth President of the United States. But the regular chain of history must not be anticipated; and in order to bring Billy fairly and with sufficient clearness before the public, it is necessary to dwell for a few moments upon the history of Bill Snub, the shoemaker, and Sally Snub, his wife.

For a few years Bill Snub was the leading shoemaker in a quiet New England village. Indeed, he took the lead from necessity, for he had no competitor; the field was all his own, and being allowed to have his own way, and fix his own prices, he managed to get a comfortable living. Being well to do in the world, and much given to whistling and singing, his shop gradually became the favorite resort of all the idlers in the village. Bill's importance was magnified in his own eyes by this gathering around him almost every evening, to say nothing of the rainy afternoons. Unconsciously to himself he encouraged this lounging habit of his neighbors by administering to their little idle comforts. In one corner of his shop was a broken chair for an extra seat, in another a square block of timber left from the frame of the new school-house, and in still another corner was a stout side of sole leather, rolled up and snugly tied, which answered very well for a seat for three. A half-peck of apples, and a mug or two of cider, always at Bill's expense, frequently added to the allurements of the place, and Bill's songs, and Bill's jokes, no matter how little music or wit they contained, were always applauded.

This state of things silently, but gradually, made sad encroachments upon Bill's habits of industry. His customers were put off from day to day, and when Saturday night came, a bushel basket full of boots and shoes remained in his shop waiting repairs, to say nothing of Sunday new ones that had been promised, but not touched. Many of his customers had to stay at home on the Sabbath, or go to meeting barefoot. The result of all this was, that an interloper soon came into the place, and opened a shop directly opposite to that of Bill. The way was already open for him for a good run of business. Bill's customers, exasperated at their numerous disappointments, discarded him at once, and flocked to the new comer. In a week's time, Bill had nothing to do. He might be seen standing in his shop door, or with his head out of the window, hour after hour, watching his old customers as they entered the shop of his rival. He would go home to his meals in ill-humor, and scold his wife for his bad luck. And if little Billy, then six years old, came round him with his accustomed prattle and play, he was pretty sure to be silenced with a smart box on the ear. Things grew worse and worse with him, and in a few months want was not only staring him in the face, but had actually seized him with such a firm gripe as to bring him to a full stand. Something must be done; Bill was uncomfortable. Whistling or singing to the bare walls of his shop, produced an echo that chilled and annoyed him exceedingly. Food and clothing began to be among the missing, and he soon discovered that walking the streets did but little towards replenishing his wardrobe; nor would scolding or even beating his wife supply his table.

At last, throwing the whole blame upon the place and its people where he lived, he resolved at once to pull up stakes and be off.

" And where are you going, Bill?" said his wife, wiping the tears from her eyes, as she saw her husband commence the work of packing up.

" It's none of your business, Sall," said the husband gruffly. " But I'm going where there's work enough for all creation; where there's more folks to mend shoes for than you can shake a stick at."

" Well, where is it Bill? do tell us;" said Sally in an anxious tone. " If it is only where we can get victuals to eat, and clothes to wear, I shall be thankful."

"Well, then," said Bill, "I'm going to the biggest city in the United States, where there's work enough all weathers."

"Well, that's Boston," said Sally.

"No, 'taint Boston," said Bill; "it's a place as big as four Bostons. It's New York; I'm going right into the middle of New York; so pack up your duds about the quickest; for I ain't going to stop for nobody."

And sure enough, a few mornings after this, among the deck passengers of one of the steamers that arrived at New York, was no less a personage than Bill Snub, the shoemaker, with his wife Sally and his son Billy. The group landed, and stared at every object they met, with a wild and wondering expression, that seemed to indicate pretty clearly that they were not accustomed to sights and scenes like those around them. Indeed, they had never before been in a large town, and hardly out of their quiet country village. Each bore a bundle, containing the whole amount of their goods and chattels, which had been reduced to a few articles of wearing apparel, a box or two of eatables, which they had taken for their journey, and a few tools of his trade, which Bill had had the foresight to preserve in order to begin the world anew.

Bewildered by the noise and bustle, and crowds of
people on every side, they knew not which way to
turn or what to do. They knew not a person nor a
street in the city, and had no very definite object in
view. Instinctively following the principal current
of passengers that landed from the boat, they soon
found themselves in Broadway. Here, as a small stream
blends with a large one into which it flows, their company was presently merged and lost in the general
throng of that great thoroughfare. They gradually
lost sight of the familiar faces they had seen on board
the boat, and when the last one disappeared, and
they could no longer discern in the vast multitude hurrying to and fro, and down the street, a single individual they had ever seen before, a sense of solitude
and home-sickness came over them, that was most
overpowering. They stopped short on the sidewalk,
and Bill looked in his wife's face, and his wife looked
in his, and little Billy stood between them, and looked
up in the faces of both.

"What are you going to do?" said Sally.

"Going to do?" said Bill; "I'm going to hire out;
or else hire a shop and work on my own hook."

Just at that moment a gentleman brushed past his
elbow, and Bill hailed him.

"I say, mister, you don't know of nobody that wants to hire a shoemaker, do ye?"

The gentleman turned and glanced at him a moment, and then hurried on without saying a word.

"I should think he might have manners enough to answer a civil question," muttered Bill to himself, as he shouldered his bag and moved on up the street. Presently they passed a large shoe store.

"Ah, here's the place!" said Bill; "we've found it at last. O, Sall, did you ever see such an allfired sight of shoes? Lay down your bundle, and stop here to the door, while I go in and make a bargain for work. So in Bill went, and addressed himself to one of the clerks.

"I say, mister, you've got sich an everlastin' lot of shoes here, I guess may be you'd like to hire a good shoemaker; and if you do, I'm the boy for you."

The clerk laughed, and told him he must ask the boss about that.

"Ask the what?" said Bill.

"Ask the boss," said the clerk, who began to relish the conversation.

"I shan't do no sich thing," said Bill; "I did n't come to New York to talk with bossy-calves nor pigs; and if you are a calf I don't want any more to say to

13

you ; but if you want to hire a good shoemaker, I tell you I'm the chap for you." Here the proprietor of the store, seeing the clerks gathering round Bill, to the neglect of their customers, came forward and told him he did not wish to hire any workmen, and he had better go along.

"But I'll work cheap," said Bill, "and I'm a first-rate workman. Here's a pair of shoes on my feet I've wore for four months, and they han't ripped a stitch yet."

"But I don't want to hire," said the man of the store, with some impatience; "so you had better go along."

"But maybe we can make a bargain," said Bill; "I tell ye, I'll work cheap."

"I tell you, I don't want to hire," said the man; "so go out of the store."

"You need n't be so touchy," said Bill; "I guess I've seen as good folks as you are, before to-day. Come now, what'll you give me a month?"

"I'll give you what you won't want," said the man, "if you are not out of this store in one minute." As he said this, he approached Bill with such a menacing appearance, that the shoemaker thought it time to retreat, and hastened out of the door. As he reached the sidewalk, he turned round and hailed the man of the store again.

" I say, mister, hav n't you got a shoemaker's shop you'll let to me ?"

The man said he had a good room for that purpose.

" Well, what do you ask a year for it ?" said Bill.

" Three hundred dollars, with good security," replied the shopman.

" Three hundred dollars ! My gracious ! Come now, none of your jokes. Tell us how much you ask for it, 'cause I want to hire."

" I tell you I ask three hundred dollars," said the man; " but it's of no use for you to talk about it; you can't give the security."

" Oh, you go to grass," said Bill; " I don't want none of your jokes. I've hired as good a shop as ever a man waxed a thread in, for fifteen dollars a year ; and if you are a mind to let me have yourn for the same, I'll go and look at it."

The man laughed in his face, and turned away to wait upon his customers ; and a little waggish boy, who had been standing by and listening to the conversation, placed his finger against his nose, and looking up askance at Bill, exclaimed, " Ain't ye green?"

Poor Bill began to think he had got among a

strange set of people, and, shouldering his bag, he marched up Broadway with his wife and Billy at his heels, till he came to the Astor House. Here he made a halt, for it looked to him like a sort of place for head-quarters. The building was so imposing in its appearance, and so many people were going in and coming out, and everything around was so brisk and busy, he thought surely it must be just the place to look for business. So laying down their baggage, he and Sally and Billy quietly took a seat on the broad granite steps. He soon began to ply his inquiries to all sorts of people, asking if they could tell him of anybody that wanted to hire a shoemaker, or that had a shoemaker's shop to let. Most of them would hurry by him without any further notice than a hasty glance; others would laugh, and some would stop, and ask a few questions, or crack a few heartless jokes, and then turn away. After a while a throng of boys had gathered around him, and by various annoyances rendered his position so uncomfortable, that he was glad to escape, and shouldering his baggage, he and his group wandered on with heavy hearts up the street.

Most of the day passed in this way without any profitable result, and as night approached they grew weary and desponding. They had no money left to provide themselves with a home for the night, though they had provision enough for a meal or two remaining in their wallets. Bill had found it utterly impossible to make any impression upon any one he had met in the city, except so far as to be laughed at. He could get no one's ear to listen to his story, and he could see no prospect of employment. Sally had several times suggested that this great road which they had been up and down so much—for they had been almost the whole length of Broadway two or three times—was not exactly the best road for them to go in, and she did n't think but what they might be likely to do better to go into one of the smaller roads, where the folks didn't look so grand. And, though Bill had been of different opinion through the day, he now began to think that Sally might be right. Looking down one of the cross streets that seemed to descend into a sort of valley, quite a different country appeared to open to them. They could see old decayed-looking houses, with broken windows and dirty sidewalks; they could see half-naked children, running about and playing in the street; they could see bareheaded women and ragged men lounging about the doors, and numerous swine rooting in the gutters. The prospect was too inviting to be resisted. They felt at once that there they could find sympathy, and hastened down the street. Arriving in the midst of this paradise, they deliberately laid down their luggage on the sidewalk, and seating themselves on the steps of an old wooden house, felt as if they had at last found a place of rest. They opened their bundles and began to partake of a little food. Heads were out of a hundred windows in the neighborhood gazing at them. Children stopped short in the midst of their running, and stood around them; and leisurely, one after another, a stout woman or a sturdy loafer came nigh and entered into conversation. As Bill related his simple story, a universal sympathy was at once awakened in the hearts of all the hearers. They all declared he should have a shop in the neighborhood and they would give him their patronage.

Patrick O'Flannegan, who lived in the basement of the old house on whose steps they were seated, at once invited them to partake of the hospitalities of his mansion, saying he had but nine in his family, and his room was large, and they should be welcome to occupy a corner of it till they could find a better home. Of course the invitation was accepted, and the group followed Patrick down the steep dirty steps that led to his damp apartment. The tops of the low windows were about upon a level with the sidewalk, bringing almost the entire apartment below the surface of the ground. The dim light that struggled down through the little boxed-up dusty windows, showed a straw-bed in two several corners of the room, three or four rickety chairs, a rough bench, small table, tea-kettle, frying-pan, and several other articles of household comforts.

"You can lay your things in that corner," said Patrick, pointing to a vacant corner of the room, "and we'll soon get up some good straw for you to sleep on." In short, Bill and his family at once became domesticated in this subterranean tenement, which proved to be not merely a temporary residence, but their home for years. The limits of this history will not allow space to follow the fortunes of Bill through three or four of the first years of his city life. It must be sufficient to state generally, that though he found kindness and sympathy in his new associates, he found little else that was beneficial. The atmos-phere around him was not favorable to industry, and his habits in that respect never improved, but rather grew worse. His neighbors did not work, and why should he? His neighbors were fond of listening to his songs, and why should he not sing to them? His neighbors drank beer, and porter, and sling, and gin toddy, and Bill needed but little coaxing to drink with them. And he did drink with them, moderately at first, but deeper and oftener from month to month, and in three years' time he became a perfect sot.

The schooling that little Bill received during these three years was eminently calculated to fit him for his future profession. He had slept on the floor, lying down late and rising up early, till his frame was as hardy and elastic as that of a young panther. He had been flogged so much by a drunken father, and had his ears boxed so often by a fretted and desponding mother, that he had lost all fear of their blows, and even felt a sort of uneasiness, as though matters were not all right, if by any chance the day passed by without receiving them. He had lived on such poor diet, and so little of it, that potato-skins had a fine relish, and a crust of bread was a luxury. He had battled with boys in the street till he had become such an adept at fisticuffs, that boys of nearly twice his size stood in fear of him. And he had so often been harshly driven from the doors of the wealthy, where he had been sent to beg cold victuals, that he had come to regard mankind in general as a set of

ferocious animals, against whose fangs it was necessary to be constantly on his guard. In short, Billy
had been beaten about from post to pillar, and pillar
to post so much, and had rubbed his head against so
many sorts of people, that it had become pretty well
filled with ideas of the hardest kind.

When Billy was about ten years old, he came running in one day in great glee, with a sixpence in his
hand, which he had found in the street. As soon as
his father heard the announcement of it, he started
up, and took down a junk bottle from a little shelf
against the wall, and told Billy to take the sixpence,
and go to the grocer's on the corner, and get the
worth of it in rum. Sally begged that he would not
send for rum, but let little Billy go to the baker's and
get a loaf of bread, for she had not had a mouthful of
anything to eat for the day, and it was then noon.
But Bill insisted upon having the rum, and told Billy
to go along and get it, and be quick about it, or he
would give him such a licking as he had not had for
six months. Billy took the bottle, and started; but
as he left the door, his cheek reddened, and his lip
curled with an expression of determination which it
had not been accustomed to wear. He walked down
the street, thinking of the consequences that would

13*

result from carrying home a bottle of rum. His father would be drunk all the afternoon, and through the night. His mother and himself would have to go without food, probably be abused and beaten, and when night came, would find no repose.

He arrived at the grocer's, but he could not go in. He passed on a little farther, in anxious, deep thought. At last he stopped suddenly, lifted the bottle above his head, and then dashed it upon the pavement with all his might, breaking it into a thousand pieces.

"There," said Billy to himself, "I'll never carry any more rum home as long as I live. But I s'pose father 'll lick me half to death; but I don't care if he does, I'll never carry any more rum home as long as I live."

He brushed a tear from his eye, and bit his lips, as he stood looking at the fragments of the bottle a moment, and then passed on farther down the street. But now the question of what he should do, came home to him with painful force. If he returned back to the house, and encountered his enraged father, he was sure to be half killed. He wandered on, unconcious where he went, till he reached the Park. Here he met a newsboy crying papers, with great earnestness and tremendous force of lungs. Billy watched him for the space of ten minutes, and saw him sell half-a-dozen papers. They contained important news by a foreign arrival, and people seemed eager to get hold of them. A new idea flashed across Billy's mind. Why could not he sell newspapers, and get money, as well as that boy! His resolution was at once formed, with almost the strength and firmness of manhood. It required capital, to be sure, to start with, but luckily he had the capital in his pocket. The rum bottle had been broken, and he still retained the sixpence. He hastened immediately to the publishing office of the paper he had just seen sold. When he arrived there, he found quite a crowd of newsboys pressing up to the counter, and clamorous for papers; for the publisher could not supply them fast enough to meet the demand. Billy edged his way in among them, and endeavored to approach the counter. But he was suddenly pushed back by two or three boys at once, who exclaimed, "What new-comer is this? Here's boys enough here now, so you better be off."

Another sung out "Go home, you ragbag, your mother don't know you're out!"

At this, one of the boys looked round that happen-ed to know Billy, and he cried out, "Ah, Billy Snub, clear out of this; here's no place for you! No boys comes to this office that don't wear no hats and shoes?"

Billy felt the force of this argument, for he was bareheaded and barefooted, besides being sadly out at knees and elbows; and looking around, he perceived that all the boys in the room had something on their heads, and something on their feet. He began to feel as though he had perhaps got among the aristocracy of the newsboys, and shrank back a little, and stood in a corner of the room. The boys, however, were not disposed to let him rest in peace there. Several of them gathered around him, taunting him with jokes and jeers, and began to crowd against him to hustle him out of the room.

"Now take care," said Billy, "for I won't stand that from none of you."

"You won't, will you?" said the boys, bursting out into a roar of laughter; and one of them took Billy by the nose, and attempted to pull him to the door. Billy sprang like a young catamount; and although he was considerably smaller and younger than his assailant, he gave him such a well-directed blow upon the chest that he laid him sprawling upon the floor. Upon this, two or three more came at him with great fury; but Billy's sleight of hand was exhibited with so much force and skill, that he made his way through them, and kept his coast clear; and when a stronger reinforcement was about to attack him, the publisher interfered, and ordered them to let that boy alone. Still they were disposed to continue their persecutions, till the publisher took up a long whip, and cracked it over their heads, and told them he would horsewhip the first one that dared to meddle with him. And in order to make amends to Billy for the ill-treatment he had received, he said he should now be served with papers before any of the rest. He accordingly took Billy's six cents, and handed him three papers, and told him to sell them at three cents apiece.

Billy eagerly grasped his papers, and ran into the street. He had not been gone more than fifteen minutes, before he returned with nine cents, which he had received for the papers, and one more, which he had found in the street. This enabled him to purchase five papers; and he found the publisher ready to wait upon him in preference to the other boys; so he was soon dispatched on his second cruise. He was not many minutes in turning his five papers into fifteen cents cash. This operation was repeated some half dozen times in the course of the afternoon, and when night came, Billy found his stock of cash had increased to about a dollar.

This was a great overturn in Billy's fortune, sufficient to upset the heads of most boys of his age; but though his head swam a little on first ascertaining the great amount of money in his pocket, his strength and firmness of character sustained him, so that he was enabled to bear it with a good degree of composure. As the shadows of night gathered around him, Billy began to turn his thoughts homeward. But what could he do? He knew his father too well to venture himself in his presence, and had no hesitation in coming to the conclusion that he must now, for the first time in his life, spend the night away from home. Still he instinctively wandered on through the streets that led him towards home, for the thought that his mother had probably been without food the whole day, pressed heavily upon his mind, and he was anxious to contrive some way to afford her relief. As he approached the neighborhood of his home, or rather the place where his parents resided, for it was no longer a home to him, he stopped at a grocer's, and purchased a sixpenny loaf of bread, sixpence worth of gingerbread, and half a dozen herrings, for which he paid another sixpence. With these he turned into the street, and walked thoughtfully and carefully towards the house, hesitating, and looking frequently around him, lest his father might be out, and suddenly seize him. At last he reached the house. He stopped cautiously on the sidewalk, and looked, and listened. There was a dim light in the basement, but he heard no sound. He stepped lightly down the steps as far as the first window, and through the sash, which had lost a pane of glass, he dropped his bundle of provisions, and then ran with all his speed down the street. When he reached the first corner he stopped and looked back, and by the light of the street lamps, he saw his father and mother come out, and stand on the sidewalk two or three minutes, looking earnestly around them in every direction. They then went quietly back to their room, and Billy cautiously returned again to the house. He placed himself as near the window as he could, without being discovered from within, and listened to what was going on. His mother took the little bundle to the table, and opened it. Her eyes filled with tears the moment she saw what it contained, for her first thought rested upon Billy. She could not divine by what means she had received such a timely gift, but somehow or other, she could not help thinking that Billy was in some way connected with it.

"Come, Bill," said Sally to her husband, "we've got a good supper at last; now set down and eat some."

Bill drew up to the table, and ate as one who had been fasting for twenty-four hours. After his appetite began to be satisfied, said he, "Now, Sall, where do you think all this come from?"

"Well, I'm sure I can't tell anything about it," said Sally; "but I should n't be afraid to lay my life on it, that Billy knows something about it."

"So does your granny know something about it, as much as Billy," said Snub, contemptuously. "All Billy cares about is to spend that sixpence, and eat it up; and now he dares n't come home. I wish I had hold of the little rascal, I'd shake his daylights out; I'd lick him till he could n't stand."

"Oh, you're too cruel to that boy," said Sally; "Billy's a good child, and would do anything for me, and for you too, for all you whip him so much. And I believe it's his means that got somebody to give us this good supper to night. I hope the dear child will come home pretty soon, for I feel worried 'most to death about him."

"I hope he'll come, too," said Snub, "and I've a

good mind to go and take a look after him, for I want to lick him most awfully."

At this, Billy began to feel as though it would be hazardous for him to remain any longer, so he hastened away down the street to seek a resting-place for the night. This he found at last, in the loft of a livery stable, where he crept away unobserved, and slept quietly till morning. True, he had one or two golden dreams, excited by his remarkable fortune the previous day, and when he woke his first impulse was to put his hand in his pocket, and ascertain whether he was really in possession of the fortune he had been dreaming of, or whether he was the same poor Billy Snub that he was two days before. The three hard silver quarters which he felt in his pocket roused him to the reality of his situation, and he sprang from his hard couch, soon after daylight, resolved to renew the labors he had so successfully followed the day before. He had now a good capital to start with, and could work to a better advantage than the previous day. He accordingly soon supplied himself with an armful of papers, and placed himself on the best routes, and at the best hours. The result was, that though it was not properly a news-day, there being no subject of special interest to give a demand for papers, yet, by his diligence and perseverance, he managed to clear, in the course of the day almost another dollar, leaving in his pocket, when night came on, nearly a dollar and three quarters.

Having completed his work for the day, his thoughts instinctively turned to the home of his parents. He felt an intense desire to go and share with them the joys of his good fortune; but he dared not meet his father, for he knew well that a severe punishment would be inflicted upon him, and that his money would be taken from him to purchase rum. He could not, however, go to rest for the night without getting a sight of his mother, if it were possible, and purchasing something for her comfort. He accordingly went and purchased some articles of provision, to the amount of a quarter of a dollar, rolled them in a paper, and made his way homeward. The evening was rather dark, and gave him a favorable opportunity to approach the house without being discovered. He saw his mother, through the window, sitting on a bench on the opposite side of the room, with her head reclining on her hand, and apparently weeping. He could also hear his father walking in another part of the room, though he could not see him. He crept carefully to the window, dropped his paper of provisions into the room, and turned away down the street as fast as he could run.

He went again to his solitary lodgings, and rested till morning, when he arose with fresh vigor, and resumed the labors of the day. The same exertions and perseverance produced the same successful results he had met with the two previous days; and the evenings saw the table of his parents again spread with a comfortable meal, which was improved this time by the addition of a little fruit.

Thus, day after day, and week after week, Billy successfully followed his new profession of newsboy, working hard and faring hard, in season and out of season, early and late, rain or shine. His lodging was sometimes in a stable, sometimes among the open market stalls, and sometimes under a portico of some public building. His food was of the coarsest and cheapest kind, bread and cheese, and potatoes and fish; and sometimes, when he had done a good day's work, he would treat himself to an apple or two, or some other fruit that happened to be in season.

But Billy never forgot his parents. Regularly every night he contrived to supply them with a quantity of food sufficient for the following day; sometimes carrying it himself, and dropping it in the window, and sometimes, when the evening was light, and he was afraid of being discovered, employing another boy to carry it for him, while he stood at the corner, and watched to see that his errand was faithfully executed. At the end of three months, Billy found himself in possession of thirty dollars in cash, notwithstanding he had in the meantime purchased himself a pretty good second-hand cap, a little too small to be sure, but nevertheless he managed to keep it on the top of his head; also a second-hand frock coat, which was somewhat too large, but whose capacious pockets he found exceedingly convenient for carrying his surplus gingerbread and apples. He had also, in the meantime, sent his mother calico sufficient to make her a gown, besides sundry other little articles of wearing apparel. He had been careful all this time not to come in contact with his father, though he once came very near falling into his hands. His father discovered him at a little distance in the street, and ran to seize him, but Billy saw him in time to flee round a corner, and through an alley way that led to another street, and so escaped.

Bill Snub at last came to the conclusion that his son Billy was doing a pretty fair business in something or other, for he had become satisfied that the food which he and his wife daily received was furnished by Billy, as well as occasional articles of his wife's clothing. And when he ascertained from some of the boys of Billy's acquaintance, that he had probably laid up some thirty or forty dollars in cash, Bill at once conceived the design of getting possession of the money. As he could not catch Billy in the street, he formed a plan to get the aid of police officers; and, in order to do that, he found it necessary to make charges against Billy. He accordingly repaired to the police office, and entered a complaint against his boy for having stolen thirty or forty dollars of his money, which he was spending about the streets. He described the boy to the police officers, who were soon dispatched in search of him, with orders to arrest him, and see if any money could be found upon him. As Billy was flying about in all parts of the city, selling his papers, it was nearly night before the officers came across him. He had just sold his last paper, and was walking leisurely along the street, eating a piece of gingerbread and an apple, when a policeman came suddenly behind him and seized him by the shoulder. Billy looked up with surprise, and asked the man what he wanted.

" I'll let you know what I want, you little rascal!"

said the officer, harshly. "Where did you get all that gingerbread and apples, sir?"

"I bought it," said Billy.

"You bought it, did ye? and where did you get the money, sir?"

"I earnt it," said Billy.

"You earnt it did ye? and how did you earn it, sir?"

"By selling newspapers," said Billy.

"Tell me none of your lies, sir?" said the man, giving him an extra shake by the shoulder. "Now, sir, how much money have you got in your pockets?"

"I've got some," said Billy, trembling and trying to pull away from the man.

"Got some, have you?" said the officer, holding him by a still firmer gripe. "How much have you got, sir? Let me see it?"

"I shan't show my money to nobody," said Billy, "so you let me alone."

"We'll see about that, sir, when we get to the police office," said the man, dragging Billy away by the shoulder.

It was so late in the day when they arrived at the office, that the examining magistrates had left, and gone home. The constable, therefore, with one of his

fellow-officers, proceeded to search Billy, and found
something over thirty dollars of good money in his
pockets. Billy persisted that he had earned the
money by selling papers; but the officers, with much
severity, told him to leave off his lying, for boys that
sold papers did n't have so much money as that.
They knew all about it; he had stolen the money,
and he must be locked up till next morning, when he
would have his trial. So they took Billy's money
from him, and locked him up in a dark gloomy room
for the night. A sad night was this for poor Billy.
At first he was so bewildered and shocked at the
thought of being locked up alone all night, that he
hardly realized where he was, or what was going on.
As they pushed him into his solitary apartment, and
closed the door upon him, and turned the large
grating key, he instinctively clung to the door latch,
and tried to pull it open. He called to them as loud
as he could scream, to open the door and let him out,
and they might have all the money in welcome. He
could get no answer, however, to his calls; and when
he stopped and listened, the silence around him
pressed upon him with such appalling power, that he
almost fell to the floor. He reeled across the room
two or three times, and returned again to the door;

but there was no chance to escape, and the conviction was forced upon him that he was indeed locked up, and all alone, without the power of speaking to any living being. He sank down upon a bench in a corner of the room, and wept a long time most bitterly. When his tears had somewhat subsided, and he roused himself up again so as to look about, the night had closed in and left him in such deep darkness that he could not see across the room. He rose and walked about, feeling his way by the walls, and continued to walk a great part of the night, for there was nothing to rest on but the floor or the little bench, and he could not have slept if he had had the softest bed in the world. He could not imagine the cause of his imprisonment, for he was sure he had injured no one ; but what grieved him most, was the thought that his poor father and mother were probably without food, as he had been prevented from carrying anything home that evening. At the thought of his mother, his tears gushed forth again in a copious flood.

Towards morning he sank down exhausted upon the floor, and fell into a short sleep. Still he was awake again by daylight, and up and walking the room. The morning seemed long, very long, to him, for it was ten o'clock before the officers came to take him before the magistrate. He was glad to see the door open again, even though it was to carry him to court, for the idea of being tried for stealing was not so horrible to him as being locked up there alone in that dark room.

The money was given to the magistrate, and Billy was placed at the bar to answer to the charge against him. The officer stated that he had found the boy in the street by the description he had of him, and on searching him, the money was found in his pockets.

"Well, that's a clear case," said the magistrate; "precious rogue—large amount for a boy—thirty dollars—that's worth three months' imprisonment; the boy must be locked up for three months."

Billy shuddered, and began to weep.

"It's too late to cry now," said the magistrate, "you should have thought of that before; but, after committing the crime, there's no way to escape the punishment. What induced you to steal this money?"

"I did n't steal it, sir," said Billy, very earnestly.

"Ah, that is only making a bad matter worse," said the magistrate; "the best way for you is to confess the whole, and resolve to reform and do better in future."

14

"But I did n't steal it," said Billy with increasing energy; "I earnt it, every cent of it!"

"You earnt it!" said the magistrate, peering over his spectacles at Billy; "and how did you earn it?"

"By selling newspapers," said Billy.

There was something so frank and open in the boy's appearance, that the magistrate began to wake up to the subject a little. He asked the officer if the money had been identified by the loser. The officer replied that the particular money had not been identified, only the amount.

"Well, bring the man forward," said the magistrate; "he must identify his money."

The officer then called up Bill Snub, who was stowed away in a distant corner of the room, apparently desirous of keeping out of sight. This was the first intimation that Billy had that his father was his accuser, and it gave him such a shock that he sank down upon the seat, and almost fainted away. The magistrate asked Snub if that was his money, found on the boy. Snub said it was.

"Well, what sort of money was it that you lost?" said the magistrate. "You must describe it."

"Oh, it was—it was all good money," said Snub, coloring.

"But you must be particular," said the magistrate, "and describe the money. What kind of money was it?"

"Well, some of it was paper money, and some of it was hard money," said Snub; "it's all good money."

"But how much of it was hard money?" said the magistrate.

"Well, considerable of it," said Bill; "I don't know exactly how much."

"What banks were the bills on?" said the magistrate.

"Well, I don't know exactly," said Bill, "but I believe it was some of the banks of this city."

"How large were the bills?" said the magistrate.

"Well, some of 'em was larger, and some smaller," said Bill.

"This business does not look very clear," said the magistrate. "What is your name, sir?"

"Bill Snub," was the answer.

"And what is the boy's name?"

"His name is Billy Snub, Sir."

"Is he any connection of yours?" said the magistrate.

"I'm sorry to own it, sir, but he's my only son, bad as he is."

The magistrate, who had been looking over the top of his spectacles some time, now took them off, and fixed his eyes sternly on Bill.

"This business must be unravelled, sir. There is no evidence as yet on either side; but there is something mysterious about it. It must be unravelled, sir."

At this, a little boy of about Billy's age, came forward, and told the magistrate that he knew something about the matter.

"Let him be sworn," said the magistrate; "and now tell all you know about it."

"Well, I've seen Billy Snub selling newspapers 'most every day this three or four months; and I've known him to make as much as a dollar a-day a good many times. And I've known he's been laying up his money all the time, only a little, jest enough to buy his victuals with, and about a quarter of a dollar a day that he took to buy victuals with for his father and mother. And I've been a good many times in the evening, and put the victuals into the window where his father and mother lived, because Billy did n't dare to go himself, for fear his father would catch him, and lick him 'most to death for breaking the rum-bottle when he sent him to get some rum.

And I know Billy had got up to about thirty dollars, for I've seen him count it a good many times. And yesterday his father was asking me what Billy was about all the time; and said Billy was a lazy feller, and never would earn anything in the world. And I told him Billy was n't lazy, for he'd got more than thirty dollars now, that he'd earnt selling papers. And then he said, if Billy had got thirty dollars, he'd have it somehow or other before he was two days older."

"You may stop there," said the magistrate; "the evidence is full and clear enough." Then turning to Bill, he continued, with great severity of manner, "and, as for you, sir, for this inhuman and wicked attempt to ruin your own son, you stand committed to prison, and at hard labor for the term of one year." Then he turned to Billy, and said, "Here, my noble lad, take your money and go home and take care of your mother. Continue to be industrious and honest, and never fear but that you will prosper."

The rest of this history is soon told. Billy was really rejoiced at the opportunity of visiting his mother in peace and safety again, and of once more having a home where he could rest in quietness at night. Bill Snub had to serve out his year in prison, but Billy constantly supplied him with all the comforts and necessaries of life which his situation admitted, and always visited him as often as once a week. And when he came out of prison he was an altered man. He joined the temperance society, and quitted the rum-bottle forever. He became more industrious, worked at his trade, and earned enough to support himself and Sally comfortably.

Billy still pursued his profession with untiring industry and great success. He some time since purchased a small house and lot in the outskirts of the city for a residence for his parents; and at this present writing he has several hundred dollars in the savings bank, besides many loose coins profitably invested in various other ways. He is active, healthy, honest, and persevering, and destined beyond doubt to become a man of wealth and honorable distinction, whose name will shine on the page of history as the illustrious head of an illustrious line of Snubs.

CHAPTER XIII.

THE PUMPKIN FRESHET.

AUNT PATTY STOW is sixty-seven years old; not quite as spry as a girl of sixteen, but a great deal tougher —she has seen tough times in her day. She can do as good a day's work as any woman within twenty miles of her, and as for walking, she can beat a regiment. General Taylor's army on the march moved about fifteen miles a day, but Aunt Patty, on a pinch, could walk twenty. She has been spending the summer with her niece in New York; for Aunt Patty has nieces, abundance of them, though she has no children; she never had any. Aunt Patty never was married, and, for the last thirty years, whenever the question has been asked her, why she did not get married, her invariable reply has been, "she would not have the best man that ever trod shoe-leather." Aunt Patty has been spending the summer in New York, but she does n't *live* there; not she! she would as soon live on the top of the Rocky Mountains. If

you ask her where she does live, she always an-
swers,

"On Susquehanna's side, fair Wyoming."

This, to be sure, is a poetical license, and before you
get the sober prose answer to your question, Aunt
Patty will tell you that she is "a great hand for
poetry," though the line above is the only one she has
ever been known to quote, even by the oldest inhabi-
tant. When you get at the truth of the matter, you
find she does live "on Susquehanna's side," but a
good ways from "fair Wyoming," that being in Penn-
sylvania, while her residence, for fifty-eight years, has
been in the old Indian valley of Oquago, now Wind-
sor, in Broome county, New York. There, in that
beautiful bend of the Susquehanna, some miles before
it receives the waters of the Chenango, Aunt Patty
has been "a fixture" ever since the white inhabitants
first penetrated that part of the wilderness, and sat
down by the side of the red man. There, when a
child, she wandered over the meadows and by the
brook-side to catch trout, and clambered up the mountains to gather blueberries, and down into the valleys
for wild lillies.

  This valley of Oquago, before the revolutionary

war, was the favorite residence of an Indian tribe, and a sort of half-way ground, a resting-place for the "six nations" at the north, and the tribes of Wyoming at the south, in visiting each other. It was to the Indians in Oquago valley, that the celebrated Dr Edwards, while a minister in Stockbridge, Mass., sent the Rev. Mr. Hawley as a missionary; and also sent with him his little son, nine years old, to learn the Indian language, with a view of preparing him for an Indian missionary. And when the French war broke out, a faithful and friendly Indian took charge of the lad, and conveyed him home to his father, carrying him a good part of the way on his back. But all this happened before Aunt Patty's time, and before any white family, except the missionary's, resided within a long distance of Oquago.

About the year of 1788, some families came in from Connecticut, and settled in the valley, and Aunt Patty's father and mother were among the first. Thus brought up to experience the hardships and privations of a pioneer life in the wilderness, no wonder Aunt Patty should be much struck on viewing for the first time the profusion and luxury and mode of life in a city. The servant girl was sent out for some bread, and in five minutes she returned with a basket of

wheat loaves, fresh biscuit and French rolls. Aunt
Patty rolled up her eyes and lifted up both
hands.

"Dear me!" says she, "do you call that bread?
And where, for massy sake, did it come from so quick
now? Does bread rain down from heaven here in
New York, jest as the manna in the Bible did to the
children of Israel?"

"Oh, no, Aunt Patty, there's a baker only a few
steps off, just round the next corner, who bakes more
than a hundred bushels a day; so that we can always
have hot bread and hot cakes there, half a dozen
times a day if we want it."

"A hundred bushels a day!" screamed Aunt Patty,
at the top of her voice; "the massy preserve us!
Well, if you had only been at Oquago at the time of
the great punkin freshet, you would think a good deal
of having bread so handy, I can tell you."

Aunt Patty's niece took her with her to the Wash-
ington Market of a Saturday evening, and showed
her the profusion of fruits and vegetables and meats,
that covered an area of two or three acres.

"The Lord be praised!" said Aunt Patty, "why,
here is victuals enough to feed a whole nation. Who
would have thought that I should a-lived through the

punkin freshet to come to see such a sight as this before I die ?"

At the tea table, Mrs. Jones, for that was the name of Aunt Patty's niece, had many apologies to make about the food ; the bread was too hard and the butter was too salt, and the fruit was too stale, and something else was too something or other. At the expression of each apology, Aunt Patty looked up with wonderment ; she knew not how to understand Mrs. Jones ; for, to her view, a most grand and rich and dainty feast was spread before her. But when Mrs. Jones summed up the whole by declaring to Aunt Patty she was afraid she would not be able to make out a supper of their poor fare, Aunt Patty laid down her knife, and sat back in her chair, and looked up at Mrs. Jones with perfect astonishment.

"Why, Sally Jones!" said she, " are you making fun of me all this time, or what is it you mean !"

"No, indeed, Aunt Patty, I only meant just what I said; we have rather a poor table to night, and I was afraid you would hardly make a comfortable tea."

Aunt Patty looked at Mrs. Jones about a minute without saying a word. At last she said, with most decided emphasis, "Well, Sally Jones, I can't tell how it is some folks get such strange notions in their heads ;

but I can tell you, if you had seed what I seed, and gone through what I have gone through, in the punkin freshet, when I was a child, and afterwards come to set down to sich a table as this, you'd think you was in heaven."

Here Mr. Jones burst out into a broad laugh. "Well done, Aunt Patty!" said he, shoving back his cup and shaking his sides; "the history of that *pumpkin freshet* we must have; you have excited my curiosity about it to the highest pitch. Let us have the whole story now, by way of seasoning for our poor supper. What was the pumpkin freshet? and when was it, and where was it, and what did you have to do with it? Let us have the whole story from first to last, will you?"

"Well, Mr. Jones, you ask me a great question," said Aunt Patty, "but if I can't answer it, I don't know who can—for I seed the punkin freshet with my own eyes, and lived on the punkins that we pulled out of the river for two months afterwards. Let me see—it was in the year 1794; that makes it sixty years ago. Bless me, how the time slips away. I was only about seven years old then. It was a woodsy place, Oquago Valley was. There was only six families in our neighborhood then, though there was some more settled away further up the river. Major Stow, my uncle, was the head man of the neighborhood. He had the best farm, and was the smartest hand to work, and was the stoutest and toughest man there was in them parts. Major Buck was the minister. They always called him Major Buck, because he'd been a major in the revolutionary war, and when the war was over he took to preaching, and come and lived in Oquago. He was a nice man; everybody sot store by Major Buck."

"Oh, well, I don't care about Major Buck, nor Major Stow," said Mr. Jones, "I want to hear about the pumpkin freshet. What was it that made the pumpkin freshet?"

"Why, the rain, I suppose," said Aunt Patty, looking up very quietly.

"The rain?" said Mr. Jones; "did it rain pumpkins in your younger days, in the Oquago Valley!"

"I guess you'd a-thought so," said Aunt Patty "if you had seen the punkins come floating down the river, and rolling along the shore, and over the meadows. It had been a great year for punkins that year. All the corn-fields and potato-fields up and down the river was spotted all over with 'em, as yellow as goold. The corn was jest beginning to turn hard, and the potatoes was ripe enough to pull. And then, one day, it begun to rain, kind of easy at first; we thought it was only going to be a shower; but it did n't hold up all day, and in the night it kept raining harder and harder, and in the morning it come down with a power. Well, it rained steady all that day. Nobody went out into the fields to work, but all staid in the house and looked out to see if it would n't hold up. When it come night, it was dark as Egypt, and the rain still poured down. Father took down the Bible and read the account about the flood, and then we went to bed. In the morning, a little after daylight, Uncle Major Stow come to the window and hollowed to us, and says he, turn out all hands, or ye'll all be in the river in a heap.

"I guess we was out of bed about the quickest. There was father, and mother, and John, and Jacob, and Hannah, and Suzy, and Mike, and me, and Sally, and Jim, and Rachel, all running to the door as hard as we could pull. We didn't stand much about clothes. When father unbarred the door and opened it—'oh,' says Uncle Major, says he, 'you may go back and dress yourselves, you'll have time enough for that; but there's no knowing how long you'll be safe, for the Susquehanna has got her head up, and is running like a race-horse. Your hen-house has gone now. At that Hannah fetched a scream that you might a heard her half a mile, for half the chickens was her'n. As soon as we got our clothes on, we all run out, and there we see a sight. It still rained a little, but not very hard. The river, that used to be away down in the holler, ten rods from the house, had now filled the holler full, and was up within two rods of our door. The chicken-house was gone, and all the hens and chickens with it, and we never seed nor heard nothin' of it afterwards.

"While we stood there talking and mourning about the loss of the chickens, father he looked off upon the river, for it begun to be so light that we could see across it now, and father spoke, and says he, 'what upon airth is all them yellow spots floating along down the river?'

"At that we all turned round and looked, and Uncle Major, says he, 'by King George, them's punkins! If the Susquehanna has n't been robbing the punkin fields in the upper neighborhood, there's no snakes in Oquago.'

"And sure enough, they was punkins; and they kept coming along thicker and thicker, spreading away across the river, and up and down as far as we

could see. And bime-by Mr. Williams, from the
upper neighborhood, come riding down a horseback
as hard as he could ride, to tell us to look out, for the
river was coming down like a roaring lion, seeking
whom he may devour. He said it had run over the
meadows and the low grounds, and swept off the
corn-fields, and washed out the potatoes, and was
carrying off acres and acres of punkins on its back.
The whole river, he said, was turned into a great
punkin-field. He advised father to move out what he
could out of the house, for he thought the water
would come into it, if it did n't carry the house away.
So we all went to work as tight as we could spring,
and Uncle Major he put to and helped us, and we
carried out what things we could, and carried them
back a little ways, where the ground was so high we
thought the river could n't reach 'em. And then we
went home with Uncle Major Stow, and got some
breakfast. Uncle Major's house was on higher
ground, and we felt safe there.

"After breakfast, father went down to the house
again, to see how it looked, and presently he come
running back, and said the water was up to the door-
sill. Then they began to think the house would go,
and we all went down as quick as we could, to watch

it. When we got there, the water was running into the door, and was all the time rising. 'That house is a gone goose,' says Uncle Major, says he, 'it's got to take a journey down the river to look after the hens and chickens.'

"At that, mother begun to cry, and took on about it as though her heart would break. But father, says he, 'la, Patty,' mother's name was Patty, and I was named after her; father, says he, 'la, Patty, it's no use crying for spilt milk, so you may as well wipe up your tears. The house aint gone yet, and if it should go, there's logs enough all handy here, and we can build another as good as that in a week.'

"'Yes,' says Uncle Major, says he, 'if the house goes down stream, we'll all turn to and knock another one together in short order.' So mother begun to be pacified. Father went and got a couple of bed-cords and hitched on to one corner of the house, and tied it to a stump; for, he said, if the water come up only jest high enough to start the house, maybe the cords would keep it from going. The water kept a-rising, and in a little more than an hour after we got back from uncle's, it was two foot deep on the floor.

"'One foot more,' says Uncle Major, says he, 'will take the house off its legs.'

" But, as good luck would have it, one foot more
did n't come. We watched and watched an hour
longer, and the water kept rising a little, but not so
fast as it did, and at last we could n't see as it ris any
more. And, as it had done raining, after we found
it did n't rise any for an hour, Uncle Major he pronounced his opinion that the house would stand it.
Then did n't we feel glad enough? Before noon the
water begun to settle away a little, and before night
it was clear of the house. But Uncle Major said it
was so wet, it would never do for us to stay in it that
night, without we wanted to ketch our death a-cold.
So we all went up to his house, and made a great camp
bed on the floor, and there we all staid till morning.
That day we got our things back into the house again,
and the river kept going down a little all day.

" But oh, such a melancholy sight as it was to see
the fields, you don't know. All the low grounds had
been washed over by the river, and everything that
was growing had been washed away and carried
down stream, or else covered up with sand and mud.
Then in a few weeks after that, come on the starving
time. Most all the crops was cut off by the freshet;
and there we was in the wilderness, as it were, forty
miles from any place where we could get any help,

and no road only a blind footpath through the woods. Well, provisions began to grow short. We had a good many punkins that the boys pulled out of the river as they floated along the bank. And it was boiled punkins in the morning, and boiled punkins at noon, and boiled punkins at night. But that wasn't very solid food, and we hankered for something else. We had some meat, though not very plenty, and we got some roots and berries in the woods. But as for bread, we didn't see any from one week's end to another.

"There was but very little corn or grain in the neighborhood, and what little there was couldn't be ground, for the hand-mill had been carried away by the freshet. At last, when we had toughed it out five or six weeks, one day Uncle Major Stow, says he, 'well, I aint agoing to stand this starving operation any longer. I am going to have some bread and flour cake, let it cost what 'twill.'

"We all stared and wondered what he meant.

"'I tell ye,' says he, 'I'm a-going to have some bread and flour cake before the week's out, or else there's no snakes in Oquago.'

"'Well, I should like to know how you are a-going to get it,' says father, says he.

" ' I'm a-going to mill,' says Uncle Major, says he. ' I've got a half bushel of wheat thrashed out, and if any of the neighbors will put in enough to make up another half bushel, I'll shoulder it and carry it down to Wattle's ferry to mill, and we'll have one feast before we starve to death. It's only about forty miles, and I can go and get back again in three or four days.'

" They tried to persuade him off the notion of it, 'twould be such a long tiresome journey ; but he said it was no use ; his half bushel of wheat had got to go, and he could as well carry a bushel as a half bushel, for it would only jest make a clever weight to balance him. So Major Buck and three other neighbors, who had a little wheat, put in half a peck apiece, and that made up the bushel. And the next morning at daylight, Uncle Major shouldered the bushel of wheat, and started for Wattle's ferry, forty miles, to mill.

" Every night and morning while he was gone, Major Buck used to mention him in his prayers, and pray for his safe return. The fourth day, about noon, we see Uncle Major coming out of the woods with a bag on his shoulder ; and then, if there was n't a jumping and running all over the neighborhood, I won't guess again. They all sot out and run for Uncle Major's house, as tight as they could leg it, and the whole neighborhood got there about as soon as he did. In come Uncle Major, all of a puff, and rolled the bag off his shoulder on to the bench.

"'There, Molly,' says he; that was his wife, his wife's name was Molly; 'there, Molly, is as good a bushel of flour meal as you ever put your hands into. Now go to work and try your skill at a short cake. If we don't have a regular feast this afternoon, there's no snakes in Oquago. Bake two milk-pans full, so as to have enough for the whole neighborhood.'

"'A short cake, Mr. Stow,' says Aunt Molly, says she, 'why what are you a thinking about? Don't you know we have n't got a bit of shortnin' in the house; not a mite of butter, nor hog's fat, nor nothin'? How can we make a short cake?'

"'Well, maybe some of the neighbors has got some,' says Uncle Major, says he.

"'No,' says Aunt Molly, 'I don't believe there's a bit in the neighborhood.'

"Then they asked Major Buck, and father, and all round, and there wasn't one that had a bit of butter or hog's fat.

" ' So your short cake is all dough agin,' says Aunt Molly, says she.

" ' No taint, nother,' says Uncle Major, 'I never got agin a stump yet, but what I got round it some way or other. There's some of that bear's grease left yet, and there's no better shortnin' in the world. Do let us have the short cake as soon as you can make it. Come, boys, stir round and have a good fire ready to bake it.'

" Then Aunt Molly stripped up her sleeves, and went at it, and the boys knocked round and made up a fire, and there was a brisk business carried on there for awhile, I can tell you. While Aunt was going on with the short cakes, Uncle Major was uncommon lively. He went along and whispered to Major Buck, and Major Buck looked up at him with a wild kind of a stare, and says he, ' you don't say so !'

" Then Uncle Major whispered to mother, and mother says she, ' why, Brother Stow, I don't believe you.'

" ' You may believe it or not,' says Uncle Major, says he, ' but 'tis true as Major Buck's preachin'.'

" Then Uncle Major walked up and down the room, whistlin' and snappin' his fingers, and sometimes strikin' up into Yankee Doodle.

" ' Here,' says Uncle Major, says he, pulling out a little paper bundle out of
his pocket, and holding it up to Aunt Molly's face: 'here, smell of that,' says he

"Aunt Molly she dropped her work, and took her hands out of the dough, and says she, 'Mr. Stow, I wonder what's got into you; it must be something more than the short cakes I'm sure, that's put such life into you.'

"'To be sure 'tis,' says Uncle, 'for the short cakes hain't got into me yet.' And then he turned round and give a wink to mother and Major Buck.

"'Well, there now,' says Aunt Molly, says she, 'I know you've got some kind of a secret that you've been telling these folks here, and I declare I won't touch the short cakes again till I know what 'tis.'

"When Aunt Molly put her foot down, there 'twas, and nobody could move her. So Uncle Major knew he might as well come to it first as last; and says he, 'well, Molly, it's no use keeping a secret from you; but I've got something will make you stare worse than the short cakes.'

"'Well, what is it, Mr. Stow?' says Aunt Molly, 'out with it, and let us know the worst of it.'

"'Here,' says Uncle Major, says he, pulling out a little paper bundle out of his pocket, and holding it up to Aunt Molly's face; 'here, smell of that,' says he.

"As soon as Aunt Molly smelt of it, she jumped

right up and kissed Uncle Major right before the whole company, and says she, 'it's tea! as true as I'm alive, it's the real bohea. I have n't smelt any before for three years, but I knew it in a moment.'

" ' Yes,' says Uncle Major, 'it's tea; there's a quarter of a pound of the real stuff. While my grist was grinding, I went into the store, and there I found they had some tea; and, thinks I, we'll have one dish for all hands, to go with the short cakes, if it takes the last copper I've got. So I knocked up a bargain with the man, and bought a quarter of a pound; and here 'tis. Now, Molly, set your wits to work, and give us a good dish of tea with the short cakes, and we'll have a real thanksgiving; we'll make it seem like old Connecticut times again.'

" ' Well, now, Mr. Stow, what shall we do?' says Aunt Molly, 'for there isn't a tea-kettle, nor a tea-pot, nor no cups and sarcers in the neighborhood.'

" And that was true enough; they had n't had any tea since they moved from Connecticut, so they had n't got any tea-dishes.

" ' Well, I don't care,' says Uncle Major, says he, 'we'll have the tea, any how. There's the dish-kettle, you can boil the water in that, and you can

steep the tea in the same, and when it's done I guess
we'll contrive some way or other to drink it.'

"So Aunt Molly dashed round and drove on with
the work, and got the short-cakes made, and the boys
got the fire made, and they got the cakes down to
baking, and about four quarts of water hung on in the
dish-kettle to boil for tea, and when it began to boil,
the whole quarter of a pound of tea was put into it
to steep. Bime-by they had the table set out, and a
long bench on one side, and chairs on the other side,
and there was two milk-pans set on the table filled up
heaping full of short-cakes, and the old folks all sot
down, and fell to eating, and we children stood behind
them with our hands full, eating tu. And oh, them
short-cakes, seems to me, I never shall forget how
good they tasted the longest day I live.

"After they eat a little while, Uncle Major called
for the tea; and what do you think they did for tea-
cups? Why, they took a two quart wooden bowl,
and turned off tea enough to fill it, and sot it on to
the table. They handed it up to Major Buck first, as
he was the minister, and sot to the head of the table,
and he took a drink, and handed it to Uncle Major
Stow, and he took a drink, and then they passed it all
round the table, from one to t'other, and they all took

15

a drink; and when that was gone, they turned out
the rest of the tea, and filled the bowl up, and drinked
round again.   Then they poured some more water
into the dish-kettle, and steeped the tea over again a
few minutes, and turned out a bowlful, and passed
it round for us children to taste of.   But if it want
for the name of tea, we had a good deal rather have
water, for it was such bitter, miserable stuff, it spoilt
the taste of the short-cakes.   But the old folks said if
we did n't love it, we need n't drink it; so they took
it and drinkt up the rest of it.

"And there they sot all the afternoon, eating short-
cakes, and drinking tea, and telling stories, and having
a merry thanksgiving of it.   And that's the way we
lived at the time of the punkin freshet in the valley
of Oquago."

NOTE—The main incidents in this sketch, in relation to the early
settlement of Oquago Valley, the "pumpkin freshet," Major Stow's
pedestrian journey of forty miles to mill, the bushel of wheat, the
short-cakes and the tea, are all historically true.

CHAPTER XIV.

A RACE FOR A SWEETHEART.

HARDLY any event creates a stronger sensation in a thinly settled New England village, especially among the young folks, than the arrival of a fresh and blooming miss, who comes to make her abode in the neighborhood. When, therefore, Squire Johnson, the only lawyer in the place, and a very respectable man of course, told Farmer Jones one afternoon that his wife's sister, a smart girl of eighteen, was coming in a few days to reside in his family, the news flew like wildfire through Pond Village, and was the principal topic of conversation for a week. Pond Village is situated upon the margin of one of those numerous and beautiful sheets of water that gem the whole surface of New England, like the bright stars in an evening sky, and received its appellation to distinguish it from two or three other villages in the same town, which could not boast of a similar location. When Farmer Jones came in to his supper, about sunset that afternoon, and took his seat at the table, the eyes of the whole family were upon him, for there was a peculiar working about his mouth, and a knowing glance of his eye, that always told them when he had anything of interest to communicate. But Farmer Jones' secretiveness was large, and his temperament not the most active, and he would probably have rolled the important secret as a sweet morsel under his tongue for a long time, had not Mrs. Jones, who was rather of an impatient and prying turn of mind, contrived to draw it from him.

"Now, Mr. Jones," said she, as she handed him his cup of tea, "what is it you are going to say? Do out with it; for you've been chawing something or other over in your mind ever since you came into the house."

"It's my tobacher, I s'spose," said Mr. Jones, with another knowing glance of his eye.

"Now, father, what is the use?" said Susan; "we all know you've got something or other you want to say, and why can't you tell us what 'tis."

"La, who cares what 'tis?" said Mrs. Jones; "if it was anything worth telling, we shouldn't have to wait for it, I dare say."

Hereupon Mrs. Joues assumed an air of the most

perfect indifference, as the surest way of conquering what she was pleased to call Mr. Jones's obstinacy, which, by the way, was a very improper term to apply in the case; for it was purely the working of secretiveness, without the least particle of obstinacy attached to it.

There was a pause of two or three minutes in the conversation, till Mr. Jones passed his cup to be filled a second time, when, with a couple of preparatory hems, he began to let out the secret.

"We are to have a new neighbor here in a few days," said Mr. Jones, stopping short when he had uttered thus much, and sipping his tea and filling his mouth with food.

Mrs. Jones, who was perfect in her tactics, said not a word, but attended to the affairs of her table, as though she had not noticed what was said. The farmer's secretiveness had at last worked itself out, and he began again.

"Squire Johnson's wife's sister is coming here in a few days, and is going to live with 'em."

The news being thus fairly divulged, it left free scope for conversation.

"Well, I wonder if she is a proud, stuck-up piece," said Mrs. Jones.

"I should n't think she would be," said Susan, "for there aint a more sociabler woman in the neighborhood than Miss Johnson. So if she is at all like her sister, I think we shall like her."

"I wonder how old she is?" said Stephen, who was just verging toward the close of his twenty-first year.

"The squire called her eighteen," said Mr. Jones, giving a wink to his wife, as much as to say, that's about the right age for Stephen.

"I wonder if she is handsome," said Susan, who was somewhat vain of her own looks, and having been a sort of reigning belle in Pond Village, for some time, she felt a little alarm at the idea of a rival.

"I dare be bound she's handsome," said Mrs. Jones, "if she's a sister to Miss Johnson, for where'll you find a handsomer woman than Miss Johnson, go the town through?"

After supper, Stephen went down to Mr. Robinson's store, and told the news to young Charles Robinson, and all the young fellows, who were gathered there for a game at quoits, and a ring at wrestling. And Susan went directly over to Mr. Bean's and told Patty, and Patty went round to the Widow Davis' and told Sally, and before nine o'clock, the matter was pretty well understood in about every house in the village.

At the close of the fourth day, a little before sunset, a chaise was seen to drive up to Squire Johnson's door. Of course the eyes of the whole village were turned in that direction. Sally Davis, who was just coming in from milking, set her pail down on the grass by the side of the road, as soon as the chaise came in sight, and watched it till it reached the squire's door, and the gentleman and lady had got out and gone into the house. Patty Bean was doing up the ironing that afternoon, and she had just taken a hot iron from the fire as the chaise passed the door, and she ran with it in her hand, and stood on the door-steps till the whole ceremony of alighting, greeting, and entering the house was over. Old Mrs. Bean stood with her head out of the window, her iron-bowed spectacles resting up on the top of her forehead, her shriveled hand placed across her eyebrows, to defend her red eyes from the rays of the setting sun, and her skinny chin protruding about three inches in advance of a couple of stubs of teeth, which her open mouth exposed fairly to view.

" It seems to me, they are dreadful loving," said old Mrs. Bean, as she saw Mrs. Johnson descend the steps and welcome her sister with a kiss.

" La me, if there is n't the squire kissing of her tu,"

said Patty; "well, I declare, I would a-waited till I got into the house, I'll die if I would n't. It looks so vulgar to be kissing afore folks, and out of doors tu; I should think Squire Johnson would be ashamed of himself."

"Well, I should n't," said young John Bean, who came up at the moment, and who had passed the chaise just as the young lady alighted from it. "I should n't be ashamed to kiss sich a pretty gal as that anyhow; I'd kiss her wherever I could catch her, if it was in the meetin-house."

"Why, is she handsome, Jack?" said Patty.

"Yes, she's got the prettiest little puckery mouth I've seen these six months. Her cheeks are red, and her eyes shine like new buttons."

"Well," replied Patty, "if she'll only take the shine off Susan Jones when she goes to meetin', Sunday, I sha'nt care."

While these observations were going on at old Mr. Bean's, Charles Robinson, and a group of young fellows with him, where standing in front of Robinson's store, a little farther down the road, and watching the scenes that was passing at Squire Johnson's. They witnessed the whole with becoming decorum, now and then making a remark upon the fine horse and the handsome chaise, till they saw the tall squire bend his head down, and give the young lady a kiss, when they all burst out into a loud laugh. In a moment, being conscious that their laugh must be heard and noticed at the squire's, they, in order to do away the impression it must necessarily make, at once turned their heads the other way, and, Charles Robinson who was quick at an expedient, knocked off the hat of the lad who was standing next to him, and then they all laughed louder than before.

"Here comes Jack Bean," said Charles, "now we shall hear something about her, for Jack was coming by the squire's when she got out of the chaise. How does she look, Jack?"

"Handsome as a pictur," said Jack. "I haint seen a prettier gal since last Thanksgiving Day, when Jane Ford was here to visit Susan Jones."

"Black eyes or blue?" said Charles.

"Blue," said Jack, "but all-fired bright."

"Tall or short?" said Stephen Jones, who was rather short himself, and therefore felt a particular interest on that point.

"Rather short," said Jack, "but straight and round as a young colt."

"Do you know what her name is?" said Charles.

15*

"They called her Lucy when she got out of the chaise," said Jack, "and as Miss Johnson's name was Brown before she was married, I s'pose her name must be Lucy Brown."

"Just such a name as I like," said Charles Robinson; "Lucy Brown sounds well. Now suppose in order to get acquainted with her, we all hands take a sail to-morrow night, about this time, on the pond, and invite her to go with us."

"Agreed," said Stephen Jones. "Agreed," said Jack Bean. "Agreed," said all hands.

The question then arose who should carry the invitation to her; and the young men being rather bashful on that score, it was finally settled that Susan Jones should bear the invitation, and accompany her to the boat, where they should all be in waiting to receive her. The next day was a very long day, at least to most of the young men of Pond village; and promptly an hour before sunset, most of them were assembled, with a half a score of their sisters and female cousins, by a little stone wharf on the margin of the pond, for the proposed sail. All the girls in the village of a suitable age were there, except Patty Bean. She had undergone a good deal of fidgeting and fussing during the day, to prepare for the sail, but had been disappointed. Her new bonnet was not done; and as to wearing her old flap-sided bonnet, she declared she would not, if she never went. Presently Susan Jones and Miss Lucy Brown were seen coming down the road.

In a moment, all was quiet, the laugh and joke were hushed, and each one put on his best looks. When they arrived, Susan went through the ceremony of introducing Miss Brown to each of the ladies and gentlemen present.

"But how in the world are you going to sail?" said Miss Brown, "for there isn't a breath of wind; and I don't see any sail-boat, neither."

"Oh, the less wind we have, the better, when we sail here," said Charles Robinson, "and there is our sail-boat," pointing to a flat-bottomed scow-boat, some twenty feet long by ten wide.

"We don't use no sails," said Jack Bean; "some-times, when the wind is fair, we put up a bush to help pull along a little, and when 'tis n't, we row."

The party were soon embarked on board the scow, and a couple of oars were set in motion, and they gli-ded slowly and pleasantly over as lovely a sheet of water as ever glowed in the sunsetting ray. In one hour's time, the whole party felt perfectly acquainted with Miss Lucy Brown. She had talked in the most lively and fascinating manner; she had told stories and sung songs. Among others, she had given Moore's boat song with the sweetest possible effect; and by the time they returned to the landing, it would hardly be too much to say that half the young men in the party were decidedly in love with her.

A stern regard to truth requires a remark to be made here, not altogether favorable to Susan Jones, which is the more to be regretted, as she was in the main an excellent hearted girl, and highly esteemed by the whole village. It was observed that as the company grew more and more pleased with Miss Lucy Brown, Susan Jones was less and less animated, till at last she became quite reserved, and apparently sad. She, however, on landing, treated Miss Brown with respectful attention, accompanied her home to Squire Johnson's door, and cordially bade her good night.

The casual glimpses which the young men of Pond village had of Miss Brown during the remainder of the week, as she occasionally stood at the door, or looked out at the window, or once or twice when she walked out with Susan Jones, and the fair view they all had of her at meeting on the Sabbath, served but to increase their admiration, and to render her more and more an object of attraction. She was regarded by all as a prize, and several of them were already planning what steps it was best to take in order to win her. The two most prominent candidates, however, for Miss Brown's favor, were Charles Robinson and Stephen Jones. Their position and standing among the young men of the village seemed to put all others in the back-ground. Charles, whose father was wealthy, had every advantage which money could procure. But Stephen, though poor, had decidedly the advantage of Charles in personal recommendations. He had more talent, was more sprightly and intelligent, and more pleasing in his address. From the evening of the sail on the pond, they had both watched every movement of Miss Brown with the most intense interest; and, as nothing can deceive a lover, each had, with an interest no less intense, watched every movement of the other. They had ceased to speak to each other about her, and if her name was mentioned in their presence, both were always observed to color.

The second week after her arrival, through the influence of Squire Johnson, the district school was offered to Miss Brown on the other side of the pond, which offer was accepted, and she went immediately to take charge of it. This announcement at first threw something of a damper upon the spirits of the young people of Pond village. But when it was understood that the school would continue but a few weeks, and being but a mile and a half distant, Miss Brown would come home every Saturday afternoon, and spend the Sabbath, it was not very difficult to be reconciled to the temporary arrangement. The week wore away heavily, especially to Charles Robinson and Stephen Jones. They counted the days impatiently till Saturday, and on Saturday they counted the long and lagging hours till noon. They had both made up their minds that it would be dangerous to wait longer, and they had both resolved not to let another Sabbath pass without making direct proposals to Miss Brown.

Stephen Jones was too early a riser for Charles Robinson, and, in any enterprize where both were concerned, was pretty sure to take the lead, except where money could carry the palm, and then, of course, it was always borne away by Charles. As Miss Lucy had been absent most of the week, and was to be at home that afternoon, Charles Robinson had made an arrangement with his mother and sister to have a little tea party in the evening, for the purpose

of inviting Miss Brown ; and then, of course, he
should walk home with her in the evening ; and then,
of course, would be a good opportunity to break the
ice, and make known to her his feelings and his wishes.
Stephen Jones, however, was more prompt in his
movements. He had got wind of the proposed tea
party, although himself and sister, for obvious reasons,
had not been invited, and he resolved not to risk the
arrival of Miss Brown and her visit to Mr. Robinson's
before he should see her. She would dismiss her
school at noon, and come the distance of a mile and
a half round the pond home. His mind was at once
made up. He would go round and meet her at the
school-house, and accompany her on her walk. There,
in that winding road, around those delightful waters,
with the tall and shady trees over-head, and the wild
grape-vines twining round their trunks, and climbing
to the branches, while the wild birds were singing
through the woods, and the wild ducks playing in the
coves along the shore, surely there, if anywhere in
the world, could a man bring his mind up to the point
of speaking of love.

Accordingly, a little before noon, Stephen washed
and brushed himself up, and put on his Sunday
clothes, and started on his expedition. In order to

avoid observation, he took a back route across the
field, intending to come into the road by the pond, a
little out of the village. As ill-luck would have it,
Charles Robinson had been out in the same direction,
and was returning with an armful of green boughs
and wild flowers, to ornament the parlor for the evening. He saw Stephen, and noticed his dress, and the
direction he was going, and he at once smoked the
whole business. His first impulse was to rush upon
him and collar him, and demand that he should
return back. But then he recollected that in the last
scratch he had with Stephen, two or three years
before, he had a little the worst of it, and he instinctively stood still, while Stephen passed on without
seeing him. It flashed upon his mind at once that
the question must now be reduced to a game of speed.
If he could by any means gain the school-house first,
and engage Miss Lucy to walk home with him, he
should consider himself safe. But if Stephen should
reach the school-house first, he should feel a good deal
of uneasiness for the consequences. Stephen was
walking, very leisurely, and unconscious that he was
in any danger of a competitor on the course, and it
was important that his suspicions should not be
awakened. Charles therefore remained perfectly

quiet till Stephen had got a little out of hearing, and then threw down his bushes and flowers, and ran to the wharf below the store with his utmost speed. He had one advantage over Stephen. He was ready at a moment's warning to start on an expedition of this kind, for Sunday clothes was an every day affair with him.

There was a light canoe belonging to his father lying at the wharf, and a couple of stout boys were there fishing. Charles hailed them, and told them if they would row him across the pond as quick as they possibly could, he would give them a quarter of a dollar a-piece. This, in their view, was a splendid offer for their services, and they jumped on board with alacrity and manned the oars. Charles took a paddle and stood in the stern to steer the boat, and help propel her ahead. The distance by water was a little less than by land, and although Stephen had considerably the start of him, he believed he should be able to reach the school-house first, especially if Stephen should not see him and quicken his pace. In one minute after he arrived at the wharf, the boat was under full way. The boys laid down to the oars with right good will, and Charles put out all his strength upon the paddle. They were shooting over the water twice as fast as a man could walk, and Charles already felt sure of the victory. But when they had gone about half a mile, they came in the range of a little opening in the trees on the shore, where the road was exposed to view, and there, at that critical moment, was Stephen pursuing his easy walk. Charles's heart was in his mouth. Still it was possible Stephen might not see them, for he had not yet looked around. Lest the sound of the oars might attract his attention, Charles had instantly, on coming in sight, ordered the boys to stop rowing, and he grasped his paddle with breathless anxiety, and waited for Stephen again to disappear. But just as he was upon the point of passing behind some trees, where the boat would be out of his sight, Stephen turned his head and looked round. He stopped short, turned square round, and stood for the space of a minute looking steadily at the boat. Then lifting his hand, and shaking his fist resolutely at Charles, as much as to say, I understand you, he started into a quick run.

"Now, boys," said Charles, "buckle to your oars for your lives, and if you get to the shore so I can reach the school-house before Stephen does, I'll **give** you a half a dollar a-piece."

This, of course, added new life to the boys, and increased speed to the boat. Their little canoe flew over the water almost like a bird, carrying a white bone in her mouth, and leaving a long ripple on the glassy wave behind her. Charles' hands trembled, but still he did good execution with his paddle. Although Stephen upon the run was a very different thing from Stephen at a slow walk, Charles still had strong hopes of winning the race, and gaining his point.   He several times caught glimpses of Stephen through the trees, and, as well as he could judge, the boat had a little the best of it. But when they came out into the last opening, where for a little way they had a fair view of each other—Charles thought Stephen ran faster than ever ; and although he was now considerably nearer the school-house than Stephen was, he still trembled for the result. They were now within fifty rods of the shore, and Charles appealed again to the boys' love of money.

" Now," said he, " we have not a minute to spare. If we gain the point, I'll give you a dollar a-piece."

The boys strained every nerve, and Charles' paddle made the water fly like the tail of a wounded shark. When within half a dozen rods of the shore, Charles urged them again to spring with all their might, and one of the boys making a desperate plunge upon his oar, snapped it in two. The first pull of the other oar headed the boat from land. Charles saw at once that the delay must be fatal, if he depended on the boat to carry him ashore. The water was but two feet deep, and the bottom was sandy. He sprang from the boat, and rushed toward the shore as fast as he was able to press through the water. He flew up the bank, and along the road, till he reached the school-house. The door was open, but he could see no one within. Several children were at play round the door, who, having seen Charles approach with such haste, stood with mouths and eyes wide open, staring at him.

" Where's the schoolma'am ?" said Charles, hastily, to one of the largest boys.

" Why," said the boy, opening his eyes still wider, " is any of the folks dead ?"

" You little rascal, I say, where's the school ma'am ?"

" She just went down that road," said the boy, " two or three minutes ago."

" Was she alone ?" said Charles.

" She started alone," said the boy, " and a man met her out there a little ways, and turned about and went with her."

Charles felt that his cake was all dough again, and that he might as well give it up for a bad job, and go home. Stephen Jones and Lucy Brown walked very leisurely home through the woods, and Charles and the boys went very leisurely in the boat across the pond. They even stopped by the way, and caught a mess of fish, since the boys had thrown their lines into the boat when they started. And when they reached the wharf, Charles, in order to show that he had been a fishing, took a large string of the fish in his hand, and carried them up to the house. Miss Lucy Brown, on her way home through the woods, had undoubtedly been informed of the proposed tea-party for the evening, to which she was to be invited, and to which Stephen Jones and Susan Jones were not invited; and when Miss Lucy's invitation came, she sent word back that she was *engaged*.

CHAPTER XV.

OLD MYERS.

IN a country like ours, of boundless forests, rapidly filling up with a growing and widely spreading population, the pioneers of the wilderness, those hardy and daring spirits who take their lives in their hands, and march, in advance of civilization, into the wild woods, to endure privations among the wild animals, and run the hazard of wild warfare among the savage tribes, form a very peculiar and interesting class. Whether it is a natural hardihood and boldness, and love of adventure, or a desire for retirement, or a wish to be free from the restraints of civilized society, that thus leads this peculiar class of people into the wilderness, it matters not now to inquire. Probably all these motives, in a greater or less degree, go to make up the moving principle.

At the head of this class is the renowned Daniel Boone, whose name will live as long as his Old Kentucky shall find a place on the page of history. He was the great Napoleon among the pioneers of the wilderness. But there are many others of less note, whose lives were also filled with remarkable adventures, and curious and interesting incidents. Indeed, every State in the Union has had more or less of these characters, which go to make up the class. One of these was Old Myers, the Panther; a man of iron constitution, of great power of bone and muscle, and an indomitable courage that knew no mixture of fear.

Four times, in four different States, had Myers pitched his lonely tent in the wilderness, among savage tribes, and waited for the tide of white population to overtake him; and four times he had " pulled up stakes " and marched still deeper into the forest, where he might enjoy more elbow-room, and exclaim with Selkirk,

> "I am monarch of all I survey—
> My right there is none to dispute."

And now, at the time of which we speak, he had a fifth time pitched his tent and struck his fire on the banks of the Illinois river, in the territory which afterwards grew up to a State of the same name. Having lived so much in the wilderness, and associated so much with the aborigines, he had acquired much of their habits and mode of life, and by his location on the Illinois river, he soon became rather a favorite among the Indian tribes around him. His skill with the rifle and the bow, and his personal feats of strength and agility, were well calculated to excite their admiration and applause. He often took the lead among them in their games of sport. It was on one of these occasions that he acquired the additional name of the Panther.

A party of eight or ten Indians, accompanied by Myers, had been out two or three days on a hunting excursion, and were returning, laden with the spoils of the chase, consisting of various kinds of wild fowl, squirrels, racoons and buffalo-skins. They had used all their ammunition except a single charge, which was reserved in the rifle of the chief for any emergency, or choice game which might present itself on the way home. A river lay in the way, which could be crossed only at one point, without subjecting them to an extra journey of some ten miles round. When they arrived at this point, they suddenly came upon a huge panther, which had taken possession of the pass, and, like a skilful general, confident of his strong position, seemed determined to hold it. The party retreated a little, and stood at bay for a while, and consulted what should be done.

Various methods were attempted to decoy or frighten the creature from his position, but without success. He growled defiance whenever they came in sight, as much as to say, " If you want this stronghold come and take it !" The animal appeared to be very powerful and fierce. The trembling Indians hardly dared to come in sight of him, and all the reconnoitering had to be done by Myers. The majority were in favor of retreating as fast as possible, and taking the long journey of ten miles round for home ; but Myers resolutely resisted. He urged the chief, whose rifle was loaded, to march up to the panther, take good aim and shoot him down ; promising that the rest of the party would back him up closely with their knives and tomahawks, in case of a miss-fire. But the chief refused ; he knew too well the nature and power of the animal. The creature, he contended, was exceedingly hard to kill. Not one shot in twenty, however well aimed, would dispatch him ; and if one shot failed, it was a sure death to the shooter, for the infuriated animal would spring upon him in an instant, and tear him to pieces. For similar reasons every Indian in the party declined to hazard a battle with the enemy in any shape.

At last Myers, in a burst of anger and impatience,

16

called them all a set of cowards, and snatching the
loaded rifle from the hands of the chief, to the amazement of the whole party, marched deliberately towards
the panther. The Indians kept at a cautious distance,
to watch the result of the fearful battle. Myers
walked steadily up to within about two rods of the
panther, keeping his eyes fixed upon him, while the
eyes of the panther flashed fire, and his heavy growl
betokened at once the power and firmness of the
animal. At about two rods distance, Myers levelled
his rifle, took deliberate aim, and fired. The shot
inflicted a heavy wound, but not a fatal one; and
the furious animal, maddened with the pain, made
but two leaps before he reached his assailant. Myers
met him with the butt end of his rifle, and staggered
him a little with two or three heavy blows, but the
rifle broke, and the animal grappled him, apparently
with his full power. The Indians at once gave Myers
up for dead, and only thought of making a timely
retreat for themselves.

Fearful was the struggle between Myers and the
panther, but the animal had the best of it at first, for
they soon came to the ground, and Myers underneath,
suffering under the joint operation of sharp claws and
teeth, applied by the most powerful muscles. In fall-

ing, however, Myers, whose right hand was at liberty, had drawn a long knife. As soon as they came to the ground, his right arm being free, he made a desperate plunge at the vitals of the animal, and, as his good luck would have it, reached his heart. The loud shrieks of the panther showed that it was a death-wound. He quivered convulsively, shook his victim with a spasmodic leap and plunge, then loosened his hold, and fell powerless by his side. Myers, whose wounds were severe but not mortal, rose to his feet, bleeding, and much exhausted, but with life and strength to give a grand whoop, which conveyed the news of his victory to his trembling Indian friends.

They now came up to him with shouting and joy, and so full of admiration that they were almost ready to worship him. They dressed and bound up his wounds, and were now ready to pursue their journey home without the least impediment. Before crossing the river, however, Myers cut off the head of the panther, which he took home with him, and fastened it up by the side of his cabin-door, where it remained for years, a memorial of a deed that excited the admiration of the Indians in all that region. From that time forth they gave Myers that name, and always called him the Panther.

Time rolled on, and the Panther continued to occupy his hut in the wilderness, on the banks of the Illinois river, a general favorite among the savages, and exercising great influence over them. At last the tide of white population again overtook him, and he found himself once more surrounded by white neighbors. Still, however, he seemed loth to forsake the noble Illinois, on whose banks he had been so long a fixture, and he held on, forming a sort of connecting link between the white settlers and the Indians.

At length hostilities broke out, which resulted in the memorable Black Hawk War, that spread desolation through that part of the country. Parties of Indians committed the most wanton and cruel depredations, often murdering old friends and companions, with whom they had held long conversation. The white settlers, for some distance round, flocked to the cabin of the Panther for protection. His cabin was transformed into a sort of garrison, and was filled by more than a hundred men, women, and children, who rested almost their only hope of safety on the prowess of the Panther, and his influence over the savages.

At this time a party of about nine hundred of the Iroquois tribe were on the banks of the Illinois, about a mile from the garrison of Myers, and nearly opposite the present town of La Salle. One day news was brought to the camp of Myers, that his brother-in-law and wife, and their three children, had been cruelly murdered by some of the Indians. The Panther heard the sad news in silence. The eyes of the people were upon him, to see what he would do. Presently they beheld him with a deliberate and determined air, putting himself in battle array. He girded on his tomahawk and scalping-knife, and shouldered his loaded rifle, and, at open mid-day, silently and alone, bent his steps towards the Indian encampment. With a fearless and firm tread, he marched directly into the midst of the assembly, elevated his rifle at the head of the principal chief present, and shot him dead on the spot. He then deliberately severed the head from the trunk, and holding it up by the hair before the awe-struck multitude, he exclaimed, "You have murdered my brother-in-law, his wife and their little ones; and now I have murdered your chief. I am now even with you. But now mind, every one of you that is found here to-morrow morning at sunrise, is a dead Indian!"

All this was accomplished without the least molestation from the Indians. These people are accustomed to regard any remarkable deed of daring as the result of some supernatural agency; and doubtless so considered the present incident. Believing their chief had fallen a victim to some unseen power, they were stupified with terror, and looked on without even a thought of resistance. Myers bore off the head in triumph to his cabin, where he was welcomed by his anxious friends, almost as one returning from the dead. The next morning not an Indian was to be found anywhere in the vicinity. Their camps were deserted, and they left forever their ancient haunts and their dead, and that part of the State was not molested by them afterwards.

The last account we have of Old Myers, the Panther, was in 1838. The old man was eighty years of age, but his form was still erect, and his steps were firm; his eyes were not dim, nor his natural force abated. Up to that time he had remained on the banks of his favorite Illinois. But now the old veteran pioneer grew discontented. The State was rapidly filling up with inhabitants, and the forms and restraints of civilization pressed upon him. The wildness and freshness of the country were destroyed. He looked abroad from his old favorite hills, and he saw that in every direction the march of civilization had broken in upon the repose of the old forest, and his heart again yearned

> "For a lodge in some vast wilderness,
> Some boundless contiguity of shade,
> Where rumor of oppression and deceit,
> Of unsuccessful or successful war,
> Might never reach him more."

The old man talked about selling out and once more "pulling up stakes" to be off.

"What?" said a neighbor, "you are not going to leave us, Father Myers, and take yourself to the woods again in your old age?"

"Yes," said Myers, "I can't stand this eternal bustle of the world around me. I must be off in the woods, where it is quiet, and as soon as I can sell out my improvements, I shall make tracks."

The venerable "squatter" had no fee in the land he occupied, but the improvements on it were his own, and it was not long before a gentleman appeared who offered a fair equivalent for these, with a right to purchase the soil. The bargain was completed, and the money counted out, and the Panther began to prepare for his departure.

"Where are you going, Father Myers?" said the neighbor.

"Well, I reckon," said the old Panther, "I shall go away off somewhere to the further side of Missouri; I understand the people haint got there yet, and there's plenty of woods there."

He proceeded to array himself for his journey. He put on the same hunting-shirt which he wore when he killed the Indian chief. He loaded his rifle and girded on his tomahawk and scalping-knife; and, having filled his knapsack with such articles as he chose to carry with him, he buckled it upon his shoulders, and giving a farewell glance round the cabin, he sallied forth and took the western road for Missouri. When he had reached a little eminence some rods distant, he was observed to hesitate, and stop, and look back. Presently he returned slowly to the cabin.

"Have you forgot anything, Father Myers?" said the occupant.

"I believe," said the old man, "I must take the head of the panther along with me, if you have no objections."

"Certainly," said the gentleman; "any personal matters you have a perfect right to."

The old man took down the dried-up remains of the panther's head from the wall, where it had hung for many years, and fastened it to his knapsack. Then taking one last lingering look of the premises, he turned to the occupant, and asked if he was willing he should give his "grand yell" before he started on his journey.

"Certainly, Father Myers," said the gentleman; "I wish you to exercise the utmost freedom in all personal matters before you leave."

At this the old Panther gave a long, and loud, shrill whoop, that rang through the welkin, and was echoed by forest and hills for miles around.

"There," said the old man, "now my blessing is on the land and on you. Your ground will always yield an abundance, and you will always prosper."

Then Old Myers, the Panther, turned his face to the westward, and took up his solitary march for the distant wilderness.

CHAPTER XVI.

SETH WOODSUM'S WIFE.

As Mr. Seth Woodsum was mowing one morning in his lower haying field, and his eldest son, Obediah, a smart boy of thirteen, was opening the mown grass to the sun, Mr. Woodsum looked up towards his house, and beheld his little daughter Harriet, ten years of age, running towards him with her utmost speed. As she came up, he perceived she was greatly agitated; tears were running down her cheeks, and she had scarcely breath enough to speak.

"O, father," she faintly articulated, "mother is dreadful sick; she's on the bed, and says she shall die before you get there."

Mr. Woodsum was a man of a sober, sound mind, and calm nerves; but he had, what sometimes happens in this cold and loveless world of ours, a tender attachment for his wife, which made the message of the little girl fall upon his heart like a dagger. He dropped his scythe, and ran with great haste to the house. Obediah, who was at the other end of the field, seeing this unusual movement of his father, dropped his fork, and ran with all his might, and the two entered the house almost at the same time.

Mr. Woodsum hastened to the bedside, and took his wife's hand. "My dear Sally," said he, "what is the matter?"

"What is the matter?" echoed Mrs. Woodsum, with a plaintive groan. "I should n't think you would need to ask what is the matter, Mr. Woodsum. Don't you see I am dying?"

"Why, no, Sally, you don't look as if you was dying. What *is* the matter? how do you feel?"

"Oh, I shan't live till night," said Mrs. Woodsum with a heavy sigh; "I am going fast."

Mr. Woodsum, without waiting to make further inquiries, told Obediah to run and jump on to the horse, and ride over after Doctor Fairfield, and get him to come over as quick as he can come. "Tell him I am afraid your mother is dying. If the doctor's horse is away off in the pasture, ask him to take our horse and come right away over, while you go and catch his."

Obediah, with tears in his eyes, and his heart in his mouth, flew as though he had wings added to his feet, and in three minutes' time was mounted upon Old Grey, and galloping with full speed towards Doctor Fairfield's.

"My dear," said Mr. Woodsum, leaning his head upon the pillow, "how *do* you feel? What makes you think you are dying?" And he tenderly kissed her forehead as he spoke, and pressed her hand to his bosom.

"Oh, Samuel," for she generally called him by his Christian name, when under the influence of tender emotions; "Oh, Samuel, I feel dreadfully. I have pains darting through my head, and most all over me; and I feel dizzy, and can't hardly see; and my heart beats as though it would come through my side. And besides, I feel as though I was dying. I'm sure I can't live till night; and what will become of my poor children?" And she sobbed heavily and burst into a flood of tears.

Mr. Woodsum was affected. He could not bring himself to believe that his wife was in such immediate danger of dissolution as she seemed to apprehend. He thought she had no appearance of a dying person; but still her earnest and positive declarations, that she should not live through the day, sent a thrill through his veins, and a sinking to his heart that no

language has power to describe. Mr. Woodsum was
as ignorant of medicine as a child ; he therefore did
not attempt to do anything to relieve his wife, except
to try to soothe her feelings by kind and encouraging
words, till the doctor arrived. The half hour which
elapsed, from the time Obediah left till the doctor
came, seemed to Mr. Woodsum almost an age. He
repeatedly went from the bedside to the door, to look
and see if the doctor was anywhere near, and as
often returned to hear his wife groan, and say she was
sinking fast, and could not stand it many minutes
longer.

At length Doctor Fairfield rode up to the door, on
Mr. Woodsum's Old Grey, and with saddle-bags in
hand, hastened into the house. A brief examination
of the patient convinced him that it was a decided
case of hypochondria, and he soon spoke encouraging
words to her, and told her although she was considerably unwell, he did not doubt she would be better in
a little while.

"Oh, Doctor, how can you say so?" said Mrs.
Woodsum ; "don't you see I am dying? I can't
possibly live till night; I am sinking very fast, Doctor,
and I shall never see the sun rise again. My heart
sometimes almost stops its beating now, and my feet

and hands are growing cold. But I *must* see my dear children once more; do let 'em come in and bid me farewell." Here she was so overwhelmed with sobs and tears as to prevent her saying more.

The doctor, perceiving it was in vain to talk or try to reason with her, assured her that as long as there was life there was hope, and told her he would give her some medicine that he did not doubt would help her. He accordingly administered the drugs usually approved by the faculty in such cases, and telling her that he would call and see her again in a day or two, he left the room. As he went out, Mr. Woodsum followed him, and desired to know, in private. his real opinion of the case. The doctor assured him he did not consider it at all alarming. It was only an ordinary case of hypochondria, and with proper treatment the patient would undoubtedly get better.

"It is a case," continued the doctor, "in which the mind needs to be administered to as much as the body. Divert her attention as much as possible by cheerful objects; let her be surrounded by agreeable company; give her a light, but generous and nutritive diet; and as soon as may be, get her to take gentle exercise in the open air, by riding on horseback, or running about the fields and gathering fruits and flowers in company with lively and congenial companions. Follow these directions, and continue to administer the medicines I have ordered, and I think Mrs. Woodsum will soon enjoy good health again."

Mr. Woodsum felt much relieved after hearing the doctor's opinion and prescriptions, and bade the kind physician good morning with a tolerably cheerful countenance. Most assiduously did he follow the doctor's directions, and in a few days he had the happiness to see his beloved wife again enjoying tolerable health, and pursuing her domestic duties with cheerfulness.

But alas! his sunshine of hope was destined soon to be obscured again by the clouds of sorrow and disappointment. It was not long before some change in the weather, and changes in her habits of living, and neglect of proper exercise in the open air, brought on a return of Mrs. Woodsum's gloom and despondency, in all their terrific power. Again she was sighing and weeping on the bed, and again Mr. Woodsum was hastily summoned from the field, and leaving his plough in mid-furrow, ran with breathless anxiety to the house, where the same scenes were again witnessed which we have already described.

Not only once or twice, but repeatedly week after week, and month after month, these exhibitions were given, and followed by similar results. Each relapse seemed to be more severe than the previous one, and on each occasion Mrs. Woodsum was more positive than ever that she was on her death-bed, and that there was no longer any help for her.

On one of these occasions, so strong was her impression that her dissolution was near, and so anxious did she appear to make every preparation for death, and with such solemn earnestness did she attend to certain details, preparatory to leaving her family for ever, that Mr. Woodsum almost lost the hope that usually attended him through these scenes, and felt, more than ever before, that what he had so often feared, was indeed about to become a painful and awful reality. Most tenderly did Mrs. Woodsum touch upon the subject of her separation from her husband and children.

"Our poor children—what will become of them when I am gone? And you, dear Samuel, how can I bear the thought of leaving you? I could feel reconciled to dying, if it was not for the thoughts of leaving you and the children. They will have nobody to take care of them, as a mother would, poor

things; and then you will be so lonesome—it breaks
my heart to think of it."

Here, her feelings overpowered her, and she was
unable to proceed any further. Mr. Woodsum was
for some time too much affected to make any reply.
At last, summoning all his fortitude, and as much
calmness as he could, he told her if it was the will
of Providence that she should be separated from
them, he hoped her last hours would not be pained
with anxious solicitude about the future welfare of
the family. It was true, the world would be a dreary
place to him when she was gone; but he should keep
the children with him, and with the blessing of
heaven, he thought he should be able to make them
comfortable and happy.

"Well, there's one thing, dear Samuel," said Mrs.
Woodsum, "that I feel it my duty to speak to you
about." And she pressed his hand in hers, and
looked most solemnly and earnestly in his face.
"You know, my dear," she continued, "how sad and
desolate a family of children always is, when deprived
of a mother. They may have a kind father, and kind
friends, but nobody can supply the place of a mother.
I feel as if it would be your duty—and I could not
die in peace, if I did n't speak of it—I feel, dear

Samuel, as if it would be your duty as soon after I am gone as would appear decent, to marry some good and kind woman, and bring her into the family to be the mother of our poor children, and to make your home happy. Promise me that you will do this, and I think it will relieve me of some of the distress I feel at the thought of dying."

This remark was, to Mr. Woodsum, most unexpected and most painful. It threw an anguish into his heart, such as he had never experienced till that moment. It forced upon his contemplation a thought that had never before occurred to him. The idea of being bereaved of the wife of his bosom, whom he had loved and cherished for fifteen years with the ardent attachment of a fond husband, had overwhelmed him with all the bitterness of woe; but the thought of transferring that attachment to another object, brought with it a double desolation. His associations before had all clothed his love for his wife with a feeling of immortality. She might be removed from him to another world, but he had not felt as though that would dissolve the holy bond that united them. His love would soon follow her to those eternal realms of bliss, and rest upon her like a mantle for ever. But this new and startling idea, of love for

another, came to him, as comes to the wicked the idea
of annihilation of the soul—an idea, compared with
which no degree of misery imaginable is half so
terrible. A cloud of intense darkness seemed for a
moment to overshadow him, his heart sank within
him, and his whole frame trembled with agitation. It
was some minutes before he could find power to speak.
And when he did, it was only to beseech his wife, in
a solemn tone, not to allude to so distressing a subject
again, a subject which he could not think of nor speak
of, without suffering more than a thousand deaths.

The strong mental anguish of Mr. Woodsum
seemed to have the effect to divert his wife's attention from her own sufferings, and by turning her
emotions into a new channel, gave her system an
opportunity to rally. She gradually grew better, as
she had done in like cases before, and even before
night was able to sit up, and became quite cheerful.

But her malady was only suspended, not cured;
and again and again it returned upon her, and again
and again her friends were summoned to witness her
last sickness, and take their last farewell. And on
these occasions, she had so often slightly and delicately hinted to Mr. Woodsum the propriety of his
marrying a second wife, that even *he* could at last

listen to the suggestion with a degree of indifference which he had once thought he could never feel.

At last, the sober saddening days of autumn came on. Mr. Woodsum was in the midst of his "fall work," which had been several times interrupted by these periodical turns of despondency in his wife. One morning he went to his field early, for he had a heavy day's work to do, and had engaged one of his neighbors to come with two yoke of oxen and a plough to help him "break up" an old mowing field. His neighbor could only help him that day, and he was very anxious to plough the whole field. He accordingly had left the children and nurse in the house, with strict charges to take good care of their mother. Mr. Woodsum was driving the team and his neighbor was holding the plough, and things went on to their mind till about ten o'clock in the forenoon, when little Harriet came running to the field, and told her father that her mother was "dreadful sick" and wanted him to come in as quick as he could, for she was certainly dying now. Mr. Woodsum, without saying a word, drove his team to the end of the furrow; but he looked thoughtful and perplexed. Although he felt persuaded that her danger was imaginary, as it had always proved to be before, still, the idea of the bare possibility that this sickness *might* be unto death, pressed upon him with such power, that he laid down his goad-stick, and telling his neighbor to let the cattle breathe awhile, walked deliberately towards the house. Before he had accomplished the whole distance, however, his own imagination had added such wings to his speed, that he found himself moving at a quick run. He entered the house, and found his wife as he had so often found her before, in her own estimation, almost ready to breathe her last. Her voice was faint and low, and her pillow was wet with tears. She had already taken her leave of her dear children, and waited only to exchange a few parting words with her beloved husband. Mr. Woodsum approached the bedside, and took her hand tenderly, as he had ever been wont to do, but he could not perceive any symptoms of approaching dissolution, different from what he had witnessed on a dozen former occasions.

"Now, my dear," said Mrs. Woodsum, faintly, "the time has come at last. I feel that I am on my death-bed, and have but a short time longer to stay with you. But I hope we shall feel resigned to the will of Heaven. I would go cheerfully, dear, if it was not for my anxiety about you and the children.

Now, don't you think, my dear," she continued, with increasing tenderness, "don't you think it would be best for you to be married again to some kind good woman, that would be a mother to our dear little ones, and make your home pleasant for all of you ?"

She paused, and looked earnestly in his face.

" Well, I've sometimes thought, of late, it might be best," said Mr. Woodsum, with a very solemn air.

" Then you have been thinking about it," said Mrs. Woodsum, with a slight contraction of the muscles of the face.

" Why, yes," said Mr. Woodsum, "I have sometimes thought about it, since you've had spells of being so very sick. It makes me feel dreadfully to think of it, but I don't know but it might be my duty."

" Well, I do think it would," said Mrs. Woodsum, " if you can only get the right sort of a person. Everything depends upon that, my dear, and I hope you will be very particular about who you get, very."

"I certainly shall," said Mr. Woodsum ; " don't give yourself any uneasiness about that, my dear, for I assure you I shall be very particular. The person I shall probably have is one of the kindest and best tempered women in the world."

" But have you been thinking of any one in particular, my dear?" said Mrs. Woodsum, with a manifest look of uneasiness.

"Why, yes," said Mr. Woodsum, "there is one, that I have thought for some time past, I should probably marry, if it should be the will of Providence to take you from us."

"And pray, Mr. Woodsum, who can it be?" said the wife, with an expression, more of earth than heaven, returning to her eye. "Who is it, Mr. Wood sum? You have n't named it to her, have you?"

"Oh, by no means," said Mr. Woodsum; "but my dear, we had better drop the subject; it agitates you too much."

"But, Mr. Woodsum, you must tell me who it is; I never could die in peace till you do."

"It is a subject too painful to think about," said Mr. Woodsum, "and it don't appear to me it would be best to call names."

"But I insist upon it," said Mrs. Woodsum, who had by this time raised herself up with great earnestness and was leaning on her elbow, while her searching glance was reading every muscle in her husband's face. "Mr. Woodsum, I insist upon it!"

"Well, then," said Mr. Woodsum, with a sigh, "if you insist upon it, my dear—I have thought if it should be the will of Providence to take you from us, to be here no more, I have thought I should marry for my second wife, Hannah Lovejoy."

An earthly fire once more flashed from Mrs. Woodsum's eyes—she leaped from the bed like a cat; walked across the room, and seated herself in a chair.

"What!" she exclaimed, in a trembling voice almost choked with agitation—"what! marry that idle, sleepy slut of a Hannah Lovejoy! Mr. Woodsum, that is too much for flesh and blood to bear—I can't endure that, nor I won't. Hannah Lovejoy to be the mother of my children! No, that's what she never shall. So you may go to your ploughing, Mr. Woodsum, and set your heart at rest. Susan," she continued, "make up more fire under that dinner pot."

Mr. Woodsum went to the field, and pursued his work, and when he returned at noon, he found dinner well prepared, and his wife ready to do the honors of the table. Mrs. Woodsum's health from that day continued to improve, and she was never afterward visited by the terrible affliction of hypochondria.

THE END.